FROM THE AUTHOR

Sam Sarkisian's
The Institute

Hi folks,

I hope you enjoy *The Institute* as much as I did writing it. I had gotten so dazed by information overload these past few years, that I decided to write a book about it. Just like scouring social media trying to verify sources, it was a trip.

If you like the book, don't worry, I plan on publishing more. You can check out my pages to stay up to date with my writing projects and other content previews, if you'd like:

Website: sam-sarkisian.com
Instagram: @theinstitutenovel @samsarkisiann
Twitter: @sammiesark

LaunchTeam Press
A division of LaunchTeam, Inc.

1128 Ocean Park Blvd, Suite 314
Santa Monica, CA 90405

LT PRESS

Published by LaunchTeam Press
in the United States of America.
sam-sarkisian.com

Set in Adobe Garamond Pro

Cover design by Flor Figueroa
Interior design by Matthew Revert
Author photo by David Harris

Praise for Sam Sarkisian's *The Institute*

"George Orwell has returned, this time with a dark sense of humor. Throughout The Institute, in a pastiche of social media posts, press releases, and dramatic set pieces, Sarkisian describes the iPhone 32B era as not very different from our own, as a newly formed government agency tries to seize control of that elusive currency, the truth. But both the *National Enquirer* and *The Onion* have survived, which is something that Orwell never would have considered."

—Jay Atkinson, author of *Ice Time, Legends of Winter Hill, City in Amber*, and *Massacre on the Merrimack*.

"*The Institute* is a futuristic novel that may in many ways be prescient. The world Sarkisian portrays is original, yet recognizable as one that could evolve, or devolve out of our own. Satire? Dystopia? A cautionary tale? All of these, and a fascinating read."

—Stephen O'Connor, author of *Smokestack Lightning, The Spy in the City of Books, This Is No Time to Quit Drinking*

"When all 'news' is clickbait for dark, conflicting agendas and we've reached the stasis of dysfunction, there's only one solution: Total Government control of media. With this debut novel, Sam Sarkisian offers a probing and wildly imaginative vivisection of the Post-Trumpocalyptic world. *The Institute* is by turns antic, cluey, and absolutely harrowing."

—David Daniel, bestselling author of *The Tuesday Man* and *Inflections & Innuendos*

"In the tradition of Jonathan Swift, Voltaire and my personal favorite, Lewis Carroll...Sarkisian has taken us through the Trumpian looking glass."

—Elizabeth Mehren, author of *Born Too Soon* and *After the Darkest Hour the Sun Will Shine Again: A Parent's Guide to Coping with the Loss of a Child*

For my dad, Pete Sarkisian—what do you think of the book, pop?

The INSTITUTE

a novel by
sam sarkisian

LT PRESS

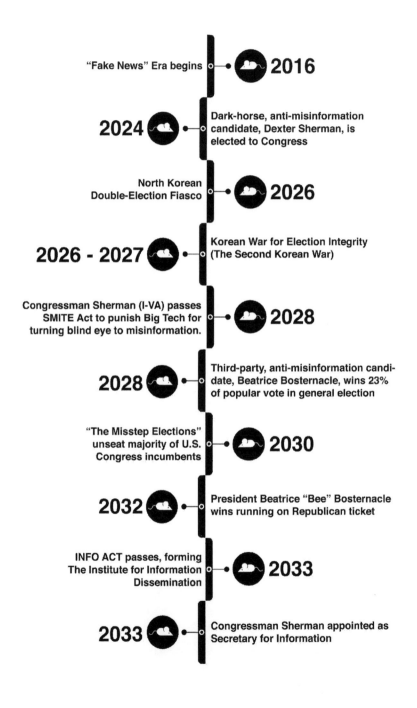

"Fake News" Era begins — 2016

2024 — Dark-horse, anti-misinformation candidate, Dexter Sherman, is elected to Congress

North Korean Double-Election Fiasco — 2026

2026 - 2027 — Korean War for Election Integrity (The Second Korean War)

Congressman Sherman (I-VA) passes SMITE Act to punish Big Tech for turning blind eye to misinformation. — 2028

2028 — Third-party, anti-misinformation candidate, Beatrice Bosternacle, wins 23% of popular vote in general election

"The Misstep Elections" unseat majority of U.S. Congress incumbents — 2030

2032 — President Beatrice "Bee" Bosternacle wins running on Republican ticket

INFO ACT passes, forming The Institute for Information Dissemination — 2033

2033 — Congressman Sherman appointed as Secretary for Information

"A free press can of course be good or bad, but, most certainly, without freedom it will never be anything but bad."

Albert Camus

PART I: WHERE WE HAVE BEEN

Chapter 1: Away We Go

Washington D.C.
Outside the Institute for Information Dissemination
August 10, 2035—the day of the escape
Around 6:30 p.m.

To a little rat on the run—
This is what I know:
They're coming.

I hear them creep, creep, creeping through the mist—after me. They are. The ones who lie and carry sentry guns, the ones led by she who loves those purses and reds and truthful snubs, she who loves her pet toad who might not return that love.

You'd know if you'd only listen. LISTEN. Damn it. You never *listen*. Voices are big and tall and loud and small. Why can't you see? How can't you see what they've done to me? Why can't I see what they've done to me?

I see myself crouching—furtively, mind you, behind a slew of pepperbush like a rat slinking through cracked and impressed pavement—watchful, observant, skirting amongst the shit and grime. The spotlights sweep, searching for a little rodent rat. Their sentries lie on their guts; they search and beg for control!

A voice pounds belligerent: I'm not a rat. I am no rat. I am no rodent of any kind. Her voice enraptures, enchanting and bewitching; oh, my little rat is scampering away, yes, he is, she says with her big red eyes and slender fingers that clack-snap-snap. They always listen when she snaps. Believe it.

Am I really in this field? No! Shhhh...

I haven't been a very good boy. Some might say I've been bad. They told me it's bad, but I don't know why. I don't *remember* why. Help. Please. She isn't here anymore.

Stay away, devil! Imps, spritely, all—get out of my mind. If only the barking would stop. The scratching and scathing barks, coarse and guttural and to no godly end!

Need to know why I was and am and what will be.

They're coming.

There might be lights across the field, but I'm not certain of much anymore, aside from my ripped beige slacks and torn sport coat. I see only smudges through thick, black frames clinging to my face, and beaded sweat slithers to a drip and lands on my beige undershirt. It once was the outfit of a man seeking Truth. I don't remember that man anymore, but I do know I need to remember.

But here, here in this field, truth doesn't exist. Lies, a manipulating succubus, disguise gentle truth, beat her down to a broken and battered near-miss. All here. They've tried to drink the truth from me, to spit my brain out, a swiveling and swirling and droplet-twirling down the drain. Coagulated and nasty sewage lathered on each and every one, to poison us all, a septic and specious excuse for truth. Intoxicated and loud. Intoxicatingly loud!

Hush now. I still hear them.

Chapter 2: A New Government Agency

It began with a title card:

Washington D.C.
Introductory Press Conference
The Institute for Information Dissemination
October 11, 2033

A stout, smug man with razor-thin glasses and a chiseled chin covered by a thick, auburn beard was about to approach a mahogany podium in front of a room of reporters equipped with notepads, audio recording devices, cameras and other tools of their information trade. The man took his time backstage, sauntering, waiting for a cue from a little gray man in little gray suspenders wearing a little gray hat to cover what is left of his little gray hair. The little gray man stood meekly at the podium as the stout man stood offstage to his right, waiting for the little gray man to introduce him in a high-pitched voice that the stout man always thought too nasally for public service. It reminded him of his nephews playing the kazoo, and he didn't much like his nephews.

The man hadn't had time for children, as he dedicated himself to an ambitious career serving the public. And despite the raw, animal appeal of his auburn beard and chiseled chin, his loveless marriage was only for appearances to keep the Sharons and Sheilas, Dons and Dans of his constituency happy. Hell, he'd be the first to admit that he sacrificed a lot in his personal life, but working his damn ass off to change America was well worth it—whenever his thoughts went sour, he'd simply remember his adoring public. You could almost call them "fans," but there were few fans of politicians anymore. Nobody truly had been for as long as anyone could remember.

But now the auburn-bearded man's charged dream, a dream the naysayers discarded like moldy leftover soup, just might come true: he may finally be able to root out political corruption for good. Misinformation no longer could be a tool for the wicked to dupe Americans.

His dream sprang from a strong distaste for misinformation and consequently the media in general, feeling their questions pointed in all the wrong directions, were laden with faulty implications that coaxed the public into a rabbit hole of lies (he still refused to speak with his brother who worked for *The Miami Herald* at family Christmases). In fact, combatting misinformation was the central tenet of his platform during his early years as a congressman for Richmond County, VA. It had seemed to work. With four consecutive congressional victories (the last two in landslides by over 63 percentage points), he'd earned his spot behind the podium and was ready to serve a dogged public who were damn tired of biased media and silver-tongued leaders.

But how did he get here? Some days his success felt like a waking dream to the vibrant, 42-year-old Congressman from Virginia. He'd only come into the public sphere under ten years ago in the elections of 2024, winning his district as an anti-establishment, anti-media dark horse, but his rise to prominence in American politics seemed to happen overnight. It must have been his grit and charisma, not to mention his iron-thick skin. He scoffed at the disavowal from both the Democrats and Republicans; he'd run as an Independent, didn't want their money, and didn't care about their relentless smears. They blabbered about him because they feared his ambition and success would unseat them. And it had.

For the first few years, most of his opponents wrote off his anti-misinformation platform as idealistic and narrow-minded, but after avid supporter, Beatrice "Bee" Bosternacle—pronounced: BAH-stur-nah-ckle, campaign slogan, "Bee-line your way to truth!"—won a significant minority of the popular vote in the 2028 Election as a third-party candidate (after being barred from the primaries of both parties, no less), many of his anti-misinformation protégés followed in a stampede two years later, running and winning both historically Democratic and Republican seats in the House and Senate during the 2030 Midterm Elections. He and his supporters had successfully wheedled their way into indubitable significance on both sides of the aisle.

Their victories only added to the sore egos of political pundits and seventh-term senators, who had so desperately and foolishly clung to the hope that single-issue platforms couldn't win. His critics went so far as to try and insult him out of office, presumptuously discarding his supporters as "Mistaken information Missionaries" (MiMs) and their rise to power as the "Misstep" of

2030. Too bad the man didn't care. How many other politicians had an election year named after their movement, in praise or not? This was his moment, and he was ready.

"I'd like to introduce to the American people the newly elected Secretary for Information, the Honorable Dexter Sherman," the little gray man squeaked.

Secretary Sherman, after wiping a smudge from his glasses in a manner as nonchalant as a long day's yawn, smiled for the cameras, and uplifted his stubbled cheeks. The reporters peered on in anticipation, perhaps fooled by the typical politician's ploy—all smiles!—or perhaps convincing themselves this stout man might surprise them and be sincere. Journalists tended to view Sherman with skepticism and annoyance; he was endlessly critical of media and reporting in general. Any criticism of him, then, made the reporter seem unreliable and personally motivated. The public, on the other hand, liked Sherman even though journalists found him crass; his philanthropy work helping rural America was tight and focused, and his four campaigns for Congress made it a point to release every morsel of information, from email logs to detailed expense reports. Heck, they even knew he bought a $5 beer at O'Hoolihan's the night after a tough debate!

All of the American media were present, eager to record and report on what promised to be a momentous occasion. There were penpoints resting anxiously on notepads, microphones nose up for the best acoustics. This was a *big deal* all right. The public had finally achieved a major victory against misinformation, but perhaps not so much a victory against disinformation as they or Sherman thought.

Fascinated or frustrated or both, the awaiting journalists' dedication to the tenets of Newsworthiness meant they had no choice but to listen to the school-boy charisma of the stout Secretary Sherman:

"Ladies and gentlemen of the media, it is my sincere pleasure to announce the opening of the newest department of the United States Government: The Institute for Information Dissemination. In this age of information overload, an era with seemingly infinite opportunities to consume information via the web, Congress and our President believe a department dedicated to streamlining essential policy updates was in order. We have seen what can happen when such important news is unjustly filtered through the media, their job only made more difficult when government officials omit crucial details, hard-pressed by lobbyists and private interests. So, here we are.

As Americans, I know we stand firm in our belief that the public must be informed, as an informed public is the crux of our democracy. As Thomas Jefferson so eloquently said in the formative years of our great nation, 'If a nation expects to be ignorant and free in a state of civilization, it expects what never was and never will be. If we are to guard against ignorance and remain free, it is the responsibility of every American to be informed.' His words resonate with us now more than ever. And we should heed his insightful warnings to a T!"

Secretary Sherman then raised and lowered his chest in a very exaggerated sigh before furrowing his brow and abruptly pounding his fist to the podium with great force. The podium shook, the sound reverberating in echoes throughout the silent, attentive hall. The reporters' eyes spoke what could not be said, what dared not be said: "Yes, but how the hell did we get *here*, listening to you, needing to listen to you?" Sherman continued:

"But how can we be informed, truly, accurately, as a democratic populous, when we have such a gross excess of malignant, uninformed opinions riddling the very foundation of our free, self-governing nation state? Information, vast and intimidating as it may be, is our lifeblood as Americans. We know after years of foreign interference in our elections, that nowadays warfare rarely takes the form of explosive, beastly man-on-man action, and instead favors a corruption of our information highways, polluted with filth, deceit, and lies: all to divide our country.

It is no fault of the common man that today it is nearly impossible to get reliable information. In hindsight, we now see our trouble with falsified news sprouted its ugly head when the public began to seriously distrust the media during the spiraling "Fake News" Era of 2016. But we know to diagnose a problem is not to remedy it.

There is simply *too much* information, spinning and swerving in all directions. Even if a report is as accurate as can be, we may find ourselves flooded with naysaying counter-reports from just as well-meaning journalists. Americans can be fervent and shrewd in our research on happenings of the day, and still be victim to unreliable information. Why must we read competing stories—about the same topic mind you—with opposite facts, with snippets of the same source quote threaded together for opposite ends? It's only natural the American public no longer knows where to turn, no longer knows who to believe."

He then gestured to the increasingly nervous reporters who stood watching as their frantic pens spread ink on the page and their iPhone 32bs recorded audio.

"Listen. You all have an honorable craft. On behalf of the United States, we thank you for your service to our great nation. As reporters, writers, editors, photographers and videographers, your efforts have been more than commendable, but we can no longer rely on piecemeal efforts. And as I've said repeatedly, the release of American news and information cannot be patch-worked in an information age. We no longer live in cities and states separated by days, hours, or minutes, but by fractions of microseconds, where Joe in West Virginia might know what happened in downtown Seattle before Mayor Quimby does.

We must work together to spearhead where and how Americans obtain information. Our success is imperative for the health and recovery of our democracy. We understand some of you may be upset, some of you may be angry, but we at the Institute for Information Dissemination would like to walk hand-in-hand with the media to spread reliable, trustworthy information to the public. Without you, there couldn't be an Institute, and we trust you know this. You are our comrades in this war against misinformation.

As the first-appointed Secretary for Information Dissemination, it is my sincerest hope that you will all view the Institute for Information Dissemination as an ally, as a friend, as a companion in the noble pursuit of truth. We are not the enemy. We are here to help, and more importantly, need *your help* to get there together, so we can again regain the trust of Americans in what they read and what they hear.

In a time of great crisis, we might recall what President Ronald Reagan so wisely said, 'I know it is hard to understand, but sometimes painful things like this have to happen. It's all part of the process of exploration and discovery. It's all part of taking a chance and expanding man's horizons. The future doesn't belong to the fainthearted; it belongs to the brave.' The Institute for Information Dissemination is pulling us into the future, this land of the free and home of the brave. We hope you'll follow us.

Thank you all for coming today to witness this innovative development to defend and bolster our democracy."

After Secretary Sherman finished his speech, he swelled, feeling very noble indeed. There was some muffled applause from the press. They intuited that Sherman had a vendetta against them, having called media figures "misguided mis-truthers" in his previous campaigns for Congress.

The reporters seemed pensive, yet alert. Some scowled, but most were fueled by a palpable curiosity about the announcement rather than by animosity. The split second of silence was on the verge of eruption.

"I will now open the floor to questions," Secretary Sherman said, gesturing to the media with an open palm. The room exploded; reporters shouted in a dissonant orchestra. Boom!

"Mr. Secretary! Mr. Secretary! Secretary Sherman! Congressman!"

He nodded toward the crowd, singling one out to ask the first question.

"Mr. Secretary, what types of updates, specifically, can the public expect from the Institute?" called a young-buck reporter with red-rimmed, caffeinated eyes.

"Thank you for your question. The public can expect daily reports of the results of Congressional sessions, executive orders, election results, happenings in the Capitol and around our great nation, among other things. By working closely with media personnel in all corners of America, we even one day hope to be your source of local news. A source of news you can finally trust," he said.

"But what about the media outlets? Won't your institute endanger their ability to function and thrive?" the young buck said, fearlessly rearing his newly grown antlers in parry, trying to pin down a story of First Amendment violations.

"Firstly, it is *our* Institute, not mine. And, not to worry, if you look to section 4.342ab.7 of the INFO Act, the Institute for Information Dissemination is mandated to have an active and collaborative relationship with the American press, monitored and thus secured by monthly reviews and checks to ensure the Institute's goals are being met according to protocol. I'll say it again. The Institute is not here to displace the press. We are an ally. And remember, it's what the public wants," Sherman said, without missing a beat.

"How will the Institute for Information Dissemination gather its data and validate it? And what about citizen privacy?" a seasoned correspondent asked, veiling the discontent in her eyes so that she might get an honest answer.

"Let me answer your second question first. The Institute will have investigative powers similar to the FBI, but with the goal of public knowledge rather than national security. We are an entity directly serving the people. And of course, as an official government entity, we are bound by the Constitution and Bill of Rights to respect the lawfully bestowed privacy of our citizens.

And how will we attain this public knowledge to be distributed directly to Americans you ask? Why, with the most thoroughly vetted experts in every field, quadruply checked for accuracy," Secretary Sherman said before winking at his audience. "And, in a notably shameless plug, if any of you are looking for work, the Institute for Information Dissemination plans to hire the most reputable journalists to help us in our investigative efforts. Job security, good pay, benefi—"

"And how does the Institute differ from other government departments or press offices? How will they improve on what the press is already doing?" another reporter shouted.

"Well, firstly, since the Institute is not a government press office, there will be little need to report *on our reports.* Press offices release information only beneficial to their represented parties. They would not inform the press of damning information since they function as an arm of public relations. We've taken out the investigative middle man, in a sense. I am committed to keeping the Institute for Information Dissemination a non-partisan entity, fearless in the pursuit of even damaging truths," Sherman said, his smugness on full display.

"Our goal, among other things, is to scrutinize contested claims from competing media outlets, to clarify and fact-check political disagreements and statements, and relay synopses on current events. I cannot stress this enough: we are our own, non-partisan department, working closely with the Department of Justice.

The Institute for Information Dissemination will give unbiased information regardless of its potential to defame political leaders or alter public opinion in an undesirable way, so it would be counterintuitive for us to have a press office, and uninformed to call us one," Secretary Sherman responded, scoffing silently to himself at the reporter's ignorance. And then, almost inaudibly, out of earshot of the reporters:

"Green journalists will be the death of this country."

Following the Q & A exchange, some members of the press grinned at the possibility for government work, some grumbled at the risk of deceit, but few were bold enough to challenge the new, self-assured Secretary. Most only spoke with their eyes. Except one, it seemed, whose eyes and mouth were always synchronized.

A familiar-looking, fat man from *The Washington Post* stood up. He has an old-fashioned, brown-brimmed hat boasting a black-felt banner above the brim which snugly held his "press card" with dignity.

"Mr. Secretary, why would the public trust the Institute's memorandums over what filters into their social media feeds or what they search on the web? Isn't the SMITE Act of 2028 enough to regulate false information on the Internet?"

The Secretary sighed and smiled. He had been waiting eagerly for someone to bring up his revolutionary 2028 bill, but the scene did not unfold quite as planned.

"Ah, an ever-important question. Thank you, mister...uh?" the Secretary said, feigning ignorance.

"Andrews. Dr. Andrews, Mr. Secretary."

"erm, that Andrews, fine, yes, Dr. Andrews, fine—*erhrm*. Firstly, while we at the Institute clearly support the SMITE Act's strict requirements for social media outlets to remove misleading and false information—I wrote the bill for God's sake—" Sherman quipped, receiving gentle laughter from the tense audience, "that is not always where their priorities lie. Before the Institute, the government could only enforce regulation to a certain extent, crippled by our painstakingly slow legal system. Now, the public can take comfort in knowing that our memorandums will be copiously reviewed by a team of fact-checkers, researchers, and yes, like I said before, perhaps even government-employed journalists, in order to be pristine in both their presentation and credibility. No more wondering what's true and what's not, what's misleading and what's not. With the Institute's flagship memorandums, false information will be less likely to go viral before half the public has sent it to their brothers, aunts, and cousins.

Perhaps the most crucial, distinctive aspect of the Institute for Information Dissemination is that it will provide accuracy reports of all elected officials, from the President to a local town's Alderman. Elected officials who spread biased or misinformation will do so at their own risk, but of course it is up to other government departments to dole out justice.

And better yet, all avenues and steps to acquire and check the information will be provided in the reports, and if the public deems any unfit or uncertain, we will tirelessly work to correct it. We are here to serve," Sherman retorted at length, thick with confidence. He then turned to call on another reporter, but heard the fat man continue:

"That's all well and good, sir, but still, the idea of government-employed journalists is a paradox in itself. Won't you be, even with the greatest of intentions, suppressing the voice of the free, independent press? Won't your agency disseminate a one-sided view? Is not the ability to parse through information and form your opinion one of the pillars of free speech?" Andrews said with the unerring confidence of a lion's roar. He was on the hunt, not to be fooled by gilded, albeit polished prose. It looks like the young-buck reporter may have his First Amendment story after all.

The Secretary pursed his lips and winced. He seemed displeased with Dr. Andrews' sudden outburst. His ruddy cheeks then inflated, emanating the sheen of a finely taut, rosy balloon. All you'd need is a pin. Pop!

Sherman wiped his glasses and the single bead of sweat from his forehead, took a breath, tilted his chin down, and then reframed them to give himself time to think before answering.

"Well then, are you implying, if I'm hearing you correctly, of course, that the government is not composed of citizens and therefore not permitted to exercise free speech as well? Oh, Mr. Andrews, I don't mean to condescend, but surely as an educated man, you are aware that the Constitution, which, of course, we all hold dear, is a *living document*, and one that can and should be interpreted based on the social atmosphere of the era? I'll remind you, as an expression of the will of the people, the Institute for Information Dissemination is publicly funded, and heeds *no partiality*. We are truly independent, releasing scrutiny on even our own officials. I'm not sure how many more times I must repeat that," the Secretary said, clutching his note cards tightly by his waist, crumpling and creasing them to folded bits. His hatred of the press boiled within him. They were not about to squash his dream of ridding America of misinformation. They were part of the problem, a tumor needing to be removed.

"Yes, well, of course, but—" Andrews said, trying to get a word in, trying to clarify the importance of his point before the public was drowned in a voice louder than his.

"—you'd agree, that under the sheer gargantuan beast of the information highway that is the internet, we must take action to protect and guard our inalienable rights? Is biased information spewing biased speech even free speech at all? You do appreciate the evolution of our democracy, don't you...Mr. Andrews?"

Andrews was afraid of this, of Sherman getting on his high horse, spewing all his talking points that got the bill passed in the first place.

"Yes, of course, no one should doubt my—nor the press's— belief in healthy democracy, but doesn't limiting access, or, even if not limiting, then, championing a particular source, hinder the right for the average American to form his own opinions? His or her own right to choose? This smells like a dire threat to our most invaluable right as citizens," the fat *Washington Post* reporter said, receiving subtle nods from his colleagues and competition. He'd been covering Sherman's rise to national popularity for years, desperate to sniff out a shred of corruption. So far, zilch.

"Oh, you journalists and your love affair with objectivity. Don't you see that we cannot be 'balanced' in our pursuit of truth, anymore? How can we balance an entangled spider's web? The world no longer has two sides to an issue. No! We must take it into our own hands, wrestle with the infinite possibilities to streamline a unified front of information. And of course, we won't restrict access to the beloved media of the United States of America. That would be unconstitutional."

"I agree about objectivity, and I mean no offense—but—the first impression's impac—"

"I'm glad to hear you agree. No further questions. It seems we're out of time."

Chapter 3: The Institute Has Formed

Location unknown
Sometime in mid-August 2035

To a dirty ver-man scavenging through pulp in a dark place:

I must tell my friend. He told me to write to remember. I have to try. He tells me I should try even when it's loud in my head. The barking still hasn't stopped.

I don't know who I am, but what I do know is:

He must believe me about them. He tells me I'm his "old friend," but he still won't believe me. When I told him that old friends should believe what old friends tell them, that he must believe me, must know that *they're coming*, he said nothing and told me to keep writing, but not about that, not about *them*.

It's so dark in here.

I'm not quite sure why a big gray building with big gray walls and a man standing outside it with a handsome red beard is burned so deep into my brain-mind, but my good friend tells me to write down anything and everything, even "stuff not about you," (just not the stuff about *them*. He's very clear about that). But I guess he would know, he's a doctor. I think his advice has helped.

Yesterday, when I mentioned the red-bearded man's name, Sherman! When I called him the "heartthrob of the people," my doctor got very excited and went upstairs for I don't know how long. When he came back down, he had a thick folder with some papers from the big gray building, the Institute it's called I guess, and some papers of people writing about what they did in that big gray building:

From the Great Gray Lady, *The New York Times*:

NEW GOVERNMENT FACT-CHECKING AGENCY CONFIRMED BY CONGRESS

From the Beantown press, *The Boston Globe:*

AMID DISMAY FROM BOTH LEFT AND RIGHT, CONGRESS OPENS NEW FEDERAL AGENCY

From the barons of financial scrutiny, *The Wall Street Journal:*

SENATE NARROWLY PASSES BILL TO OPEN INSTITUTE FOR INFORMATION DISSEMINATION, NEWS MEDIA STOCKS FALL

From D.C.'s own beacon for democracy, *The Washington Post:*

NEW GOV'T DEPARTMENT PUTS INDEPENDENT JOURNALISM IN PERIL

And piping from just a few miles away, the Washington D.C. watch, *The Hill:*

NEW GOVERNMENT INFO AGENCY BECKONS THE PRESS'S HELP, WILL MONITOR ELECTED OFFICIALS AND MEDIA

From the big apple tabloid, *The New York Post:*

THEY'RE AFTER US! GOV'T BILL PASSES, HANDICAPPING PRESS

And with their weekly news cycles, the magazines put in their two cents a few days and few more sniffs later:

The New Yorker:

HAVE WE DEVOLVED INTO AN ORWELLIAN ABYSS?

The Atlantic:

INSTITUTE VOWS TO WORK WITH JOURNALISTS BUT MANY WORRY FOR FUTURE OF AN INDEPENDENT PRESS

National Enquirer:

IS HEARTTHROB SHERMAN IN LOVE WITH NEW DEPUTY? WHO IS THIS MYSTERIOUS LOVER?

After I told my doctor that the news media doesn't count for all media, he smiled and said "you are quite right! But of course, the news media cannot encompass *all* media. Social media and opinion pieces inundated the web that day, too."

Then he went upstairs for a little while.

When he came back, he gave me some papers that he "printed off the web from that fateful day," and told me to think hard while I read them. But it hurts to think, Doctor! Please.

From "America's Finest News Source," *The Onion*:

AREA MAN NOT CONCERNED WITH NEW GOV'T AGENCY SINCE "THEY SEEM TO BE SOME TRUSTWORTHY GUYS"

"They haven't steered us wrong much before," the man continued.

From the Facebook page of Donna Foiblicker, 37, resident of Chesterton, Indiana, and self-described, "loving mother of two boys":

Donna Foiblicker
19 m · ⊙

FINALLY. FINALLy, the government is doing something. Something for the good of all of us!!! Yes! I don't who out of my friends follows politics but let me say wow we have taken steps in the RIGHT DIRECTION. All of our work has finally paid off!

Let me give you some details. Ive been working with the local task force "Americans for Truth" to get something freaking done about public distrust with the news media and its public officials. And today, TODAY, Congress listened to us!!!!!!! I am so so happy! Love, love Congressman Sherman always fighting for the lil guy!!

The government just passed Sherman's bill forming a new department to give us all THE TRUTH. They're going to have an informed task force full of tip top researchers whose job is to find what we can trust and package it right up for us!!! Goodbye Fake News!

See ya later, Im done being lied to, and I think you all are too! I know some of my friends might not be happy about this but jeez its just so hard these days to trust the news. Someone says one thing. And then someone else says another and they both say that theyre right. Not anymore!

THANK YOU U.S. GOVERNMENT. THANK YOU AMERICA, THE GREATEST COUNTRY ON EARTH!!

⭕👍😲 29

👍 Like   💬 Comment

T.J. Clarke
Yes. Yes. Love this!

Like · Reply · 19 m

Wendell Johnson
Donna, you know I always appreciate your passion for politics and your thoughts on them, but you are oh so very wrong about this. Authoritative states always come after the press first! A government-sanctioned info disseminator lays the groundwork for FASCISM! Please pray that it buckles under outside pressure and the bill is repealed.

Like · Reply · 14 m

T.J. Clarke
Oh Wendell, I know you mean well, but I see what you post everyday. AS IF CNN CAN EVEN COUNT as "the press". You leftists are always preaching on how your beloved New York Times and Washington Post are the best of the best when they're about as liberal as they come! Anytime someone posts anything outside your circle or from an outlet you've never heard of, it's immediately FAKE. I mean how elitist can you be? We NEED THIS. BOTH SIDES NEED THIS. Not that you'll ever listen to reason anyway. So long as you have your CNN.

Like · Reply · 8 m

Tess O'Donnell
Just hearing about this today—what great news! Thank YOU, Donna, for everything you do to keep America great!

Like · Reply · 12 m

Vijayta Patel
Didn't we learn ANYTHING from Trump???

Like · Reply · 11 m

T.J. Clarke
Yes. That we can't trust the news!

Like · Reply · 4 m   3

Clarice Chen
Helloooo 1984.

Like · Reply · 4 m

Write a comment...

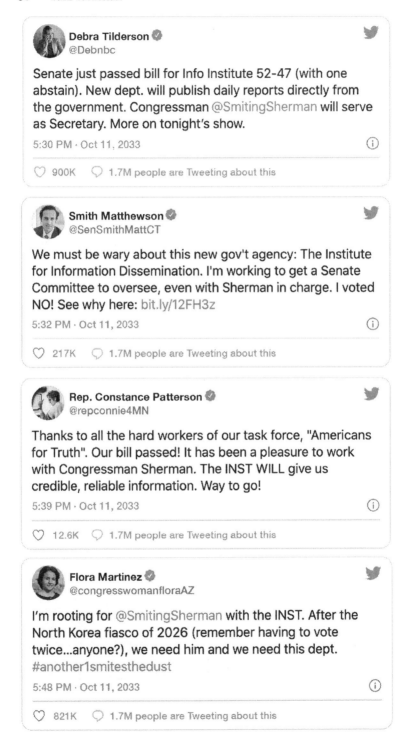

Debra Tilderson ✓
@Debnbc

Senate just passed bill for Info Institute 52-47 (with one abstain). New dept. will publish daily reports directly from the government. Congressman @SmitingSherman will serve as Secretary. More on tonight's show.

5:30 PM · Oct 11, 2033   ⓘ

♡ 900K   💬 1.7M people are Tweeting about this

Smith Matthewson ✓
@SenSmithMattCT

We must be wary about this new gov't agency: The Institute for Information Dissemination. I'm working to get a Senate Committee to oversee, even with Sherman in charge. I voted NO! See why here: bit.ly/12FH3z

5:32 PM · Oct 11, 2033   ⓘ

♡ 217K   💬 1.7M people are Tweeting about this

Rep. Constance Patterson ✓
@repconnie4MN

Thanks to all the hard workers of our task force, "Americans for Truth". Our bill passed! It has been a pleasure to work with Congressman Sherman. The INST WILL give us credible, reliable information. Way to go!

5:39 PM · Oct 11, 2033   ⓘ

♡ 12.6K   💬 1.7M people are Tweeting about this

Flora Martinez ✓
@congresswomanfloraAZ

I'm rooting for @SmitingSherman with the INST. After the North Korea fiasco of 2026 (remember having to vote twice...anyone?), we need him and we need this dept. #another1smitesthedust

5:48 PM · Oct 11, 2033   ⓘ

♡ 821K   💬 1.7M people are Tweeting about this

Stephanie Elon
@stephybabyy28

Any fellow @MiMs see Sec Sherman rip that reporter a new one at the press conference today? Dreamboattttt. #talksherman2me #heartthrob #MiMs4lyfe #marryme

6:10 PM · Oct 11, 2033

♡ 21   💬 1.7M people are Tweeting about this

Josh Mulbury ✓
@mulburycomedy

I don't normally get involved in politics, but this new Institute is some scary stuff. Be on guard here, folks.

6:10 PM · Oct 11, 2033

♡ 442   💬 1.7M people are Tweeting about this

Shawn Handelson ✓
@shawnhandelnightnews

Opponents of The Institute need to realize the overwhelming evidence that it will do good for America. Don't believe what they say. Hold officials accountable. It won't "kill the media." It'll bolster it. I'm on board!

6:32 PM · Oct 11, 2033

♡ 58K   💬 1.7M people are Tweeting about this

I told my friend that it's not fun to slog through social media, that it's dirty and unclear, told him that I don't think I ever liked it. He said to me, "We all have to do things that aren't fun sometimes, my good friend. You might not know it, but you

had quite a big role in all this. It's important that you remember. You must remember who you are. I want you to read some more papers. You can do that for me, for your good friend, right?"

I said yes but told him nothing makes any sense. He said he understood but that "nothing will ever make any sense," if I don't record how I got here. It's so dark down here.

I need my friend because I can't see. I call for him sometimes, but he tells me to read the papers and after I read the papers that he'll come and diagnose me. It's so hard to read the papers when there's only a tiny square window for light. He tells me that he knows, and that he's sorry, but it will only be for a little while longer. The sooner I get better, the sooner I can go upstairs. It's not safe right now.

He says that I start to sound better, sound like "my old self" after I read the papers. I think he's right. He told me it's ok if it's hard, ok if I get frustrated. Writing about it helps me sort my thoughts, helps me articulate like I used to, helps me retain some semblance of normalcy. After I told my doctor that writing helps me feel normal, he smiled and said, "Good. You'll need to be in the proper place for my next prescription."

Then he handed me the Institute's initial press release. He reminded me to stay calm. Here it is:

RE: INSTITUTE FOR INFORMATION DISSEMINATION

SHERMAN ANNOUNCES VICTORY OF INSTITUTE FOR
INFORMATION DISSEMINATION

FOR IMMEDIATE RELEASE

WASHINGTON—On Tuesday, October 11, 2033, the Institute for Information Dissemination was formed
by the U.S. Senate passing Bill I.N. 5643. Later
that day, President Bosternacle signed it into
law.

The Institute for Information Dissemination's
staff will consist of professional researchers,
journalists, university professors, and policy
makers whose sole goal is to provide reliable,
truthful information to citizens of the United
States. The Institute intends to recruit our nation's top communicators and media scholars to
sift through and deconstruct unreliable information, with the goal of streamlining accurate news
and policy statements directly to U.S. citizens.

Biweekly Institute reports will include accuracy
ratings of all elected officials and media outlets with detailed analyses and fact-checking.
If successful, we aim to inspire a more informed
public, one that is no longer disheartened by
their mistrust of news and the government.

The Institute will open its doors in the heart
of Washington D.C. in order to maintain a close
relationship with Congress and the President. The
Institute wants and needs the unwavering support
of all branches of the U.S. Government to ensure
its success.

"We must fight on a unified front against misinformation," Congressman Sherman said in a statement
after being appointed to the newly established
position, Secretary of Information. "I'm honored
you all understand the dire effects of rampant and
misleading facts. The Institute is our remedy for

that. The trust of our media, of public office both right and left, depends on our success."

In response to legal pundits opposed to the bill, retired Chief Justice Darby said, "The Constitution is a living document, meant to be mended for contemporary cultural needs. Congress carefully considered the potential for violating a free press in America when composing Bill I.N. 5643. Said law strives to include the press in all the Institute for Information Dissemination's decisions, memos, and research aggregation. Too, the bill requires monthly reviews by an external special counsel and the FCC to ensure the accuracy of the information spread to the public. Without reasonable doubt, the First Amendment has not been violated."

Congressman Sherman's INFO Act, which effectively creates the Institute for Information Dissemination, has garnered increasing support from the public and members of Congress since the initial House vote two weeks ago.

"We trust you know that our decision to open the Institute of Information Dissemination comes from a good place. We are continuously distraught to hear public discontent of the media and their distrust of their government officials, so we are confident that the Institute for Information Dissemination will help remedy this public ill by holding said officials and media outlets accountable," Congresswoman Patterson, Chairwoman of the House Permanent Select Committee on Intelligence, said.

According to details found in Bill I.N. 5643, the INFO Act, each U.S. residence will be forwarded a mailed survey that asks preference for information conveyance methods. Each residence may opt for email, text message, social media notification, or paper copy documents. The weekly mailer will also provide updates on Institute personnel, ranking members, and any other major or minor changes.

To coexist in harmony with the press, the Institute for Information Dissemination requests
attendance in their new headquarters with major
editors-in-chief and heads of publishing houses
in the coming weeks.

The Institute will formally open its doors by the
end of 2033. Any and all are welcome to visit
and obtain more information on this exciting new
development to help elucidate truth in American
society. It is a department made for and run by
the people.

Sincerely,

Dexter Sherman
Congressman for Richmond County, VA
Newly Appointed Secretary for Information

I don't remember much, but after the first time I read the Institute's press release, I think that I might have been mad. The
potential for these government junkies to violate basic rights
must have made me so mad that I had to do something, maybe
write something important. I remember I wanted to figure
out why people choose sides, why some barking and shouting
worked, and some didn't. Why particular combos of barks and
whines and whistles could make people follow or not.

When I told my friend about the barking and yelping, he
prescribed me some more papers and essays from the begin-
nings of the Institute to help me remember what I used to
think about it. There were a lot of people barking and a lot of
people not listening after the Institute bill passed, but I like this
one the best:

An Utter Crisis: The Institute Endangers the Press—
But Could It Be Our Fault?
by The Doctor

Appearing in the October 13, 2033 edition of *The Washington*
Post

By now, we've all heard the news: after tooth-and-nail, gritty deliberation and debate, the U.S. Senate officially ratified the House Bill forming a new government agency, The Institute for Information Dissemination. Though the name sounds like it came out of a 1950s pulp sci-fi novel, I urge you, my readers, to not ignore the gravity of this national development. We must not become numb to perils against free speech; action must be taken, but how I do not know. And yet, I will propose a *why*. Though I may sound like I'm shooting my own industry's foot, we, the press, are partially to blame for the formation of this potentially dangerous, government-sanctioned info disseminator. We did not properly educate the public on the true role of journalism's public service. And then they voted for the government to handle it. To my knowledge, this is how and why it happened.

The Institute is Congress's response to public discontent with the news and subsequently with them. We know this. Legislators have said it. Congressman Sherman (I-VA) ran four successful campaigns using the public's disgust with misinformation as his platform and has subsequently become a national hero of sorts. And of course, it wasn't at all difficult for a publicly beloved man like Sherman to rise into a non-existent cabinet position of a previously non-existent department after the Republicans smartly let his ally, another well-known Independent,

Beatrice "Bee" Bosterton, run on their ticket in 2032 (who won by the most overwhelming popular majority since Lyndon Johnson in 1964, I might add).

Her choice to appoint Sherman as the new Secretary for Information was simple, and grossly uncontested: the overgrowth of executive power had already been set as a precedent at the turn of the century, growing ever stronger with each succeeding president since 2000. After Sherman scrounged enough House and Senate votes for his revolutionary, INFO Act, his appointment was as easy as calling in a favor.

And however well-meaning Sherman's INFO Act may be, its over-reach by forming the Institute can only be called a symptom of our own ignorance, passivity, and insatiable need for instant gratification. The Information Age has incited an angry public to want change, to want it fast; we are tired; we are confused; so who could blame us for wanting some clarity?

For the last few decades, politicians have been bending every which way trying to refute partial or falsified press coverage, but they've run out of options and the citizens have run out of patience trying to determine whom to believe. At the start of our nation, our libel laws were meant to protect against politically damaging slander and misinformation, but the molasses-efficiency of our court system, unfortunately, has too little bearing on public opinion. And before the Institute, it was a slandered man's only purported system of defense.

Whether you believe it or not, the shelf-life of public memory cannot wait out legal disputes. When the Congressman first hatched his idea for the Institute, he bluntly said it was a response to our court's inefficiency in dealing with misinformation: "We must change the legal code. We don't have time to take so much time."

The public applauded. Of course they did. Before Sherman's rise,

America's confusion ran rampant and seeped much farther than our social media feeds. A confused public quickly becomes an angry one, and an angry public frequently degrades into a violent one. Americans have been pleading and begging— asking nicely with sugar on top—for some solution to their confusion for years. The only two asks were reliable, accessible information in order to make informed decisions, and for liars and cheats to be punished. They've (justifiably) had enough of the games, enough of political skirting, enough of inaction. And thus, in spite of Congress's inertia, the Institute was born.

Congressman Sherman sure did one thing right—he listened and actually tried to come up with a solution, even though I think it has too many risks. His answer was simple: take away libel and slander from the courts, and give it a faster turnaround. To create a system of accountability for the information supplied to the public. It's grown more since, and we now must take comfort or discomfort in the fact that the Institute for Information Dissemination will watch what we say and how we say it.

And that's what puts independent journalism in such a predicament.

Considering that journalism can be viewed as the "fourth branch of government," public distrust will inevitably leak into the other branches. Without fortifying some type of dam to halt the (sometimes) unfounded condemnation of public officials, the rushing cascade of public discontent has inevitably waterfalled to the Legislative, Judicial, and Executive branches. Members of Congress, reasonably, could not risk anarchy. It was this media discontent compounded with the North Korean DoubleDown Fiasco in the *elections* of 2026 that caused so many to side with Sherman in the notorious, "Misstep" midterm election of 2030. And yet, perhaps even unknown to Sherman's army of MiMs, the idea of forming a research institute gained more and more traction, speeding through the information superhighways, garnering support from Tucson to Tallahassee, all in the blink of an eye. The public, drunk on the potential for reliable, conveniently packaged information, was gung-ho on the idea, sick and tired of the "lies." The bill passed before we could shake the hangover.

The American public's distrust in the news media is not a new phenomenon, nor one that should have been ignored. Just under twenty years ago, at the beginning of the "Fake News" era of politics, the trending distrust began its downward spiral. According to a 2016 *Gallup Poll*, only 32% of Americans posited that they have a "great deal" or even a "fair amount" of trust in the U.S. mass media. This figure was pitiful then, and things only raced downhill from there. Editors-in-chief, while perplexed, allowed themselves to be placated by the public's aberrant, occasional bumps of confidence, and chalked up the chasm of distrust to a passing milieu of discontent with the political scene. This stance was as lazy as it was ignorant.

But, what do they care so long as their publications had subscribers? Sure, so long as the publishers and webmasters got some coin, it didn't matter. And why would it? Money is money. Lower trust doesn't necessarily mean lower subscription rates. Sometimes it meant more. Angry, impassioned headlines meant more clicks, and more clicks meant more money from advertisers.

And just how the press was to go about solving accusations of "Fake News," I do not know. But the media certainly had their hands full. In tandem with these "Fake News" accusations, the media were forced to spar with politicians quick to vilify and scapegoat their constituents' confusion, seeking an excuse for their own ineptitude, backtracking and waffling instead of taking accountability. The result has been a bloodied-and-beaten press who were prone to attack back, as a cornered animal would. Alas, it's much easier to point fingers than to have a sincere moment of self-reflection.

Unfortunately, to make the plight of the floundering press industry even worse, the American public tends to have idealistic demands of journalists, demands that sabotage credibility and foster belligerence toward the information trade if unmet. The political sphere happily joined in with the public lament over press credibility, adding insult to injury. This unhappy union only served to spark smoking embers of distrust into conflagration. Too bad the politicians' schemes backfired and caused the public to distrust them, too.

Now, here's what I think the American public needs to know about journalism: When we talk about credibility and reliability in the press, the typical rallying cry against "bad" journalism is that it is not "objective." When a particular piece or news outlet does not succumb to this objective ideal, the denounced article then propagates "bias" and therefore should be deemed not credible, or worse, dishonest. This misperception has terrible potential to further boggle the public, who likely will cling to the first source they read (my main concern with this gov't-sanctioned information streamline).

Too, the word "objective" has been tossed and thrown and cussed around so much that it has nearly lost all significance. It has become a moot cliché, with many dissenters using the word without truly knowing what it means, never mind what it means in relation to journalism. True objectivity, or our closest synonym, neutrality, has much more to do with reporting methods and integrity than tone and language use, but the public seems to think a strong tone automatically equals un-credible reporting. I have seen when news outlets attempt to cater to this impractical and morally perverse ideal of faux neutrality; the outcome is not that they gain credibility, but in fact lose it. Plus, lest we've forgotten, reporters have emotions, and to demand journalists mask those emotions may ironically cause them to be dishonest in their prose, robotically veiling what they believe to be important on account of a skewed, unrealistic public command.

I will say it as I always have: objective does not mean balanced. All opinions are not created equal. And so airtime in a piece should be reflected in this critical vein.

Regardless of the somewhat unfounded public discontent, I want to stress that when we consider the press as an information trade, it is then a service to the public, so, regardless of the unachievable demands laden on the industry, it is our duty to try and manage expectations and mollify slashes to credibility. For if the public thinks journalism un-credible, or our services unsatisfactory, we certainly aren't performing our main function: to inform, accurately and honestly. It'd be like going to a bar for your favorite whiskey, but the bartender keeps watering it down behind your back. You would not return to that bar and would seek to consume elsewhere.

Many have cheered at the Institute's founding, and I see why, but I still call for a recourse, call for renewed chance for the press to prove itself credible, call for the journalism industry to better cater towards its consumers, but for said consumers to scrutinize their expectations of journalists, too. If not, a government-sanctioned information source could become a juggernaut paralyzing any chance the press might have for redemption. We must have options, must not be seduced by the first things that we read.

I wish this weren't so, my readers, I really do, but here we are. And if you're looking for somewhere to point your finger, look no further. You can point it right at me.

The Doctor has a weekly column, "Malpractice," for The Washington Post. *See more of his work, here.*

This conversation is moderated according to The Post's community rules. Please read the rules before joining the discussion. Send feedback about the comments section here.

Top Comments (150k)   Viewing Options ▾

Shalese Grayson   3 hours ago
a sober piece taking credit. We thank you for your honesty as always, good doctor. I hope your wish comes true.

Like 👍 10.9k   Reply ↰   Link ∞   Report ⚑

anonymous   3 hours ago
That's right! It is all your freaking faults!!! Now we're all screwed because you couldn't get your act together. Thanks a lot. Unbelievable.

Like 👍 10 4k   Reply ↰   Link ∞   Report ⚑

Heather Lorraine   2 hours ago
While you make some solid points, doc, we can't forget the unearthly ignorance harbored by some of our "fellow Americans". Who in their right mind would think that a government-sanctioned press is a "good idea"? They've put their trust in the wrong place. Truly the epitome of "mistrust".

Like 👍 9.1k   Reply ↰   Link ∞   Report ⚑

anonymous   1 hours ago
yes, borne out of your incompetence, yes! No need to worry, no, of course, no! The Institute will come to save you all. Vile sinners!

Like 👍 8.9k   Reply ↰   Link ∞   Report ⚑

Burt Bobson   1 hours ago
ugh. We're so screwed.

Chapter 4: The Public Responds in My Dream-Mind

Location unknown
Date unknown, sometime in mid-August 2035

To a pea-brained, dreaming sewer scamp:

Something odd, something strange, something I can't explain happened to me a short time ago. I can see what I can't see, what I shouldn't see. Who are they?

Sometimes my brain-mind takes me places I don't want to be, and it hurts, pounds and pummels my head to pulp. I keep getting flashbacks. I don't know why, but my eyes get all blurry and sometimes my little feet-claws hurt, too, and then I'm somewhere else and it's not so dark anymore.

I can hear voices and see people I don't know. It's scary but my doctor tells me that I need to "write down as much as you can, dear friend. It's truly helping." He gets mad and sad when I tell him where I go, but he says that I shouldn't worry and that they are just dreams, but I think he's lying. If they're dreams why can I feel and see and think and hear in them?

Last night I went to a small liberal college in Northern Virginia in my dream.

Various locations in the United States
Mid-October 2033

Before the students attend class, the halls might have buzzed with manic chatter. They all talked so fast:

"Did you hear?"

"Did you hear?"

"Did you hear?"

"What?"

"No, I haven't...who cares anyway?"

"I *know*."

"Congress just opened a new department."

"Dude. This shit is serious."

"How can our legislators let this happen?"

"So? Why do you look like you're gonna vom?"

"It's not like there's anything we can do about it. Plus, I like that Sherman guy. He's all about truth."

"We have to try and shut this shit down. It was that fraud Sherman. They think this will make us trust them *more?*"

"They're going to streamline what we can and can't hear— I'm fucking afraid."

"We can't just roll over and die like that, man."

"Who knows, maybe Sherman's onto something and it will be legit. Remember how we had to vote *twice* a few years ago?"

"Fucking North Korea. No, fuck us for not knowing it would happen."

"Can't trust the gov't. Can't trust the news. You got any bright ideas?"

"But what if it *does* drown everything out? What's going to happen to journalism?"

"Can Congress even do that? Is it even legal?"

"They've changed the laws man."

"They keep saying that they're not the enemy of the press. That they want to work with them. What's better than accuracy reports on elected officials anyway? Keep 'em from lying their asses off."

"How can they be so stupid?"

"You think people will be dumb enough to believe them?"

"And they think we're dumb enough to believe that?"

"I don't know what to think anymore."

"When they're scared and confused, people will believe just about anything."

"They do, apparently."

After the bell, a teacher tried to calm her vociferous class.

"Quiet down now. Hey, quiet down," the teacher said.

"What can we do?"

"The free press is going to *die*. It's going to *die*."

"My pop said he's glad about it. My whole family voted for Sherman, and his support is all over America. Why are y'all freaking out? He's going to change the code for the greater good!"

"Yeah. It's not like we could trust the press anyway, bunch of lying bastards. Congressman Sherman has known that from the start. He doesn't even trust the government."

"Seriously folks, you need to be quiet. Let me take attendance and we can talk about this in a minute."

That did not console the agitated crowd. The frustrated instructor sighed and counted out her students. "How the hell am I going to defuse this situation?" she thought. At least that's what I thought.

After I saw the frazzled instructor quarrel with her students to quiet down, I saw and heard people I don't know in coffee shops and bookstores and administrative offices and Fortune 500 companies and startups say:

"This is all bullshit. No way I'm reading not-so-secret propaganda for the government. Accuracy reports? Published *by the government on the government*? You've got to be kidding me."

"Finally! Something we can *actually* trust."

"Who wouldn't want a public-record FBI? People in power think they can get away with anything!"

"I don't know, dude. It's like a dystopian novel."

"I don't read the news anyway. I guess this isn't the time to start."

"How can you not be mad? How can you just let this go? Who in the fuck voted for this?"

"Didn't they say that they'll be working with the press? Why wouldn't we want the most reliable info from the best in the business? Plus, it had overwhelming public support. Give it a shot. Sherman's got guts to stand up to others in government. Change the code!"

"Why can't people understand that the media *are*? It's not one single thing!"

"That's the damn problem."

"There must be some agenda for this...ugh why do I even vote? This shit sucks."

"Good riddance! I'm tired of not knowing what to think anymore. Tired of politicians getting away with whatever in the hell they want!"

"Time to pack my bags."

"Thank God we live in the greatest nation on earth."

"This place fucking sucks."

"It doesn't seem like they're hiding anything."

"They're hiding something. It's all right there."

In the depths of newsrooms and some unconvinced corners of Congress, I only heard one thing:

"We're fucked."

And sometime later (I don't know how long, don't ask me right now) right now, right now! Some of the rabble had been consoled, some had not. Some had taken each release from the Institute at face value, and some had viciously denied its veracity, citing as many studies and articles as they could. Fools! Don't they know what they'll do to you, what they'll do to your minds? Help me, doctor. Help me.

Soon though, echoing my doctor's concerns, the number of news articles waned, as did their credibility in the eyes of the public on account of the Institute's aggressive agenda. I feel like it's my fault, but I'm not sure. Sherman…what was it about Sherman? Not sure of much anymore. I just feel something bad about it, like I'm in trouble, like I'm about to be punished. Thanks to my doctor and his papers, I do know that the Institute played while the press was away. No one watching! No one watching except me. *They're coming.*

Chapter 5: Where am I?

A Rat's Diary #1

Location unknown
Date unknown, sometime in mid-August 2035

To a little rodent man with gray hairs on his head and gray hairs in his beard:

I have found some refuge for now, but my little rodent mind keeps running away from me. It's been happening more and more and more. Thank the gods for my doctor. And for these two! No, yes! Hush now. Hush. Stop it! Ouch, my head.

Remember what they told you. They told you to journal, told me "it'll clear your head, little professor, to focus on one mind, and shut out the rest. Remember *who you are*." Journaling helps keep me focused, helps me drown out all the other sounds and people and voices that aren't really here. Why won't they listen to me? *They're coming.*

From the videos and the papers and the digital screen-prints and all the words echoing in the chambers in my head, it sounds and looks and feels like no one is really listening to anyone at all anymore, never mind if they ever had before, and people are just more observant now with the web-ties knotting up everyone's thoughts all the time, so maybe my case isn't as peculiar as I think? We think?

How can I know what's real if I don't know whom or what or how or why to believe? Secretary Sherman thinks he's found the answer. And maybe he has. Everyone is yelling and barking at each other and saying that they're right, trying to be louder than everyone else.

But still Secretary Sherman found a way to be the loudest of all. He has some way to get people to believe him. He does seem sincere.

Wait. No time! I must remember, but I can't get too mad at myself because reflecting is a good way to remember. My doctor told me that in one of our meetings.

Start at the beginning, yes! How else could we begin? *Remember who you are.* Then they'll listen. Yes, then they will. I think they will if I remember. Try to think. How did I get here?

I remember that when I was running and scampering out from the big gray building, I must have been wetter than a tubby guy with the meat sweats after a grease-caked plate of sweet sausage. The fog comes and goes, so I might be bad at telling you what happened and how and why. This is the first time I've really tried to record my own thoughts from my own mind, from my own memory...ouch! Damn it! No... Stay here.

My head hurts so badly, so badly it hurts all the time. Please. Make it stop. Should I write about my feelings and who I am now? Will that help? I guess. Just don't stop or you'll go back and you need to remember or else he won't listen and if he won't listen then they will come to get us and there will be no time, no, no time at all for "I told you so"s or "Why didn't you listen"s.

I've been swearing more than I think I used to. I think. I like it though. It feels good. While saying bad words makes me a naughty boy, in their sweet, sexy sonics, vulgarities have little nibbles of truth. And I want that. Need that.

A little rat nibbling, yes!

As my back clung desperately to the Institute's big gray building, the sweat stung my beady eyes and got my blazer all wet under the pepperbush. I must have then crouched with my palms in the dirt, desperately trying to keep my mouth hole shut. While I couldn't think, couldn't parse through the blaring loud in my head (all those dreaded voices stinging and coming all at once!), there was one thing I did know: *They were coming. She was after me.* Yes! Is she coming now? No! Hush. *Remember who you are.*

I remember I had to breathe—"respire" is a word I used to say I think—very carefully. One puff of air too loud, or one naughty splat of sputum to scratch my gullet, and I was done for, finit, caput, as the gangsters say, "a goner." No coughing for little rats.

The episodes come and go, come and go, shifting, amorphous and cascading free, bubbling up. I can't help it and I can't stop them. Clinging for clarity. I write as fast as I can. "Kaleidoscopic" is a word I think I knew and know for it. Forgive me. The only sense I know is true is the touch of my greasy fingertips. Good thing it's not so hard to see with your hands as you might think. It's coming back. Yes! Hehehe, the little rat gets away. I sure showed that devil bitch!

My escape scene must have looked like a cliché: sirens, searchlights, the whole thing, man! Yes! No, I almost feel craven telling you. But someone *must know*. The doctor needs to help me and my little feet claws. Doctor, please. Why haven't you come? Shhh!

Right, sirens and searchlights. I must have looked down at my hands through saline-dripped lenses, and clenched my palms. I had to test if they were still numb. I remember, I remember! I remember fighting my brain-mind as I passed each watchtower that guarded the deep recesses of that terrible building with the terrible underground, watchtowers that guarded the subterranean pit where she does things no one can know and no one can talk about. Not even Mr. Sherman. Maybe he could've stopped it. Hush, hush, we mustn't let them know that we know else we all become naughty, nasty little rodent rats. My head...

I think I must have said as I was counting the guard towers perched on the corners of the building: "shhhhhHHHHHh-hhh, you fiend! You little sweet rodent. They'll get those little pink feet-claws, they will! At this rate, you'll get us all killed! Killed!"

I looked down at my feet, noticed one was bleeding. I don't think it's still bleeding, but it still hurts.

While he, she, and they may have shouted, my innermost brain-mind surely did bring up a point: there's a rat catcher on the loose. That's something I don't think I'll forget. I remember getting dizzy, remember thinking back to being hung like meat, pokes and prods and that voice tormenting me, ignoring my screams, enjoying my screams. I wasn't sure where I was going, but I was sure that I didn't think I wanted to go back. Please. Not again. Just listen, please. Where's my doctor?

What I did know was that I should keep stepping, well, crawling forward since the spotlights hurt my beady little eyes. No! Not beady. No. Yes! You are a little rat. Ouch...

The glaring thermo-search beams kept sweeping the same way: thirty feet to the right, thirty feet to the left, with a delicate three-foot gap between each trajectory's diameter. I think they were computer-programmed to scan the barren field inside their iron-fenced compound at 17 seconds per sweep (I watched them so, so many times before I felt safe enough to scamper), and then they would stop and wait before sweeping again. There was a little dark gap between each light. Lucky me! I must've counted the, I think I would call them, "periodic" sweeps, thirty times before I picked up my sweaty little palms to skulk to the next gap between lights.

As I danced like a furtive field mouse scurrying from hawks that swooped above, I could hear the echoing of the loudspeaker. It was her voice, the voice of that devil woman, the woman in charge of the underground:

"ATTENTION SECURITY AND NON-SECURITY PERSONNEL OF THE INSTITUTE. GRADE 5 BREACH. RUN RODENT RUN. I REPEAT. GRADE 5 BREACH. RUN RODENT RUN. THIS IS NOT A DRILL. I REPEAT. THIS IS NOT A DRILL. ALL FEDERAL INFORMATION BATTALION LIEUTENANTS, MAN YOUR POSITIONS. RUN RODENT RUN. ALL PERSONNEL SHOULD BE ON HIGH ALERT. RODENT MUST BE EXTERMINATED ON SIGHT."

Her voice did help me forget being so hungry. I couldn't remember the last time I'd eaten, but that was the least of my worries once I'd finally made it to the outskirts of the Institute's compound. Remember. Mole-like. Not a rat, no. A mole.

Like I said, 15-foot iron fences, and damn it they almost looked medieval. I guess the only way to control the future is to tame and train the past. These walls had guard towers fashioned at each corner, manned by the best snipers money could buy. Wait I already talked about the towers. Ouch...ugh my head...

Rocking there in the dirt, anxiously counting the lights, I imagined the lieutenants' hawk scopes scanning the dirt beneath my feet, each sentry gunner salivating for me, salivating to exterminate the naughty little rat. I think they wanted to impress *her*. Well, turns out, their drool had nothing on me, since I was at the base of the fence, underneath one of the towers. Ha! Fooled them! They couldn't see me under the tenth tower.

I must have thought fast at the base of the fence, but I was terribly confused. Still am terribly confused. Hush! No time. *They're coming.*

I remembered and saw and reminded and co-minded and felt and said all at once. My mind boggled, addled, and blurry. I remember that I didn't have anything to climb the wall. Silly little rat, rodents can't fly! That's when the thought struck me like a bully's clenched fist—but of course...my belt...

I was lucky enough to be captured with my most expensive pleather belt, adorned with a curved steel buckle that reads: "Foxy." (I still have it. I like to look at it. I think someone gave it to me).

It reminded me that I shouldn't climb like a monkey, but burrow like a fox. I started to dig with the buckle. Clawing through the heavy dirt at the base of the wall, I was nervous. I cocked my head around every thirty seconds or so. I can't remember how many "RUN RODENT RUN"s it took for me to finally get on other side of the wall, but after I did, damn it, the rodent sure did run.

The voices still ring in my head like a surgeon planted them there even as I write. I have to write them down. I can still hear the simmering sounds of her brass-like voice (but not just hers! No!). I remember but don't want to. My head gets all cloudy when I think of her. I still hear them, still hear her! Devil woman!

I must keep my voice in these dreams. I need to keep my thoughts clear in these dreams. I am not them and they are not me. They are not me and I am not them. They are not mole-rats.

Now it's getting dark again...stop...help me...plea—

Chapter 6: An Amphibious Coercion

3rd Floor of a Call Center Contracted by The Institute
Date unknown, sometime in 2034

I see a desk with papers primped and stacked meticulously: a single puff of air could spell chaos for the pile. A pale hand with an odd tint of green reaches up to fix a pair of gargantuan-framed glasses. The hands look manicured; the nails haven't a scuff and the fingers not a callous.

The thick lenses of his glasses are bringing on a headache...why can I see through his eyes? Why can I feel a bit of sweat drip-drop down the back of my neck (our neck)?

Blindly, his arm extends, reaching for the office phone, but then he stops, reaches again, stops again. More sweat. Drip. Drip. Saline beads lose their grip and slide down his oily skin, wetting the fabric that sits too tightly around his neck.

Hush now. I must watch.

The man looked down at the primped papers. A sheet bearing official importance, seals and titles, stamped "CONFIDENTIAL" in big and bold, red letters sits at the top. A sweat droplet plunged onto the paper, its wispy tendrils gradually blotching the letters "I-A-L" into a red smear.

Shhh! Someone's coming...

An important-looking woman walked right up to the gray cubicle mostly barren but for the small macrophotography shot of a salamander on a lily pad and a few plaques recognizing good performance. The woman placed her hand bracingly on the seated man's shoulder.

"Mr. Frog? Might I ask...is something wrong?"

"No, ma'am. Nothing wrong at all," the spectacled frogman said, casually. "Oh. Why do you ask? Just a bout of nausea from some bad caviar last night at my sushi place," he went on without waiting for an answer.

"Hmm. So that's why you look so green. But what concerns me is that you've fallen short of your quota every day since last week. And today, you've only confirmed three Institute recruits. Why is that?"

"The nausea..."

"I don't mean to sound curt, Earl, but this is the fourth time this month you've claimed an ailment as excuse for poor performance. The excuses are becoming, well, inexcusable. I can't have my best worker withering away. Our business with the Institute...I, well, I count on you and your recruitments, Earl. I need her to keep trusting our high performance. We need this contract."

"I apologize, Ms. Dipper. It's been a tough month for me, and sometimes my emotions bring out the worst. A cruel gift from mind to body. Scapegoating," Mr. Earl Frog said, trying to force a laugh and lighten the mood.

His boss had never been angry with him before, he thought, worrying as he looked over to the seven plaques proudly plastered to his cubicle walls that read, "Employee of the Month," "Best in the Business," "Top Tadpole of the Team," among others. He'd only been at Dipper's company for seven months and sixteen days.

"Then you must go to a doctor, Mr. Frog, and not waste my nor the Institute's time. You're still on the payroll, nauseous or not. But surely you know this already," Ms. Dipper said, her tone lined with unsubtle condescension.

"No need for the quacks' advice, Ms. Dipper, not me," he replied casually, conscious that without his continued recruitment success, Dipper's business would fail. No other callers had his track record of Institute referrals, and since he'd been hired, Dipper and Co. had taken on a work load that was hardly sustainable without him. The second-best recruiter had barely half of Earl's numbers. "I'll get back on track. You'll see. Frogs are known to have speedy recoveries. It's well-documented."

"I hope that document has been under the scrutiny of an Institute Accuracy Report. See that you do hop back on track."

Earl took this as the conversation's conclusion, and began to reposition his chair, leaning back.

"When I started this company in 2033, you'd be so kind to remember, that I recognized and jumped on an opportunity to contract for the Institute for Information Dissemination. Such a big project and so much government funding! They needed bodies on the ground to help with the Institute accuracy reports. No piece of data can be published without validation from four unrelated outside parties. Do you know how much manpower that takes? A big-time job—not for the faint of heart," Dipper said, puffing out her chicken breast with pride. This hen knew crowing wasn't made only for roosters. *Cock-a-doodle-doo!*

Our frogman sighed, trapped in his cubicle-prison, having heard this hen crow before, many times. And yet, Dipper's anxiety-provoked tirades now being directed at him made Earl nervous. Did his boss know about his budding doubts around the company mission, doubts he'd tried to keep close to his amphibian heart?

"I knew such a large endeavor would need help, and perhaps more importantly, need help outside of the government's direct purview and the Justice Department's bimonthly, constitutional investigations," Ms. Dipper paraded on. "The Institute would need some little guys to do some of the grunt work, under the radar. The only catch is that while the Deputy pays well, she's one tough cookie. If we don't maintain our weekly recruit quota, our contract is nixed and we're thrown to the gutter. You know this. Our business relies on a constant flow: a copious supply of knowledge for an important demand of useful facts and friends in high places. But that doesn't mean the supply wants to meet that demand. My employees must understand, embrace, and embody the values of our work for the greater good. We're holding people accountable. Dirty, vile citizens must give recompense for their treachery. Must be held accountable for their lies!" she exclaimed, her eyes bulging with passion and desperation like a crazed lioness on the hunt after weeks of scarcity.

"Accountable for their lies, yes," Earl said in tandem, sarcastically.

"Oh! So, you *do* remember?"

"Yes ma'am, you certainly have informed the entire office. I remember. You know, a frog has an excellent memory," he said vacantly, clenching his fists underneath his cubicle desk, outside the boss's view.

"Peculiar. An excellent memory, but you still forget what we're doing here. Or at least *why*."

Earl wanted to shout. Why? To make you your money, that's why. But he sat silent, instead waiting for the moment he'd be saved from his boss's tired speech and be able to return to work. Ms. Dipper waited too, her bloated eyeballs locked with Earl's and her lips slightly parted, revealing yellowing, grinded teeth. Her expression made Earl uncomfortable, so he chose to say nothing and pretend he'd not just seen a woman who looked possessed.

"Not a croak? Hmm. Then I just have one more question, Mr. Frog."

Earl waited some more and then glanced up from his desk, finding it harder and harder to mask his annoyance.

"...yes?"

"Are you trying to *fuck me*?"

"Wuh—huh?"

"You heard me. Are you, Earl Eustace Frog, trying to *fuck me*?"

Earl was confused. He'd never really tried to fuck anyone before. At least he didn't think he had. He was no cocking rooster. Frogs can't mate with hens.

"...no?"

"Ah! Well good! Because it sure as hell seemed like it, my boy!" Dipper said, slapping Earl's back, hard. "The Institute has exceedingly high expectations of outside contractors, especially contractors like us who report directly to the Deputy Secretary. If it were up to me, she would be the one in charge. Not that idealistic—"

"—twat with impossible notions who doesn't have a practical bone in his body, Sherman. Yes. I know."

"Thank God for our Deputy Secretary, Dee. This work is imperative for her Information Gathering Initiative. An initiative, I might add, that is of Grade—"

"—Grade Four Security Clearance. Yes, I remember," Earl replied, even more annoyed now. "We had a serious vetting process, Ms. Dipper."

"Then you best not forget! I want to see your dedication to this company, to the Institute," his boss said, peering.

Earl figured it best to get to work right away before he said something he'd regret. He checked the first paper atop the primped pile, and began to dial another client—wasn't this why his boss so ruthlessly went on and on and on?

"Bup-bup-bup, Earl. Allow me a pop-quiz. How many referral clients per day does the Deputy require of us in order to maintain our contract? How many clients must we recruit for the Institute?"

"Ninety-seven," Earl said, robotically.

"Precisely," Dipper said, struggling to keep her voice from rising in both velocity and volume. "So, without my most efficient recruiter, how in hell am I supposed to keep thirty-seven employees paid and insured, all who benefit from a generous 401K-match, when I have a floundering little frog with a damn tummy ache?! I need to stay in the Deputy's good graces, damn it!" the boss woman said and pounded Earl's desk, causing the primped papers to fall into disarray.

Perhaps because of his boss's anger, and not despite it, Earl felt he had the upper hand. Earl surmised that Dipper's boss, the Deputy Secretary for Information, was clearly not happy with Dipper and Co., and though Earl had never met her, the Deputy had an ominous reputation and little patience for incompetence. She was the greased cog spinning the Institute's engines, and had no time for mis-fitting gears slowing her operations down. This must have been why Ms. Dipper was on edge. Still, why overplay his cards? He couldn't lose this job, at least not until he had something else figured out. Plus, Dipper and Co. paid well, and on commission. How else was he to pay for his sick salamander's expensive medicine? Ms. Dipper never cared about his salamander, Salvatore, though. Sally was a dumb amphibian, in her eyes.

He stared at his boss, blankly, then gestured toward the phones.

"Good idea. Get on the damn phones, Earl. No more excuses. If you don't reach your recruitment quota for the week by the end of the day—you're fired. No severance package. Nothing. Gone. I don't like getting fucked," Ms. Dipper said, pointedly.

"My entire *week's* recruitment quota? It's only Tuesday! What if clients hang up and refuse?" Earl pleaded. Even in his best weeks, Earl's call-to-recruitment ratio hovered around fifty-seven percent. And though Institute recruitment was a nascent field, his performance broke industry records. It was why he was Top Tadpole.

Ms. Dipper turned and walked away, refusing to hear another word.

His boss's acerbic comments shook my new acquaintance, mentally and physically. It seems as if the two had been at odds before this incident. In fact, I think Earl resented how hypocritical and ridiculous Ms. Dipper tended to be, ridiculous in her faux altruism about employees' benefit-packages, and hypocritical since Dipper ignored the rampant rumors of what happened to recruits after their office sent them to the Institute.

"There's no proof they've been forced to do anything against their will. They voted for this damn Institute, after all. We must not forget the common good," Dipper would say if anyone ever brought up the taboo subject. So long as the company was successful, she didn't care to entertain "vicious, half-baked rumors" about the Deputy Secretary and her methods for the Information Gathering Initiative. Not an ounce of truth! Certainly not. Earl did not care to hide his rolling eyes whenever his boss preached like that.

But recently, Earl felt that there just might be something to those rumors about the Deputy Secretary. It could no longer be ignored that there may be something peculiar, no, dangerous, about her methods of coercion. He felt it deep in his froggy soul. Heck, the Deputy's protocol mandated his *own methods*, so each day it was getting harder and harder for Earl to lie to himself that the Institute wasn't forcing citizens to do government bidding. And that he wasn't part of that coercion.

For instance, there were but few recruitment methods signed off by the Institute for their Liaisons for Institute Escort Office branches (Dipper and Co. proudly represented

Branch #43.28b). Recruiters were only allowed to home in on four baseline elements in order to convince citizens to join the Information Gathering Initiative: patriotism; prestige from crowd acceptance (tribalism); distaste for the government; or (the worst in Earl's mind) *shame* from hiding something from a loved one or neighbor. So regimented were the Deputy Secretary's methods that each potential recruit would have bold-lettered signage in the right-hand corner of their call sheet which labelled their category or some combination of the four. A recruitment call from a citizen accuracy report labelled, "PATRIOTISM AND PRESTIGE" might go like this:

"Hello, Miss Reed (or Mr. Reynolds or Mrs. Smith or Miss Sanchez), may I steal just a few moments of your time in order for you to serve our great country? This is Earl Eustace Frog, your local representative in the Liaisons for Institute Escort Office."

"Oh…uh…hi. What can I do for you?"

"Oh, it's not what you can do for me, but for America. You are a patriot, are you not, Miss Reed? Tired of being misinformed?"

"Well, yea, but who isn't? I supported Sherman and his INFO Act or whatever, but why are you calling me? Isn't this *your job?*"

"Ma'am, we need thoughtful citizens like yourself to help with the Institute's Information Gathering Initiative. It is of paramount importance to Secretary Sherman that everyone is on board. We want the public to be informed, but we can't do it alone. We are a government department, but this is America! The United States Government has always been, always is, and always will be for, by, and of the people."

"Everybody knows that. Don't get me wrong, I want that. Really. But not everyone's cut out for politics. Jane, you know the homely gal from down the street, she became obsessed after she joined. Said she talked to a cute little frogman." Earl smiled at this imagined detail, fancying himself an adorable tadpole swim-swimming in the ponds of his youth. He, she or they might continue, "Anything else I can do for you? I have to go get back to work."

"Just one more moment and then I can let you go, but first I want to thank you for being honest about your concern for Jane. Honesty is at the crux of the Institute's mission. Our movement against misinformation fires people up sometimes. It can be hard to see a friend switch on you so quickly, especially when you've never seen why yourself. You know what they say, 'seeing is believing'."

"I guess."

Once Earl managed to get the recruit to hear his speech on honesty, recruitment rate skyrocketed to 78%.

"You're a godly man, Miss Reed?"

"Church every Sunday, but can't say I'm perfect. Try my best not to sin, hurt others."

"That's all any of us can do. Do you mind me asking how many of your congregation have joined the Information Gathering Initiative? If any?"

A misleading question, and unnecessary. The call sheets always had the numbers.

"Well, I don't know the number exactly off the top of my head."

"Take a guess, then. Please," Earl might say.

"Ah, I guess about half. Maybe more."

Maybe more was the correct answer.

"And you trust the judgement of those in your congregation? They're smart folk? Wouldn't join something dastardly or hurtful to this great country?"

"No. I guess not. No."

"Certainly not! And why would they? They just want to help make sure everyone's informed and not being lied to by those shameless politicians and media barons."

Often there would be a moment of silence while the potential recruit reflected. But then, almost as if by clockwork, they'd gradually open up their malleable, I-hope-they-let-me-sit-with-them-please-like-me minds to take the plunge in the Institute abyss (if they had yet to hang up, his recruitment rate hovered around an impressive 88%):

"You got that right. Earl, was it?"

"Yes, ma'am. But you can think of me as a patriot on a mission, one who trusts his neighbors, just like you. If you decide to join, as a member of the Information Gathering Initiative, you'll get special insider updates before they're released, an official membership certificate, and comfort knowing you've joined the tooth-and-nail fight against misinformation. If I can be so bold, by joining you'd be able to say you were on the right side of history when your grandkids ask you," Earl might say, pointedly, sensing he'd netted another, even if only in his amphibian imagination.

"All right, damn it. Sign me up. I know my partner and I were tired of not knowing what to believe before you all came around. Seems only natural I help out."

Those were the easy ones, though, and Earl had always thought it strange that most of his potential recruits mentioned how much people changed after they joined the Deputy Secretary's public team. The change always seemed to be stark, unnatural, they said.

And so, with unnatural change on his mind, he'd done a bit of reflection and investigation on what happens to his recruits after they arrived for their initiation to the Deputy Secretary's Information Gathering Initiative. Unsurprisingly, not all recruits seemed gung-ho to help the Institute when Earl first spoke to them, but when he called a week later for the mandatory follow-up, they had only sunshine-and-rainbow comments to share, chirping praise. It was almost as if their suspicions had been wiped clean. Odd. And those Americans on Earl's call sheets just *had to be onto something* when they said their friends and neighbors changed after joining. What was that Deputy up to?

First of all, why would a Deputy Secretary—in a high-level federal department, no less—want to meet with Joe Flaherty, 47, truck driver and father of three? Why in the world would the government need to give an accuracy report for any Joe

Shmoe? It's not like she had constituents of her own; Sherman appointed the high-ranking staff.

There *must be* some merit to the rampant conspiracies about the Institute for Information Dissemination, some merit to the rumors that the Institute had cameras and microphones and undercover agents roaming the streets in all 50 states and territories...right? How else would the neatly primped stacks of citizen accuracy reports arrive to Earl's desk each morning at eight o'clock, sharp? He always thought the recruitment calls helped to verify information in the Official Institute Accuracy Reports on major media outlets or on politicians, and sometimes he could clearly see how the individual could help verify information, but recently Earl started to notice that details from his previous recruitment calls were showing up on his new ones. And these people had no clear connections to anyone of note. The details were spilled to him accidently, details bordering on gossip and hearsay, details that couldn't reasonably be proven unless you knew the person intimately. Like, "Goes to bed at approximately 9:30pm on weeknights, except on Tuesdays to watch *Late Night with Billy Birdie*" or "Active crotchetier, only uses primary colors," or "Says they enjoy craft beer but usually buys Bud Light," or "Average text message response time is seventeen minutes, but response times to mother considerably longer."

Citizens valued privacy. If only they knew...if only he could *prove* the Institute was up to no good under the influence of Sherman's Deputy...

But still, some of the rumors had to be exaggerated, right? The whispers were much too farfetched, and only aired on sensational web programs and conspiracy Reddit pages. Earl thought it ridiculous that some people would think the government could be so bold, would be so willing to unabashedly torture its own citizens and surveil their every which move.

Yet he couldn't quite ignore when, just last week, *The New York Times'* article, "To Obtain Information, Man Strapped to Metal Table and Electrocuted by New Gov't Dept," was taken down just *two minutes* after its initial publication. The article made Earl feel hideously unsettled, that the darkest rumors might be true. Sure, *The New York Times* issued a public apology claiming they'd been hacked by conspirators, but when had *The Times* ever been hacked before? Even their intracity comrades, *The New York Post,* released a headline later that day (also abruptly taken down) which said, "THEY LIE! *TIMES'* JOURNALIST STANDS BY REDACTED ARTICLE." He kept looking in the next few days for more coverage, but he couldn't find any. Later he saw that the *New York Times'* journalist who worked on the article had a change of heart, and had happily taken up residence as an Information Investigator for the Institute a month later. The evidence for foul play was mounting.

These people are dirty. Dirty is bad enough, but to be dirty, have connections and use them for influence, manipulation... well, that's an invocation of the devil, Earl thought, brooding in his cubicle. He still had not made any recruitment calls. He hated this job more by the day. He was no longer the glistening, froggy-eyed novice of seven months ago.

It all smelled far too fishy. Distrust was building in Earl's gut; the deep stench of suspicion seeped into his nostrils, stinging his senses to action. But still, what could he do? It's not as if they were breaking the law. The Institute had *changed the law*, and the public had given them permission to do it. Worse yet, as has been the case time and again, any investigative morsel published by the dissenting press would no doubt be nixed by an Official Institute Media Accuracy Report, given a "D" rating.

And if his suspicions were true, the public would be heart-broken. Contrary to popular opinion, Earl suspected that Secretary Sherman wouldn't care even if there were foul play. Whenever journalists accused Sherman of Institute overreach, his responses either seemed too calculated, or too much of a blatant disavowal. He'd say, "The Institute is a non-partisan bureau of the highest integrity," or "Didn't you just see last week that we gave our own report a 'B/B+' rating on account of insufficient evidence? Sheesh! How can anyone win with you people? We're even investigating ourselves! Stop questioning the right of Americans to access reliable information."

Even though Earl had come to hate Ms. Dipper, his boss was right when she complained that Sherman was a little too into himself. Earl pegged Sherman as self-righteous and shallow; he suspected Sherman was too busy preaching lofty speeches to notice what was happening right under his nose. Sherman wouldn't, *couldn't*, believe that his brain-child had devolved into a propagandistic tool to torture and coerce the public. And even if the Institute wasn't what the public had imagined, Sherman had little incentive to make any more sweeping change. He had the American people in the palms of his sweaty hands. And power is seductive. Now as Secretary for Information, he simply had to say what the public wanted to hear.

Earl's unsettled disdain grew the more he thought about Institute foul play from his gray cubicle. Even if everyone else was duped, or pretended not to notice, he could no longer ignore his own role in Institute treachery.

If only he had evidence! Without something to hide, the Institute simply had no reason for such aggressive recruitment calls forcing honest citizens to admit to wrongdoing or appeal to their sense of tribalism and join the bandwagon. For what? To guilt them to acquiesce and report monthly for the Information Gathering Initiative without telling them their knowledge would later be put in their fellow neighbors' "accuracy reports"?

Yes, indeed, it must be very important to have an accuracy report on Jane from Idaho. Must be very important to pry at Jane's vulnerabilities until she cracked, to make her cry, to make her promise she'd be a good citizen and help the Institute's mission, to make her understand that it was her public duty, her *patriotic obligation* to help.

He felt ashamed.

"Anything you're ashamed to do in front of others, you shouldn't be doing at all," Earl remembered his sobbing mother telling him one day at the threshold of his bedroom.

Earl, as I'm learning, is not one to stand for injustice; he must have wanted to be a hero all his life, but his short stature and large eyeballs wouldn't let him believe he could. He knew that heroes had to be handsome and moral. He was only moral. You win some, you lose a lot, I guess.

"Damn Dipper, damn Sherman, and damn this horrid, thankless job," Earl said quietly to himself at his desk, not realizing how long he'd been brooding. "I joined because I thought I'd be gathering true and accurate information to help regular people, not to manipulate them. I want to help parse through the muck. But making a normal guy rat out their neighbor just isn't the way to do it. Even if it might help the Institute verify what the media and public officials say. This is all wrong."

"Earl? Why haven't I heard your voice on a call yet?" Ms. Dipper barked from her office.

He didn't realize how long he'd been entrapped in his ruminations. Jumping into a sense of urgency and remembering his sick salamander, Earl tried to ignore his bubbling discontent and so then looked down at his call sheet with determination. His eyes narrowed and his heart pounded after he saw the right-hand-corner stamp atop the report was labelled, "SHAME."

"Punching in the numbers now, ma'am. Last call didn't answer," Earl lied.

"Well get on it. No-answers don't count towards the quota."

"I know. Damn it," Earl said under his breath, jilted and angry, more at himself than Ms. Dipper.

"Something to say?"

"Of course, ma'am! On it."

Scanning the accuracy report, Earl prepared himself for his own shameful performance.

Last name: Andrews. First name: Andrea. Prefers "Mrs." not "Ms." Stay-at-home dog mom to a wily, two-year-old Great Dane pup named Strawberry Shortcake. Wears lilac-and-honeysuckle-scented perfume. And then there was the reason for the recruitment call: married to a very influential *Washington Post* reporter. "SHAME" call-reports almost always had a blatant reason for the call. A connection to a public official; the cousin to a big-time, social media influencer; a filmmaker with a big audience. It made sense to call and recruit people like this. Their connection to someone well-known meant that *by law* the Institute was to investigate the accuracy of their statements. Ms. Andrews' husband was an established opinion columnist, and it wouldn't hurt to have an ally nearby. Earl had read the husband's articles, but they had too much panache for his taste buds.

He typed in the phone number and waited, hearing only digitized ringing through his earpiece. Sighing, he tried to convince himself his work was for the greater good.

"Hello? Who's this?" the woman on the other end of the receiver said with nerve, as if she already knew.

"'Hiya, Mrs. Andrews!"

"It's *Mizz*. I'm not some notch on my husband's belt."

Dipper must be really on edge; the call sheets had never been wrong before.

"Right. My deepest apologies, Ms. Andrews. This is Earl Eustace Frog, calling as a representative from your local Liaisons for Institute Escort Office. Please, just a moment of your time, and I can tell you how you can help our country continue our fight against misinformation."

The woman was silent for a moment.

"Huh? What the hell do you want?"

"Ma'am? I'm sorry to bother you. Only two minutes of your time. Surely you know about the Institute's mission to hold public officials and the media accountable for falsified statements? Well, I'm calling because we need help from great Americans like yourself to do just that."

"What? Oh. Yes. I know who the hell you are and what you do. My husband's told me. Yeah, yeah, he works for *The Post*. You got the right person, but I'm not interested," she snapped and hung up the phone.

Earl sat, stunned. Before he could gather himself, he heard his boss shout from across the office.

"Best call back and reel that one in, Earl. You only have two misses in that entire pile. Such a pity to lose one off-the-bat. Tick-tock. One week's recruitment quota!"

"She might've stayed on the line if your call sheet wasn't wrong off the bat," Earl mumbled.

"Little comments under your breath won't help!" she shouted before continuing to type furiously at her computer.

The cubicle-bound frogman looked down at his watch and reluctantly called the number again, but this time from a different caller ID. His liaison office has 5,238 different caller IDs.

"Hello? Who's this? I'm busy," Ms. Andrews repeated.

"It's Earl again, from the Liaisons for Institute Escort office," he said, meekly.

"I told you I'm *not interested* in helping that vile Institute. You know it's against the law for the Institute to coerce citizens into its initiatives? Right? Harassment and coercion are of the same kind in my book. I know a few lawyers who agree."

He knew how to deal with people like her: setting a workingman's plea as a lure.

"Please, Ms. Andrews. Just a moment of your time. Honestly, I don't care if you don't agree with what we do here. I'm just a working man, and I want my boss off my back. Will you hear me out? Who knows, perhaps by the end of the call I can put you down as a 'maybe.'"

For a few moments, Earl's earpiece was silent except the gentle hum of buzzing feedback. He briefly thought about how he needed a new earpiece, or at least use his backup.

"Fine. But if you view Institute recruiting as just 'a job,' then you must be a hack, a stupid kid, or some kind of sick masochist."

This riled Earl more than he'd expected. His eyebrows furrowed; his chest lowered.

"What do you mean? I'm helping accomplish what the public wants, what the public has asked for and what it needs. America has overwhelmingly supported anti-misinformation laws and initiatives for at least a decade," Earl said, aiming more to convince himself than his potential recruit.

"Well, let me ask you this—what was it, Earl?"

"Yes. Earl Frog."

"Odd name. Well, Mr. Frog, do you know what happens to Institute recruits after your offices send them over? We both understand why you're calling me in particular—to get close to my husband, keep an ear on him. So, say I agree to your scheme. What the hell happens to me?"

Earl did not know what happened after he sent over recruits, though he desperately wanted to. He shook his head, trying to stay on task and not get wrapped up in unwieldy, perilous curiosity. He had a job to do, had to do this job for Sally, his sick salamander. And damn it, he was the best recruiter in the business. Earl decided it was time to use his top-tadpole, skeleton-key-like method to unlatch the veiled locks of all victims' heart-shaped boxes which were branded "SHAME." He looked for his coup d'état against Ms. Andrews, a vulnerability that might make her comply. At first, nothing, but as his froggy eyes scurried farther down the page, they lit up at item number 48: "Has committed adultery with several lovers. Husband does not know." The bait had only to be set and dipped in the water.

"I'll be blunt in saying I don't know what happens to recruits, Ms. Andrews, but not for lack of curiosity. That's Institute business, not in my department's jurisdiction. But I must say, I do respect a woman who is so defensive of her husband. You must love him very much, would never violate his trust. How admirable. Wish I had a partner who'd treat me like that," he said, playing the part, pretending he didn't feel obscenely dirty.

She was on the hook now, and he was ready to reel, waiting for her shame to overwhelm her into acquiescence.

The two sat in silence on the phone for a few moments.

"Wh—excuse me? Where do you get off saying that? Of course, I love my husband," she said. "It's too bad you don't have someone. Probably because of your sicko job. Violating trust—ha! Y'all are hypocrites."

Earl was getting more confused by the moment. His practiced methods were failing. Ms. Andrews seemed shrewd, but not so shrewd the best-in-the-business couldn't get a "maybe" out of her.

"Hmm. There are many ways to violate trust, don't you think?"

Now he had her. Confess! He had many more calls to make.

No sounds ventured into his earholes, but the feedback did get louder, almost piercing his eardrums. Ten seconds passed. It was best to wait. They always caved in time, Earl reassured himself. To his dismay, Ms. Andrews started laughing, cackling so loud the sonics in his earpiece distorted.

"Ha! Ha! Such a peach. Yeah, I cheat on my husband. But he knows what I do, so you can drop that pretty little act."

"Uh—"

"Oh, honey, you think I'd let you have dirt on me? You really have *no idea* what happens to the people you send over to the Institute? Man, they sure do run a tight ship over there. I'd think you'd want to know, but maybe it's better you don't, so you can sleep at night," she said, her voice turning to stone.

The feedback kept getting louder, but Earl would have to ignore it for now. He needed to stay on the line.

"Well, erm—I-I have my suspicions."

It was then Ms. Andrews heard a flicker of fear in his voice. After a moment of silence, she became concerned, serious.

"Hush. Don't say that word. They're always listening. My husband and I don't know for certain, but I can tell you that people who go to help that Institute initiative come back like zombies. Flat-faced zombies! All they can talk about is how wonderful the Institute is, how thankful they are our government is finally doing something for the people, how important it is everyone do their part for the greater good. These are *strong-willed* people, Earl. Dissenters. People who wouldn't be *caught dead* working for the Institute. In any way, whatsoever. Especially not for some little, trinket certificate and a pat on the back from Big Brother. And now a 180? It just doesn't make any sense. Wait. Shit! You're not hearing fee—"

"—Ms. Andrews? H-hello?"

Earl looked around with urgency, trying to snap out of his fever dream, and slammed down the phone. He tore the still buzzing headset out of his frog-face, causing his ear canals to throb with raw pain. He thrust up from his chair, grabbed his bag, and began walking with haste toward the door. It didn't matter if he were fired. He didn't know how the Institute transformed recruits into flat-faced-zombie supplicants, but he wasn't about to volunteer as a guinea pig and find out. Ms. Andrews had proven his inclination right: whatever the hell that Deputy did to change recruits into supporters was bad news. And now officials at the Institute would have something to put in *his citizen accuracy report*, something for his own stamp of "SHAME."

His chest felt tight, like he couldn't breathe. But as he was about to exit, he heard a shout from across the room, piercing with booming intensity of a foghorn:

"EARL? What have you done? What the hell did you say on that phone call? I'm ruined," his boss said furiously, tears building in her eyes.

"You know what, Ms. Dipper? I don't care if you don't like being fucked. I quit."

"Oh, Earl, my boy. You don't understand. I wouldn't worry about anyone else being fucked. You're to report to the Deputy Secretary's Office, immediately. They are waiting outside. This isn't a request to be refused," she said, ominously.

PART II: WHERE WE ARE

Chapter 7: A Dream Diary Begins
A Rat's Diary #2

Location unknown
Date unknown—sometime in mid-August 2035

To a mouse-on-the-run with bleeding feet-claws:

I think it's a good idea for me to try and write about what I hear and feel and touch in my dream-mind, not just what I see. I don't get it. I don't get why I can see and hear and feel and touch what other people touch and feel and hear and see. I heard somewhere once that everyone you've ever dreamed of you've met at least once. Bullshit. I can't remember ever seeing in real life the kids at college or the bickerers in the coffee shops and I really don't think I've ever seen Mr. Frog, though I might like to. Plus, a lot of the times it feels like I'm awake when I'm dreaming and that's not how dreaming works.

I've never *not been* in my dreams before. It's like Mr. Frog's head was inside my head so his brain was in my mind, but my mind was not in his brain. Too many layers. It's not like he can hear me. I've tried yelling, believe me.

I tried to tell him to not be so scared, to not let himself feel shame, to not do something he'd regret. They always get you if you feel regret. I think he did something he regrets.

I know I should keep writing but I'm tired now and my head hurts a lot.

Chapter 8: Waiting, Waiting, Waiting

O'Hoolihan's Bean Brew and Draught
August 15, 2035—the last day
2:01 p.m.

The air was thick and hot, cramped and jammed; it's hard to breathe. A woman's rolling and ringing fingertips echo and thud on a diner tabletop as she sat, awaiting her guests. Normally the woman with red fingernails might have sipped on a cocktail by this time of day, but people rarely came to O'Hoolihan's for the shoddily made cosmopolitans or the overpriced, watery beer. Except the Honorable Secretary for Information, of course. Most came for the cheap coffee and ambiance. And for the owner's wife, Sheila. What a doll she was to sneak a nip of whisky in your afternoon coffee. A sweet surprise for her favorite customers.

The woman with red fingernails, however, did not care for the coffee nor the ambiance. The archaic, fire-engine red booths with faded and worn tabletops always stood in venomous contrast to the polyurethane-sheen of the recently remodeled bar top in her eyes. And that Sheila woman was a bitch, always sticking her fat nose where it didn't belong.

A man sat across the table. After he took off his thick glasses, nearly blind, he carefully huffed a wisp of coffee breath onto the lenses and massaged the fog. His intermittent bean-slurping was only interrupted by an occasional high-pitched "eeeek!"

Every "eeeek" seemed to surprise him. The woman had told him it's a tick he's had since he was a boy, a symptom of his high-strung personality, but the man can't recall she ever knew him as a boy. He was nearly certain she hadn't. But every time he thought this, his eyes started to hurt.

"Freshen up your joe, Earl?" the homely waitress asked, coming by the table.

Earl! Mr. Frog, hello! It's nice to see you again even if you can't see me.

My friend Earl appealed to the red-finger-nailed woman sitting across from him. She nodded in response with the confidence of a master appeasing her dog with a treat.

"O-oh, sh-sure, Sheila, that'd be just fine. Th-thanks v-very much. You're a d-d-d-doll," he said with effort.

Earl? What's happened to your voice? And who is this woman? It certainly isn't Ms. Dipper.

The woman at Earl's table sighed heavily but managed to remain poised. You could tell she wasn't one to give out treats lightly, and she found the waitress's presence irksome.

"Well, gee honey, aren't you sweet? Now what's a gentle boy like you," Sheila said, pinching his cheek, "still doing hanging around with a gal like this?" She then gestured playfully to the woman's expensive snakeskin purse set on the table and looked at him with subtly knowing eyes.

Earl sat silent, slurping the last drop of his coffee, not making eye contact with either woman.

"Fine. Fine. Keep pretending ol' Sheila's not a good judge of character," the waitress said, only partially in jest. Earl chuckled. He liked Sheila.

The woman cocked her neck slightly toward Sheila and forced a grin, exposing her unnaturally white teeth.

"Sheila, if you would be a dear and fetch me another hibiscus tea, I'd be *eternally* grateful."

The two at the table waited for what felt like a few minutes in silence. The woman kept unwavering eye contact with Earl up to the moment Sheila returned to the table with her refill.

"Yes, that's it, sweetie. Thank you," the woman said to Sheila. After the waitress departed the tableside, the woman snapped her slender fingers as she looked to Earl.

"What a bitch, isn't she?"

"Snobby fat bitch, yes, eeek!" Earl said before slurping another glug from his quickly vanishing coffee and darting his eyes around the café. He began to look around at the mostly empty red booths, but stopped. His eyes hurt too much.

"Go easy on the damn caffeine, my sweet frog. It makes you more excitable than a toddler snorting pixie sticks. We need this job to go well. It's imperative for the lifeblood of the Institute, and I won't have my efforts torn down because of your gluttony. We've a little rat to catch," she said, peering out the window, still tap-tap-tapping her fingers.

"B-but wh-wh-what about the reporter?"

"A precocious little frog with a clever memory, yes! But how could we forget when we were so helpful in getting Momma such damning evidence on the fat cat?"

"R-r-really?"

"Of course, dearie, you certainly were my A+ amphibian helper!"

"B-but we st-st-still haven't found him."

"Such a sweet, caring little frogman. Don't worry, my sweet. Momma has a plan, but she needs to see the big-bird corporal, first. Have him see me, come straight to Dee. There's some very, *very* important information that Momma Dee must give the corporal on the nasty reporter and his little scampering rat friend. We wouldn't have known where he was hiding if it weren't for you helping Momma. But! We mustn't have any distractions, none at all. Now, no more questions!" Dee said, picking up her hand from the tabletop to snap her fingers.

"Whatever you say, boss. I wish they'd come soon. Hate seeing you wait, eeek!" Earl said, mechanically, fingering the handle of his cup, a bit dazed.

It feels like my eyeballs are rolling around in my head. Bulbous eyeballs! This lady looks more attractive than before. She's got nice eyes. Red.

"Well, you know, those two creatures-for-hire are quite the haughty pair. Dirty little predators, yes! They should know better than to be late. Unprofessional. Disappeared *for days* when we needed to add the hit on the researcher rat. What a bitch that clammy little sidekick is. The corporal and I made a little deal yesterday," Dee said, rubbing her snakeskin purse and peering inside it, and then snapping her fingers.

"Glad to hear it. He'll certainly choose you over her. I hope they come soon. Maybe they already found the fat cat, eeek!" Earl said.

"Oh, now there's an optimistic little frog, yes! Plus, we do have quite the incentive for Corporal Davis."

She then reached purposefully into her purse and pulled out a manila envelope sealed delicately with red tape. It made a heavy thud as she dropped it on the tabletop. As it dropped, Earl felt his shame churn, like a conductor-less, steaming locomotive charging straight to his chest. His goosebumps prickled to full attention. Ten-Hut!

"Is-is that wh-wh-what the k-k-k-kid stole?" Earl tried to say softly, his hurting eyeballs glancing at the classified folder and then to the ground. He began tearing at the paper napkin which guarded his lap, letting the scraps waltz to the floor.

"No need to croak so loudly, my sweet amphibian. I *simply cannot comprehend* why you wouldn't remember! No, it's not the exact one if you must know. But no more of that now, we have taken care of the interns. A brave little frog you were in the face of such dire, unexpected adversity. I know it hurts to remember. But Momma Dee is here for you, always," she said and snapped her fingers before rubbing the heaving manila envelope as if it were a puppy. At ease, goose-bump boy.

Earl relaxed at the sound of her snap, but a few guilty butterflies lingered insistently, fluttering up and down and up and down in his gullet even though he couldn't quite put his froggy finger on why.

"D-Dee, I wa-wa-want to talk to you about something. I-if it's n-n-not too much trouble."

She ignored him and glared out the window with purpose, tapping her fingers on the table, murmuring in a ritualistic cadence, "Don't listen to her, corporal. Yes, *reject* your love for that [choose-your-favorite vulgarity unfit for print]. We don't need her. All you have is love for me."

It wasn't like Dee to be anxious, and that made Earl anxious, now forgetting why he wanted to ask about the envelope. Mere moments of looking at Dee's frustration caused his own shame to fade. He became overwhelmed with compassion for his Momma Dee, and scrounged up the courage to croak and console her.

"Gosh, D-Dee, your tap-tap-uh-tapping isn't g-gonna bring them here any faster. Th-th-they won't say n-n-no t-t-tuh-oo you. Re-relax," he said and tried to smile. He did not do a very good job.

"Well, Earlie, it shouldn't be taking him this long. He's a military man. Used to taking orders," Dee said, scowling.

Earl thought Dee might be taking out her anger on the two hired hitmen since she couldn't locate the hit-target herself. She'd even given her hired assassins the wrong address, but preferred to blame the unfinished job on the fact that she hadn't heard from them for days. Regardless of the true reason, the longer the contract wore on, the more Dee would have to pay them.

A beat.

Dee then clasped her hands together and laid them gently onto the tabletop. She looked down at her hands and smirked slightly with pursed lips. She snapped her slender fingers, tilted her chin to the right, and said:

"How about this...I was thinking...since we're spending all this time waiting for these deadly folk...help me, won't you please? My mind is much too preoccupied and I'm beginning to get short with you. I can see in your eyes how much you'd like to help. Tell me a story."

Earl might have thought that this was odd, never knowing Dee to enjoy a story when agitated, but her honeyed little pleas made him feel so very good. He became agreeable, a helpless, wee babe cradled in the woods of the unknown.

"Whatever you say. And what you would like to hear, darling? eeek!" Earl blurted.

"Oh, 'darling,' are we? My, my, you're bad, yes, very bad. We're in public!" Dee said, looking into his bulging eyeballs and smiling. "Oh, what to pick...Oh! Do you happen to remember what happened the day we met? Tell me you remember."

He thought for a moment.

"Why..." he said, glancing out the window, blissful and unaware of the pressure building behind his eyes. "Sure, I remember, Dee. You know what they say: 'a frog has an excellent memory.'"

"Mmmm, I guess they sure do say that, don't they?" she said and smiled coyly, stroking his balding head.

As his frogmouth opened to croak, he noticed Dee leaning over, exposing her chest. Eeek! Sometimes she was repulsive to him, sometimes he wanted to quit the Institute for good and hop away forever, but whenever he doubted her, she would touch his hand, and look longingly with

her sanguine eyes, transfixing him. She was touching his
hand now. He liked looking in her eyes. She seemed to like
it, too, and Earl thought that he liked it that she liked it.
Then he wasn't so sure he wanted to tell the story at all.
Suddenly he wanted to race out the door. The shame had
returned.

"Erm, b-but, you t-t-tell it so much—" Earl said, his hands
beginning to shake under Dee's intensifying grip.

"Humor me," she said coldly and snapped her fingers again,
releasing his hand.

Earl's froggy forehead started to become slimy with sweat.
He paused, dazed, and then continued.

"I'd been a very bad tadpole. Almost believed a very bad
lady telling very bad lies about the Institute and my darling
Dee's Information Gathering Initiative. Sniffing in places poisonous to Institute prosperity. Lies poisonous to our mission.
Our mission for the greater good."

"Oh, sweet little frogman, no need to look so glum. I forgive
you, yes! Tell it for us as it really happened. No one's watching.
No one's listening to your croaks, my dear. Tell us like it was.
From the start."

Earl shifted his bottom in the coffee shop booth, nervous
again, unable to ignore his mounting shame. "Bu-bu-but m-m-
must you make me tell it? You already kn-know."

"We are a rambunctious little frogman today, aren't we? Haven't we learned what happens when we doubt our Momma?
You know we must get the story right, for we had a mistake the
first time," she said and snapped her fingers, getting cross and
impatient.

"Yes, right, for the underground cloud, right, eeek! Must not have any misinformation in Momma Dee's cloud," Earl said, his words monotone.

"Let's first start with how you felt the morning before we met. How's that, my charming tadpole?"

I felt Earl sigh and then his pinch to his nose. My eyes hurt really badly right now.

Earl tried to slurp more of his coffee, but the remnants mostly dripped down his chin. His drooping face then shot up, alert as a boot-camp recruit in front of his master sergeant.

"I'd been doubting the Liaisons for Institute Escort Office's methods. Especially in my branch. Subpar. Too many unanswered questions."

His hands kept slipping on the sleek tabletop. Though sweat continued to lubricate his shaking hands, with effort he gripped a paper napkin.

"Yes, good, oh, do go on," she drawled, twirling her locks and bopping her knees together underneath the table. "Tell us what happened next. Tell us!" Dee said and slid her foot up and down Earl's calf, inching closer and closer.

"I-I'd r-rather not," Earl croaked to his own surprise, becoming a bit repulsed.

"But please, little Earlie? I thought I was your darling Dee?" she said, batting her sanguine eyes and refusing to break contact.

"My boss had chastised me, told me to straighten up. My performance hadn't been up to sp-speed the p-past few weeks."

"Tsk. Tsk. How could you, Earlie? You've always been the hardest of workers. The tadpole at the tippy-est of tops!"

"It-i-it wasn't me. The c-call sheets weren't in the citizens' b-best interest."

"Well, since Ms. Dipper was such a big and mighty woman, she certainly would know how to run such an important business to your Momma Dee," she said and snapped. "I'm sure she was doing her very, *very* best."

"An incompetent fraud. Never meeting call quotas without my help!" Earl said almost snarling, beside himself.

"Oh! Juicy. Yes, very tasty, my frog, quite tasty," Dee said and let out a subtle moan while looking at Earl's eyes closely. "So, your boss, she was going about this all wrong? Not letting us do our jobs or ask right questions? The people just want help, just want to help," she said.

"Yes. They only want to help!"

"Yes, yes! We need their help, need them to fill in the blanks on our accuracy reports so they can sleep safe and sound. What a nasty, silly woman—how did Ms. Dipper have you handle these little flies' stories, my sweet?"

"With utter insufficiency!"

"Yes, yes! People can't live with their dirty, vile secrets! Too much shame from their lies. Secrets from their sons, secrets from their wives, secrets from their neighbors, secrets all their lives! It's such a dreadful scene, my sweet. That's why they need a nudge from *us*!"

That seemed to irk my old friend. Earl anxiously glanced about the coffee shop, seeing blank-faced patrons slurping and checking their watches. They looked at him with bulging eyes and smiled with slightly cocked heads. He heard a snap and Dee's electrifying voice:

"And we'd have gotten a friend outta that nasty lady if it weren't for Dipper's incompetence. Never ambitious enough to ask the hard questions. You were perfect, my sweet frog."

"No. Not even close. Ms. Andrews wouldn't budge with all of Dipper's pesky methods. Always considering citizens' privacy and comfort. Never willing to push hard enough or call anyone more than twice! Not to mention the incorrect call sheets. I even called her *Missus* Andrews!"

"*Verily*, my sweet frog. Inefficient and set up for failure. But we can't be inefficient for the greater good! She didn't believe you when you told her about all the good we do here at the Institute, did she? She could never understand all the good we're doing, trying to get the truth out to those poor people of America. She was tricked by her fat husband's *lies*!"

"Such a sad life, giving in to petty rumors. Especially rumors about my darling Dee and her underground. She only brings them underground to be reborn! Eeeek!" he croaked.

"Oh, you know Momma only wants to help them, and to help them they need to help us, too. Sometimes it hurts to help out the greater good. No one likes tattling on Jim about what he said to Barbara, but when Jim fibs to Barbara, says nasty things about the Institute, sometimes we must intervene. And I trust you know, Earlie Pearlie, that I wouldn't hurt a fly."

"A rat maybe, eeeek!" Earl snickered.

"Oh yes, yes a rat, yes! We know I don't tolerate babbling fibbers! But please...back to the story," she said and licked her lips.

"More coffee, Earl?" Sheila said, interrupting, while she passed the table, pot in hand.

"Sh-sh-sh-sure—"

"Oh hush, you brazen buffoon! Can't you see that Earl here is in the middle of a *story*?" Dee nearly spat at Sheila's feet, but kept her eyes on Earl's face and frogmouth.

"Hmph. Now do you see why you must mind your company, Earl? Hibiscus again I take it, for you," she said and glanced at Dee's empty, red-stained cup, wishing for Earl's sake that this haughty woman with red fingernails would up and disappear as fast as she burst onto the D.C. scene when the Institute opened its doors.

Sheila presumed to fill Earl's coffee cup, but Dee shot her hand over the open mug and smiled, shaking her head at the waitress. Sheila stared her down with skeptical eyes, but knew it best to not start trouble, and instead walked toward the bar, intent on eavesdropping instead.

"Remind me, sweet frogman, how did Dipper want you to recruit the fat-cat's wife?"

"I was to get Ms. Andrews to admit her little slips and dips!"

"Oh, you naughty, little frog. An adulterer? Yes. Delicious. The guilty ones *always* confess. Repent, repent, yes! Sinners. Vile, dirty sinners need to confess and feel compelled to give us the juicier gossip, yes!" Dee said and pounded the table, moaning.

This excited Earl.

"And I was right there, Momma, had her baited and hooked!" he said as Dee got more and more animated.

She shivered, hardly able to contain her excitement. She moaned again and snatched Earl's hand ferociously.

"POW! Right in the kisser! They'd know who knows, yes, who knows their vile, little dirty sins. They would have NO

CHOICE but to confess! Liars, all! But yes, no, yes, we can absolve them of sin. Nothing the good ol' Institute can't fix."

This made Earl sad but he didn't know why.

A beat.

"B-b-but I couldn't even g-g-get her to c-c-c-c-confess."

"Oh, my amphibian man, don't fret, no, don't let a single, wee tear wet your slimy cheeks. Momma Dee is here for you as you are for me..." she said, slipping her left high heel off to better massage Earl underneath the table. He felt very uncomfortable, wanting to hop, hop away. "Let me help finish you off. I know it hurts to remember."

A beating beat.

"It's not your fault my sweet. Dipper's methods were old-fashioned, useless to our cause. Anyone who cannot be shamed cannot be tamed, but you already know that don't you?"

"Y-y-yes."

"That was why you tried to run away from that office, tried to run away and tell your Momma that something else *just had to be done*—that such a shameless person can't get away with spreading such vicious lies."

"Y-yes."

"Yes! And it's your loyalty that convinced Momma to promote you to her very own top tadpole," she said and removed her foot from Earl's thighs. Dee then caressed the manila envelope sealed delicately with red tape, sighed, and locked eyes with Earl.

Earl gulped. He was sad that there was no coffee left and sad that his pants felt funny.

"Your conscience got the better of you. But we know it won't this time. Not *ever again*. Isn't that right?"

"No. Not ever again."

"You certainly aren't the same frog you once were. You make Momma so, so proud. Please don't be sad. My little heart just can't bear it. Dipper and Co. had to go. Her methods were archaic, her wherewithal thin!" she said and snapped her fingers.

"Nowhere for them with wherewithal thin but underground to face their sins, eeek!" Earl recited.

The two then sat with the manila envelope, waiting.

Chapter 9: A Rat's Diary #3

Location unknown
Date unknown—sometime in mid-August 2035

Hush now, little frogman in my mind. It is time to write:

I couldn't hear Earl as well in my last dream. It was like there was this thick cloud fogging the connection between his brain and mine. It was nothing like when he made the phone calls with Dipper and Co. where my brain was in his mind and his brain was in mind. One brain and two minds.

I don't know why, but the lady he was with gave me the creeps. He can barely talk when he's around her. He stuttered, a lot; he didn't sound like that before. Didn't think like that before. He was scared.

I can't blame him. I don't know why exactly, but her voice made me want to scamper far, far away, made my feet-claws throb and hurt and wince. I'm shaking now just trying to remember.

But why would my good friend Earl lie like that? He wanted to run away from his job, felt so much shame. What happened to Ms. Dipper? I don't understand. Help me understand.

No! Who wants to help a little treacherous and treasonous rat, a good-for-nothing ver-man?

I'm sad. I'm sad and angry that I don't know what's happening. I'm sad and angry that I can't convince my doctor that they're are coming for us.

THEY'RE COMING.

Chapter 10: They're Coming! Listen!

Streets of Washington D.C.
August 15, 2035—the last day
Around 2:00 p.m.

A rusting Chevy convertible whipped through the streets of Washington D.C., very clearly, very intentionally ignoring speed limit signs and other traffic regulations. Congested city air filtered through the open windows as the driver navigated towards his destination. I'm in the driver's seat, but when I look down, I can see much bigger muscles than I have.

Hush now. I need to see so I can tell my doctor:

The big-muscle man turned to look at his passenger, a small, extraordinarily fit woman with coal-black eyes and a dark complexion. The car roared through the streets, the driver impatient and anxious to get to his destination.

"Davey. Hey. Davis! Slow down before you kill us, damn it," the woman said, her eyes widening.

"There's a lotta cash on the line. We can't be late. She's gonna be so pissed. We shouldn't have spent this morning in bed," he said, combing his hair through his beefy fingers.

As the car raced closer toward O'Hoolihan's Bean Brew and Draught, Davis felt his head getting foggy, unable to shake a pesky headache.

"Chill the fuck out Davis, baby—it's not like you've cared about being a few minutes late for any other client. We'll be fine."

"We're already on thin ice. We ignored her for days. This job isn't like other jobs, Dahlia. You know that."

A pause.

"And what's so special about this one?"

The two sat silent in the car, Davis focusing on the road, and Dahlia focusing on him.

"Well, now that I think about it...she *did* want to see you privately yesterday before we left the Institute," she said, her tone a bit more accusatory than she would have liked.

"What of it, Dahlia? What're you trying to say?"

Dahlia angled her head toward Davis with intent, opened her mouth, but hesitated. She couldn't ignore the sweat beads speckling his forehead.

"Hmmm, oh nothing my big bird, my corporal—just maybe that she's falling for your hunky pecs. You're not gonna make me a jealous little clam, are you? My wee heart might just shatter right into pieces," Dahlia said and squeezed Corporal Davis's thigh.

"Cut it out with that shit, mollusk. She treats us good. Is gonna pay us good. Have a little respect," he said, annoyed.

"Oh my, we are spicy today. Hush about her, Davey. She's just the money machine. Still, you know I *do* like it when you get spicy—can't help myself. You talkin' dirty, gettin' mad," Dahlia said playfully, trying to ease the tension, giggling, beginning to enjoy herself. "All the blood's pumpin' into this little clam of mine."

She grabbed his hand and rested it in between her thighs.

"See? Come on, move those talons around for me."

Corporal Davis tried to ignore her, wished she would just listen, listen *for once damn it*, wished Dahlia would just listen to how important it was for them to do this job and to do it right and to do it on time. But of fucking course, she was too busy thinking about ways to get in his pants. Didn't she know how important this job was to the Deputy Secretary? How important it was *to him*?

He paused his reeling mind, a bit dazed. He'd never rejected Dahlia's advances before. His mind whimpered. He wasn't sure why he'd had such a change of heart, but he was damn sure Dahlia better get her mind out of the fucking gutter if they were to do the job right. Where was the Dahlia he met when they first teamed up to do missions together? Sure, they'd mess around, but never when there was a job to do. Wait, when had *he* ever turned down the idea to mess around? Corporal Davis wasn't sure what was happening to him. He loved Dahlia. That bitch.

"Oh, stop assaulting me, will you? I'm trying to focus on the damn road," he said getting more agitated and jarring his hand free from Dahlia's grip that pinned his fingers to her panties.

"Assault? Oh my, this hawk's really a bad boy, today. It's ok, Davey, you know I like seeing you all riled up," Dahlia said, twirling her hair seductively, perhaps pretending she didn't recognize the corporal's uniquely high-strung state. "He seems like he needs a little nap, and maybe a little love from his baby clam. Who cares if we're a little late? If she wants us, then she needs us. That little rat's got nowhere to go, can't scurry more than a few miles without any help. Pull over. Let's get that head right—no use getting intel all pent up, hungry," Dahlia said, giving him a bewitching look.

"I need a fucking drink is what I need. And I need this fucking job done is what I need. The rat *does have help*. That's the whole damn point of this meeting in the first place. To find out where the fuck they are! *She's* waiting for us, and she said every minute counts. For days we haven't even had a sniff to go on!"

"Like I need reminding. Chill the fuck out. Damn. That Deputy's the reason we haven't caught the reporter yet. Not us. She gave the address to an empty house. But, yes, you're right, I don't care about you *or* our work. We're hitmen, not P.Is. Fuck. Asshole," she said, her concern quickly turning to annoyance, and clasping her bra.

"We shoulda asked around this morning, but you wanted to fool around. We can't disappoint her."

"Just me who wanted to fool around? You sure your head's on straight? What's the matter with you? Since when do you care what clients think so long as we get the job done?"

"Head's never been on tighter," he said, peeved.

"Well, unless you got brain damage in the last 20 minutes, *you're* the one who pounced on *me* right when you got back from your special job with the Deputy last night, and wouldn't let me go. Held me tight, said you 'missed me, couldn't live without your favorite little clam,' that you didn't even want to go back to the 'hell hole of an Institute.' You looked like you were gonna cry after our first fuck," Dahlia said, crossing her arms and eyeing Davis skeptically.

Davis faced Dahlia, and looked like he was going to open

his mouth to apologize, wanting this whole argument to be buried and die, but slammed on the brakes as the car in front of them stopped abruptly for a yellow light turning red. After he loosened the tension of his seatbelt, his will to apologize disappeared as quick as a finger-snap. He could only grunt in response.

"No, Davey. Hey. It was sweet. No, I didn't mean it like that. Lighten up," she said, looking at him quizzically. "God, what's up with you? So damn sensitive…you're normally a nasty, dirty bird," Dahlia said, touching his shoulder tenderly.

Davis shirked his shoulder back and jerked his elbow to get her off.

"Don't touch me 'til the job is done, damn it."

"Seriously? I let it go last night when you were acting weird. C'mon Davey, this shit sucks. We're in this together. A hawk and his mollusk. A razor clam and her big bird. Why you gettin' all wrapped up in what she thinks? I don't fucking get it," Dahlia said before pausing to think. "You better not have been with her yesterday before you got back. You did take your sweet-ass time at the Institute after I left."

"I told you. She gave me a separate job. She told you that, too. But it was confidential, a one-man gig. I showed you the money after I got it done and the contract and everything. What the hell else do you want? A video of my afternoon? Get off my fucking back. Nothing's ever good enough."

She was unconvinced, but collected herself. She was more worried about foul play against Davis than against their relationship.

"Davey. What's going on?"

Davis looked over at her briefly, said nothing, and then looked back to the road.

"Okay, fine. I'm sorry I accused you. It wasn't right, but you know it's only because I want my hawk baby all to myself. Jealousy doesn't suit me," she relented to the silent cabin inside the roaring Chevy. A pause. "Hell, you even said she was a 'creepy bitch,'" she said and laughed. "I shouldn't have grilled you. Come on, you can talk to your favorite clam. You know you can always talk to your little clam. What's got you so worried?"

Davis seemed to want to reply, but could only let out another grunting sound.

"Fine, we don't have to talk now. You're obviously tense as hell about this job," she said, examining him again. "Hey. What the fuck's up with your eyes? They look like they're gonna pop. Jesus, your blood pressure must be through the roof. Just relax. We'll get the job done. Get it done right like we always do. Remember what we said when we started taking these jobs: 'We don't work for them; we work for us.' And we sure as hell don't work for any creepy seductress who treats her employees like dogs," she said and snapped, mimicking the Deputy Secretary.

Davis caught himself getting angry and wondered whether he could be overreacting; he considered that it might just be stress from wanting to get the hell out of this line of work.

"All right, fine. You're right. But keep your hands off me and my cock. Let's just get to the damn coffee shop. We're already late," he said.

"For a very important date. Apparently."

The rusting Chevy sped on, urgently threading the D.C. streets toward its destination.

Chapter 11: An Intern Meets the Boss

Halls of the Institute for Information Dissemination
August 10, 2035—the day of the escape
11:45 a.m.

An errand boy made his way down a long marble hall. The hallway was adorned with intricate, hand-carved statues made specifically for the Institute to help showcase their "symbiotic" relationship with the press. The statues were of Joseph Pulitzer, William Randolph Hearst, and other notable journalism tycoons from the early 20th-Century. The flighting errand boy's favorite had been the one of Arthur Sulzberger. The boy always got pissed when his boss incorrectly said "Sulzberg."

Wait. I can hear him, too?

In his hand, the young man carried a manila envelope, sealed delicately with red tape.

As he scurried through the hall, passing Dorian Greek columns every ten feet, he wondered whether the pillars were aimed to buttress the hall's structural integrity, or if they were there just for decoration. Then his thoughts were interrupted. He heard the hoarse, callous voice of his boss shout behind him:

"Danny! Hurry up, you lazy peon! If my boss gets kept waiting on this, it'll be your ass that roasts. Not mine! I fuggin' swear! You interns are a dime-a-dozen—no skin off my nose."

"Fucking ass," Danny said quietly to himself.

"I'm going to pretend I didn't just hear that," his boss bolted back while chomping gum.

That got his blood pumping. His blood pressure was already 141/102, and for a kid of nineteen, the doctors had told him that this number was "inordinately high." The docs told him to practice some breathing exercises, or to practice *something*, anything, for at least 10 minutes a day to calm his nerves. And bickering with his boss didn't seem to be helping.

But how could he calm down when he was working at a damn high-strung place like this? He thought some Xanax might help, but when he told the doctors about his new job, about how stressful it was, they had told him to piss off. Xanax was for junkies.

"Why am I sweating? Why am I always sweating at this fucking job? Christ. This is an unpaid internship," he said aloud to no one in particular. "I can't believe I sacrificed my summer for this shit...what was I thinking? Resumé-builder, my ass."

He'd taken the job to follow his favorite professor who left his post to head the Media Research Department of the Institute for Information Dissemination, but now that Danny thought about it, he hadn't seen his professor for quite a while. Danny wanted his mentor's opinion about if he should power through to the end of his internship, or quit. But every time he asked the front-desk admin, the prematurely balding man would look up from his phone screen and say, "Not sure. Think he's been out sick for a few days. Really bad cold," and then make this really weird squeaking sound—almost like a field mouse. Danny (rudely) asked him about the squeak once, ignored common etiquette and asked him what was up, but the admin just sat there, confused like a goldfish a few seconds after you'd tapped the bowl.

The fish-bowl, field-mouse admin had been giving the same answer, word-for-word, all week. It got Danny's boxers in a bunch, so to speak, bunched up enough they might start to chafe his hairless legs if he weren't careful. He did not want chafed legs, even metaphorically chafed ones. Didn't have time for it with all the weird shit going on and all the rumors he'd been hearing.

As his thoughts were speeding up, Danny compensated by slowing down to catch his breath and glance at the murals lining the walls. He needed to calm his fiercely rising blood pressure. Yet before he had any such luck, a familiar, crass voice hissed behind him.

"If you're not huffing and sweating by the time you get back here, you can kiss that recommendation for research assistant good-bye! Ya slacking chump!"

This prompted Danny to pick up the pace. His mom would kill him if he didn't get the research assistant position next semester. Danny'd have no problem living up to one piece of his boss's demands, though: he was already sweating more than usual. His stained and sticky shirt couldn't deny that, lapped and discolored on his back.

Was his boss, Dennis, so out of touch that he couldn't foresee how stressful this task would be for a young intern? Sure, no problem, deliver a "HIGHLY CONFIDENTIAL" manila envelope sealed delicately with red tape straight to Deputy Secretary's office—to *her*. An envelope that looked just like the one he saw in his professor's Personal Institute Employee File, yesterday. While he hadn't opened that particular envelope since it was sealed with red tape, a different, unsealed document in the file had used the word, "Exterminate."

You see, the urge to get some intel about his professor prompted Danny to make a regrettable decision: snap a photo of an "Institute Hit Document" that he found by sneaking into the Data and Inquiry Department. Danny couldn't help himself, things just kept getting weirder and weirder at this internship. He knew he shouldn't have snooped around, but couldn't shake the feeling that it might help him find out where his professor had gone.

His old professor had never been sick more than one day in a row before, and sure, Danny hoped it wasn't anything serious, but *of course,* his professor just *had* to be sick when Danny needed his advice. Shit always played out like that, like everyone was out to get you, like you couldn't catch a break in this messed up place. So, he had to find out, and snuck into the Data and Inquiry Department yesterday when all the guards were at a reception. But no time to think about that now...

That must be why Dennis was abundantly clear when he gave Danny the "HIGHLY CONFIDENTIAL" envelope: "Whatever you do, kid, don't you *dare* look inside or it'll be your ass that burns." Danny suspected that he currently held another "Institute Hit Document" right now. Was he about to send a person to their death?

Was he about to send himself? He'd committed a *felony* yesterday against the government entity *responsible for knowing and distributing information.* Why couldn't he quiet his curiosity and just go through the motions like everyone else? There was no way this task was a coincidence. The Deputy knew he'd snooped. The death knell rang louder and louder.

He would be stupid not to be afraid, but then again, his boss was stupid to pretend *any* Institute employee wouldn't be. No intern had ever seen the Deputy Secretary, but they'd all heard Institute veterans caution the interns to never ask about her. If an intern ever broke taboo and asked anyway, the employees who'd worked at the Institute since its inception would then dart their eyes suspiciously around the office, wince, and shake their heads and whisper, "It's easier to not know."

If this envelope was so damn important, why trust Danny-the-chump-intern to deliver it? Dennis always said any delivery to the Deputy Secretary is a "job of the most fuggin' importance." It was a point of pride for Dennis, who wanted to rise past his lowly position as Intern Supervisor, to be the one "chosen" to do it. A new envelope came by the office every couple of days, and Dennis hand-delivered them like clockwork to the Deputy. Whenever Danny's boss returned, he'd always have a shit-eating grin on his face, too. Recently, though, the envelopes had been coming in more and more. There was another on Dennis's desk when he told Danny to get his ass to the Deputy's office. How many hits was the Institute responsible for?

Danny became even more nervous, nervous because though he hadn't heard much, there were vile rumors about the Deputy Secretary, rumors he might meet face-to-face in about 1,000 feet of marble hallway. Maybe he wouldn't have to see her, could just drop the envelope off at the front admin's desk.

Danny didn't even know what the Deputy looked like. Few did. He could've passed her just a few feet back. She could've been the lady in the purple dress who waved at him and smiled every morning when he got his morning coffee!

"She probably likes to do behind the scenes work, avoid the spotlight, you know," he remembered his friend and fellow intern, Dina, saying, but he thought Dina too optimistic. He respected her opinion, but knew she'd heard the rumors too. Everyone who denied hearing the rumors *lied.*

As Danny turned the corner out of Dennis' sight, his feet slowed to a gentle stroll, so his thoughts could speed up. He couldn't stop thinking about what he had heard about the Deputy Secretary, those pretty fucked up things.

Namely, the guy you saw on TV making all the announcements, Sherman, was nothing more than a dummy microphone controlled behind the scenes. It seemed like no one had the gumption to question if the rumors were true, never mind the grit to investigate them. Their passivity made sense: friends at school were smitten by Sherman's school-boy charisma, and supported his platform to fight against misinformation, believed him whole-heartedly when he said that rampant, conflicting reports were a plague eating away modern democracy. Before Danny had started working at the Institute, he'd believed Sherman, too. Who wouldn't?

But now, with his newfound, insider knowledge, whenever Danny questioned the Institute's mission, it was as if all his social circles, especially his family, told him to pipe down, to just *relax,* that he shouldn't succumb to petty gossip from the old guard. The establishment wanted Sherman and his MiMs to fail, so they'd say just about anything to tarnish his reputation.

But Danny wasn't so sure. It was too easy a retort, bordered on denial.

The weirdest part of what he'd learned from his internship was about the personnel, though. Too many workers at the Institute walked around like drooling zombies, and never had a bad thing to say about their divine Deputy Secretary. It was like they were brainwashed. Whenever he brought it up at dinner to his parents, it wasn't uncommon for Danny to hear his straight-edge, lawyer Ma preach, "People shouldn't believe everything they hear. Congressman Sherman is a respectable man who works for the people. Brainwashed? Listen to yourself. I thought we raised you better than to chirp gossip, Daniel Umberto Hernandez. Slander is not welcome in this house." Or worse, when his wine-stinking Dad joined in, half-slurring, and said that he didn't want his son to become "one of those crazy, conspiracy kooks." These comments always tested his patience, like the universe was poking and prodding him to lash back, to tell all of them they were phonies, how hypocritical they all sounded, believing what they saw on TV and on social media without doing any research of their own. His patience won out most of the time. It just wasn't worth it. Without any solid evidence, he'd never convince them.

But when he thought about it, their hypocrisy was *fucking bullshit*. Just what was *their evidence?* How was he the conspiracy kook? Danny actually listened to people. Tried to form his own damn thoughts. He didn't even have a problem with Sherman, he just thought Sherman's head had gotten too big and had been hasty when appointing staff, that most of the strange phenomena pulsing through the Institute was a symptom of bad management rather than malicious intent. Of course, he wasn't so ignorant to believe the tinfoil theories that the Deputy controlled Sherman's mind or whatever, even though his friend from AP Lit, Daniela, wouldn't give the idea a rest. She pointed to all sorts of articles that claimed Sherman had been deceived by his Deputy—that she tricked him into giving her more and more power; or that Sherman had been seduced by her and taken advantage of; or that all the power had gone to Sherman's head and he left the Institute in his Deputy's care so he could splurge taxpayer dollars on himself.

Every media outlet had something else to say or to add or to question, but when it came down to it, they were just blindly throwing darts. The media's recklessness in reaching rushed conclusions was why Sherman wanted to form the Institute for Information in the first place. Or at least this was what Danny used to argue when his friends questioned why he would want an internship at Sherman's brain-baby Institute. He remembered the speech Sherman gave when Danny was in high school right before the "Misstep Elections of 2030." The guy really seemed sincere, that he actually wanted to give America the truth even at the expense of his political colleagues or the big-business media. But now, just two years after the Institute for Information Dissemination had formed, the media outlets were dropping like flies, and Danny wasn't so sure the Institute was living up to their promises to the American people that the Institute would walk "hand-in-hand" with the press. Danny had seen too much, heard too much to believe that. Or at least he thought he had. Then again, what did an intern with high blood pressure know? Nothing.

He needed to calm down. Regardless of all the crap he'd heard, what could he do? He couldn't refuse to deliver the envelope; there was no way he planned to embarrass himself in front of the other interns by getting screamed at, or jeopardize his research assistant position by getting a bad recommendation from his quick-to-ignite boss, Dennis. What other option was there besides walking right into the devil's den? Run out on his internship and not get the college credit?

And then again, even as his blood continued to pump, some thoughts of sick pleasure found their way into his consciousness. As masochistic as it might sound, and despite his anxiety, Danny kind of liked the fear. Liked it in a way that only fortunate young people can understand; he was thrilled by the dangerous negligence and the flirtatious tryst with mortality. He donned a devil-may-care attitude.

What were consequences, anyway?

Walking down the hall toward the Deputy Secretary's office, Danny couldn't quell this curiosity, this fearless confidence, couldn't quell his dream to rescue an America unknowingly in distress. Maybe he'd find out something important, something that'd make people believe the rumors were true. He'd make his own judgments on the Deputy and act accordingly. Who knows? He might even become the next Deep Throat. Then they'd put statues up of *him* in fancy government buildings for doing the public such a service. He'd be a hero. He could see the headline now in big, bold letters atop *The Washington Post's* homepage:

HANDSOME INTERN SAVES PUBLIC FROM GOVERNMENT MANIPULATION

How a young man uncovered one of the biggest scandals of the century

Who could say, maybe he'd even be awarded the Congressional Medal of Honor. Or be knighted or something. Whatever it was, it'd be fucking sweet. He pushed down his fear; Danny Umberto Hernandez could pull this off as well as anybody.

Soldiering on down the marble hall, he quickened his pace, continuing to be fueled by his growing, youthful confidence. He had to see this Deputy Secretary, had to talk to her, had to know why she stayed in the background, why they gave her so much control, or worse, why she had stolen so much control. What were these "Hit Documents" all about? And why would Sherman willingly give up the post he'd worked so hard for? He had *to know*.

Yes, Danny thought, now might be his chance to gather some intel, gather some intel to tell his buddies back home. Then they'll see who's the *real* conspiracy kook.

As he turned down the final corridor and reached to open the double doors to "The Office of the Esteemed, Her Honorable Deputy Secretary for Information Dissemination," Danny heard a voice call to him from inside as he turned the knob, interrupting his thoughts:

"Very good. Very good, little Danny, yes. They'll see who's the *real* conspiracy kook, yes!"

Chapter 12: Basement Shivers
A Rat's Diary #4

Location unknown
Date unknown, sometime in mid-August 2035

To a rat in a professor's clothing...

To a very messy, stinky little rodent-man:

I still don't know what day it is.
I still don't know what time it is.
I still don't know what place I'm in.
I still don't know why I'm in the place I'm in.
I still don't know who I am.
I still don't know me.
What have I done?

I hear some type of pandemonium upstairs. Ignore it. Remember: journal, journal! They told me, "it'll clear your head, little professor, focus on one mind, and shut out the rest. Remember *who you are*." I am getting my words back, getting better every day though, getting better every time I remember. I shouldn't get ahead of myself though. My doctor says I have good days and I have bad days. Today is a very OK day.

I met some more people in my dream-trips last night. There was this young errand boy who doesn't get paid walking around a building—yes!—walking around The Institute for Information Dissemination. He doesn't really like his job and feels skeptical about the people who work there and all their secrets. My doctor hates the Institute, too, so I bet he and my new intern friend would get along.

There was something...oh! Something important. The lady's voice that talked to Danny at the end of my dream sounds a lot like the same lady Earl sat with at the coffee shop. That must mean—Earl works...with her? At the Institute? What happened to him? Why's he such a big baby, blathering stutterer now? I guess because the lady with red fingernails is menacing and scary and I don't like her and don't want to ever see her again in my dreams. Ouch! My feet-claws hurt...

But *they're coming.* I know bad people are after me and I know they hate me but I don't know why. No one will listen. No one will listen to the nutty professor even if he does get more articulate each day. It's hard to convince my doctor when I can't tell him who's coming after me or when they'll be here, but I know he's getting more and more nervous about it, says that I have to remember soon or else our goose is cooked, that *he needs me to remember for both our sakes.*

The past few hours I've been a very messy little rat. Chaos. Dirt and grime. I'm only allowed to shit and piss in a bucket because my doctor says that I'm not allowed to go upstairs even though he's "truly sorry" about it. But I keep spilling it and then the doctor's wife gets mad and tells me to be more careful. I don't think she likes me.

Why am I sweating in this dank basement if my doctor says *they're not coming* for me? He's scared for me. I must have done something really, really wrong. I always ask him what I did but he doesn't know.

I know *they're coming*, doctor!

Maybe I *should* scamper off. Maybe it would help him if I weren't here anymore.

Ugh. It's so hot, so hot. Just turn it on, the switch, all's it takes is a switch to cool the house. Don't they know? "There's something off with the system, little professor," they say with perfect confidence, like I am some deaf and dumb child. They're probably right. It's easier to be dumb and deaf, I think.

Little tattle rats have to sweat. No. Stop talking like that. You know it doesn't help at all to speak like that and it hurts my head and my eyes.

Oh, hush, would you? You've no right to complain. No right at all, since my friend, Dr. Andrews, is sticking out his neck for me, and I'm not about to complain. No.

Please don't misunderstand me. There have been some good things among the shit and grime and basement dank. Like the other day in between my dream-fits and mind-splits, I went rummaging—as any little rat would—through some dusty boxes stowed away in a corner. What? I was bored and it's not like there's much to do around here except sleep and think and dream and believe and sit and stare and think. So, rummaging I went!

You'll never guess what was in the box! Go ahead. Guess!

It's okay that you didn't guess it right. I certainly couldn't. So then, why would you? Stupid little rat-man with stupid little-rat-man expectations. Hush!

I'll just tell you. For I must tell you, little rat's journal, before I forget. That way, even if I do forget, you can remind me by squeaking in my ears. Okay, you've convinced me.

I wiped the dust clean off the box and saw its top had an insignia imprint, almost like, uh, what are they called…a coat of arms! It had phrases in a dead language I think I used to know and had some *fleur-de-lis* and other fancy stuff on it. Very regal. When I opened the box, I saw the shortest little book I'd ever read. Only one page! It was a cute, leather-bound booklet with the same coat-of-arms crest on the outside, and only had one, thick and heavy, oaktag page slipped into a laminated seal. It had big and flamboyant flowing letters and said:

*THE TRUSTEES UPON THE
RECOMMENDATION OF THE FACULTY OF
THE COLLEGE OF COMMUNICATION
Hereby Confer Upon*

DREW VIRGIL ANDREWS

The Degree Of

*BACHELOR OF SCIENCE
JOURNALISM*

It made sense to me since my doctor is also a journalist. It makes sense that a doctor would go to college. Doctors *have to* go to college or else they can't be doctors. It makes me feel good to know that my doctor finished his degree.

But you'll never guess what else, little rat journal, what else I found right under that little leather book! I found a picture. A funny picture of my doctor from the day the college told him he couldn't go there anymore unless he paid them more money, the same day that he got "Hereby Conferred Upon." Everyone in the picture looks so happy!

I wish I was happy. I wish my doctor was happy. I wish I could get out of this basement and frolic and play and laugh upstairs. At least every time I get sad I can look at the picture of my doctor and his friend.

In the picture, my young doctor holds the same little leather book in his hand and wears a big, light-blue dress and an old-fashioned, black-brimmed hat that holds a card reading, "PRESS." He's smiling a lot and I can tell he's my doctor because the photo looks just like him only younger and with an afro (now my doctor is a bit chubbier and bald! Haha! …but shhhh! Don't tell him we said that, and especially don't tell him we laughed because he's bald).

He's standing with some smug-looking, stick-thin guy with shaggy hair and a scraggly, sparse beard (if you can even call it that). The guy with my doctor smiles too, and holds an identical, leather-bound book in one of his hands that he has resting on my doctor's shoulder in camaraderie. His outfit is very similar to my doctor's: a long, light-blue dress. But the only difference is that this scraggly guy has a square hat on with a single frill hanging off the side, and it looks like his dress has a big rip in the front. I think it's because he wants to show off his favorite belt since he's pointing to it with his other hand, the hand not around my doctor.

I have to say, it's a very shiny, nice-looking belt with a silver buckle. A shiny, silver belt-buckle with a huge imprint that says "FOXY" in bold letters. They look so happy...

I'm starting to feel sad. I wish I had a belt like that.

Wait, what's that, little rat journal? I *do* have a belt like that? I used it to dig my way out from the sentry guns when I scurried my tail away from the shrill lady screaming "RUN RODENT RUN"? The lady who sounds a lot like the lady with red finger nails in the coffee shop and the lady who talked to Danny from inside the office before he could see her? That's my belt!

Yes! No...No! Why would she be after me? What would she want with a dirty, vile, little rodent-rat? Run rodent, RUN!!!

No! Don't go dark again. I need to think as me—

Ouch! My head, my little hurting feet-claws.

Please...no...I need to tell my doctor...I remember...

Doctor! *They're comi—*

Chapter 13: Danny's Lament

Intern Office of the Institute for Information Dissemination
August 10, 2035—the day of the escape
About 1:00 p.m.

I could feel the tension in my shoulder blades, knotting up, tight. Unrelenting. I could see that the meeting with the lady with red fingernails (I assume, I couldn't see her) had shaken him. I think I heard him say something along the lines of "Fuck, there's no way I'm joining that crazy bitch," before beginning his shame-scuttle back toward the Institute's Intern Office.

You know the drill. I must watch and listen:

Danny looked down at his feet as he wandered the hallways, taking the long way back to the Institute's Intern Office. His mind raced, worried. He couldn't fathom why the Deputy Secretary chose him out of all the other, much more qualified and hardworking, interns.

Seriously. Why did the Deputy Secretary want to see him, want him to join her Information Gathering Initiative instead of someone way smarter, like Dina? The Deputy for Information had never mentioned that Danny had snuck into the Data and Inquiry Department; he was at least thankful for that, but he would be ignorant to believe she wouldn't find out soon.

The Deputy gave him the creeps, had this uncomfortable stare and a rich, entrancing tone to her voice. Almost bewitching. Had Danny said anything he shouldn't have? No. He barely even had an opportunity to speak since the Deputy commandeered the conversation.

Thank God, Dina didn't have to deal with that weird shit. He'd have to save her from worrying about it, for her own sake. He'd have to play it cool when he got back to the office, even though she was the only person he'd want to vent to, want to bounce ideas off of.

No! There was no way he could tell her, else that bitch Secretary would have Dina on her radar. Danny feared he could no longer pretend the rumors were just rumors. The Deputy must have eyes everywhere, was up to some shady shit.

Sure, Dina would give him some good advice about it; she was always up to date on the news, even news that hadn't been released to the public yet. Stop! He couldn't even *think* about telling Dina, no matter how much he wanted to. He'd have to fight the desire, just like he fought to get this internship in order to impress her.

In almost a haze, as he continued to slowly wade back to the Institute's Intern Office, he couldn't help but remember the day they both had gotten their acceptance letters. How did he get here? He wished he could go back and shout to Dina, beg her to understand that this place was bad news.

The day went like this...

"Jesus," he remembered whispering as he winced and tensed, trying his best to halt, or the very least, delay, his pending pitcher-sized puke. He had awoken to a buzz on his nightstand. Turning over to check his phone, he found his nausea-battle lost, and so the beer-whisky-tequila-rum cocktail that had fermented all night in his stomach, fountained and foamed from his pale mouth, splashing a brown brew onto the floor. After which, Danny grimaced, belched, and then wiped clean his lower lip of residue with the folded thumb-joint of his right hand. As his depravity pooled beside his nightstand (he'd put in no more effort than tossing a dirty towel over it, hoping it would absorb the mess), he foggily peered at his illuminated phone screen and saw a text from Dina:

●●○○○ InTel   LTE   2:10PM   28% 🔋

‹ Messages   **Dina**   Details

The letters!!! The letters
came!! From the
Institute! They're
hereeeee. PLEASE,
please wait to open
yours. Get your butt
down over here. We've
got to open them. NOW!"

Groggy and pissed at his irresponsible bender, at his childish disregard for his health and well-being, Danny slapped on some khaki slacks and a white t-shirt equipped with deodorant pit-stains and readied himself to go over to Dina's. He looked in the mirror, shrugged at the deodorant stains, and left after he brushed his teeth and rinsed his face.

Meandering as slowly as possible down the street, trying hard to calm his pounding headache, he wondered about how badly Dina wanted the government internship. He had pretended it was his dream, too, since his professor had told him about it after Danny asked after class one day, about the great opportunities for future research assistantships. Danny had texted Dina the minute after to see if she'd heard about it. He had patted himself on the back for how he talked up his interest in the Institute and their mission, how in the text he said that he hoped that either they both got it, or they both didn't. There was no way in hell he was going to have a different schedule than Dina. She was on his mind most of freshman year; he pined for what could have been a lost opportunity. He missed her, missed hanging out with her, missed stealing looks at her.

Fuck, they almost kissed once (and seriously, they both really wanted to, bad) but they were at Senior Prom with other dates and wanted to be respectful. Danny ragged on himself a lot for waiting so long to ask Dina to prom. He wasn't about to miss *another* opportunity by not getting this internship. Hell, Danny talked up Dina so much his college roommate was sick and tired of hearing about her. "We get it. She's real cool man. You had to take that other girl with great legs to prom. Sounds like it was terrible, D," his roommate would say while browsing social media. Yes, Danny did have to take Darlene to prom instead, but his roommate's sarcasm always bothered him. Darlene is nothing compared to Dina, even if Danny did have to admit that Darlene has better legs. Still, his roommate could shut the fuck up about it, okay? (Danny repeatedly told himself that Dina's chicken legs were cute and shut down anyone who talked trash about Dina or her legs. They usually only had bad things to say about her legs. Everything else was perfect.)

Danny was not about to fuck this up; he had to get this internship; Dina had to get this internship. Because if they did, on this particular—hungover—summer morning, he just may get the chance to act on his adolescent desire. Or better yet, if he bided his time, get a summer filled with chances.

This wasn't to say Dina was his only reason for applying for the internship. When the Institute for Information Dissemination formed during their senior year of high school, Congressman-turned-Secretary Sherman had issued a public call for "any and all diligent, patriotic American citizens who deem it their civil duty to fight against the plight of rampant misinformation."

Danny hadn't paid much attention to Sherman and his Institute during high school, but he sure started paying more attention when his mom said he'd better get a respectable internship, else she wasn't going to keep helping pay for his tuition. A hard bargainer, his Ma. The next day, he said to his mom that he supposed it was worth checking out the hype over at the Institute. Dina served as the icing on the cake; any time he could talk with her was time well spent.

After his queasy and staggered stroll to Dina's neighborhood, during which he cursed 23 times, Danny arrived at the front door, albeit with frightfully pale skin and clammy palms. A little credit was due though: at least he brought the Institute letter, unopened, which was tucked snugly in a back pocket. Before he'd composed himself enough to knock on Dina's door, it swung open, revealing his animated friend.

"Ah! It took you fucking long enough! Now, let's open— wow, you look terrible."

"Thanks," Danny had replied. "I went out with the boys to—"

"Who the hell cares why you're hungover? I'll get you a glass of water. But first, we gotta open these letters. Now!"

So, while standing on Dina's front stoop, distracted by the gentle May breeze dancing through Dina's burgundy hair, the two tore into the letters, her hungry for the verdict, and him hungry for her to think that he was hungry for the verdict.

Though the Institute requires interns to destroy their acceptance letters upon their first day in office, it read something like this:

```
THE INSTITUTE FOR INFORMATION DISSEMINATION
WASHINTON D.C.

Dear Treasured Applicant:

We are delighted to inform you of your acceptance
to the prestige of the Institute for Information
Dissemination's INFO WARRIORS Internship Program.
```

As you well know, the United States has been plagued by the malignant cancer of false information pervading through the fabric of our nation. As a brazen and unflinching leader on the global stage, the United States Government has decided to fight falsity tooth-and-nail, in part with the day-to-day duties enacted by the Institute for Information Dissemination. This is where YOU come in, treasured applicant. YOU are needed in this fight.

During each day at the Institute, YOU will bolster the brigade dedicated to the eradication of misinformation. Believing in our motto, "no patriot too meek, and no patriot too small," YOU can and will aid in this battle for Truth.

Please inform the Institute of your acceptance or denial no later than midnight, May 24, 2035. You can inform us by:

1. Visiting our website at:
whitehouse.gov/internships/BattleForTruth
2. Entering your registry number listed at the bottom of this letter

We at the Institute for Information Dissemination cannot wait to hear from you. We trust you will make the right decision for the citizens of our country. For all the INFO WARRIORS out there, past and present and future, we say: "Veritas Omnia Vincit."

Battle on.

Sincerely,

Dexter Sherman
Secretary for Information Dissemination

He snapped out of it, and stepped hastily back to the Institute's Intern Office, pacing past the admins before taking a seat at a worktable populated by some of his fellow wage-free workers. They got up when he sat down, scoffing at him. They knew where he'd been. One auburn-haired girl with not-chicken legs stayed in her seat.

"Danny, what's up? You look like you've seen a ghost. Did Dennis send you where I think he did?"

Oh, what he'd seen was worse than a ghost. He'd seen *her*. The behind-the-scenes boss with sanguine eyes.

"What I saw was alive and well—thriving, even," Danny said and again looked to the floor.

She placed her hand on his and gave it a light, consoling squeeze.

"I'm sure it will be all right, whatever you saw," Dina said quietly.

She darted her eyes right, then left, center, then right again, scanning the room for Institute employees, scanning for anyone listening. She didn't seem overly concerned, but conjectured Danny had gone to the Deputy Secretary's office, so she had to remain vigilant if they were to say anything about it, no matter how covertly. Good thing it was lunch break. She judged the two could at least talk candidly, if not explicitly.

"Well, did you see her? You were gone for over an hour," she whispered.

Danny's eyes widened. That's how long it was? Danny could have sworn it wasn't more than five minutes. What had he said, two, three sentences the entire time?

Nearly paralyzed by the implications of his introduction to the Deputy Secretary, all Danny could muster was a head nod. It was as if he were stunned, in shock and unable to speak. The only part he remembered with any clarity was some type of job offer to join the Information Gathering Initiative, an offer that Danny Umberto Hernandez was *not interested* in accepting. Talk of that group harkened the most brutal of rumors about the Institute. Underground torment, for one.

What was worse, he felt that the Deputy knew he wouldn't accept her offer, but she asked him anyway in some sort of perverted power play. Yes. It was like she knew he'd gone into the Data and Inquiry Department yesterday to snoop out information, but was waiting for him to admit it. *She'd wanted him to feel shame about it.* He remembered her luring sanguine eyes that locked with his, relentlessly; her unnaturally white teeth; and how she kept exposing her chest to distract him.

And what was that shit about when *she replied aloud to Danny's own thoughts?* Those "conspiracy kooks" who talk from their soapboxes about how the Deputy can "control minds," might not be kooks at all. Danny *swore* he wasn't talking aloud to himself, regardless of what that lying bitch said. He felt sick to his stomach.

"You've got to tell me. What if you need an ally?" Dina said, interrupting his reeling mind, and taking careful consideration of his face.

"I wouldn't need your cotton-candy help if that's what you're implying," Danny scowled, quite beside himself, holding his hands on his stomach.

"What the fuck is wrong with you? I'm not implying. I'm telling you that I'm here for you. If you'd need someone—someone to help you out of this mess—"

"Shhh!"

As subtly as possible, Danny then looked to the man who had bulging eyes and was slurping an unhealthy amount of coffee across the room. It was his fourth cup of the day, a modest number compared to his usual thirteen cups.

Though he liked Dina, Danny was pissed she'd be so simple to talk so openly. The rumors, damn it! The place could be bugged, and the weird big-eyed dude was right fucking there, pretending to talk to reception. Danny always saw that guy in and out of the Deputy's office. Danny knew no one would willingly talk to blubbering Donna, the receptionist. No doubt, he was there, spying, waiting to see if Danny would do anything rash.

The frogman saw Danny glaring knowingly, and so coughed up a bit of his coffee, sputtering specks of brown liquid onto his shirt. Blubbering Donna took care of the rest and told the man to clean his ass up and get out of her office.

Now a bit more relaxed, Danny did feel bad about being so curt to Dina. It was nice that she cared. He just didn't want the guilt of getting her involved in something that might put her in danger.

"I'm serious Danny. Let me help. You clearly saw her. Something's obviously up. But why would she want—"

"Obviously? What in the fuck about this hell hole of a place ever let on that anything, anything at all, is *obvious*? Their whole schtick is that *nothing is obvious*. And they're right! We're spoon-fed ideas, thoughts and theories of men long dead, some loose-leaf, semi-conscious shit that's the product of electric wires tangled and sparking from their dead heads. And we all just shout about it, can't change people's minds for shit! Reading whatever we *think* is right."

"Woah, Danny, easy," Dina said, concerned.

"Anything but easy! How can we *know* anything? Because it's been agreed upon by a bunch of dudes at a table? Because a bunch of loud people say that's the way it is? Nothing you ever know can even remotely exist in the way that I know it. If we're lucky, our ideas might, *might*, resemble one another, and that's only if the neuron-electric sparks are wired the same from what we saw, smelt, heard, touched, or tasted in our lives. Only if we've had similar experiences."

"Danny—"

"No. No! Seriously, all you gotta do is just convince someone else that they're thinking what you're thinking, regardless of if it's the total opposite, man. I guess, if we're goddamn lucky, maybe those fleeting electric sparks will pair to ignite something new. But it's all still based on a pitiful, broken foundation—that any neuron firing has any basis in the first place!"

He was shouting now. Too loudly.

"Shhh! Chill. That's pretty dark, Danny. And if you did know anything, you'd keep that kind of talk far from here," Dina said, giving Danny a fierce, but perplexed look. "Listen, we can talk and debate epistemological bullshit later on, for the rest of our damn lives if you want, but right now—" she continued, and squared Danny's face to look her in the eyes, "—but right now—I need you to get your shit together and tell me what's going on."

Danny stared blankly, his eyes now frighteningly void of concern.

"Danny?"

"Deputy Secretary."

"Yeah. I know. You—"

"She knows that I—that I—"

"Spit it out."

"We gotta get out of here," Danny said abruptly. "We've gotta get out of this place, now!"

He charged throughout the room in a fever dream, all the while mumbling, "Out. Out! Gotta get out." Each passing step electrified poor Danny all the more, his thumping soles pounding the floorboards which sent pulsing, throbbing pains up his (and my) legs. His face tingled and his fingers trembled. Sweat beaded and roller-coastered down his pug-like nose, diving in sprinkled plunges onto the moistening floor like Olympic acrobats.

Ten-out-of-ten, according to this rat-judge.

Smack! Boom! Pow!

Danny's face had been bluntly introduced to the unforgiving palm of his good friend, Dina. It stung badly, and the smack had had enough force that Danny felt his very own lifeblood drip down from his left nostril.

"What the hell?" Danny yelped, clutching his injured nose. "You *hit* me, Dina!"

"Don't 'what the hell' me. What the hell do you think you're doing? Snap out of it, Danny. Put your ass in that chair. You're freaking me out. Calm the fuck down."

"We don't have time. We have to leave, now!"

"Listen. I'm not just going to—Listen. Damn it, listen! I'm not going anywhere until you tell me what's going on. Are you in trouble? Danger?"

"She wants me. I think the rumors about her are true. And she knows I know. And now she probably knows that you know."

"Oh, Christ."

They both locked eyes, frightened, and unaware that the big-eyed frogman slurping coffee had reentered the room.

PART III:
BUT HOW DID WE GET HERE?

Chapter 14: The Doctor Is In
A Professor's Diary #1

Location unknown
Date unknown, sometime in mid-August 2035

To a sorry excuse for a man who has gray hairs in his beard:
p.s. at least it's not a scraggly beard anymore

Sometimes the doctor comes down and talks to me. He started to more and more after I realized we were friends in college. Because of him, I finally remembered being a professor who wrote papers about language and how it affects people and what they believe, and that he's a reporter for *The Washington Post*. How about them apples, little rat journal?! Did you know that *Good Will Hunting* is my favorite movie? I got to watch it yesterday, three times! My doctor says I need to listen to Robin Williams more: "It's not your fault."

My doctor still gets sad sometimes even though he likes talking to me. He usually looks sad when I tell him that *they're coming* for us and that we don't have much time. He says if I stop telling him those "ridiculous dream conclusions," of mine that he'd come down to talk to me more. So, I stopped. For now. I don't believe him that he doesn't believe me though.

When he asks me questions about the last few weeks or even the last year and I tell him that I don't know he says, "Oh, you poor sap. I'm so sorry. The bastards! This is why we must take them down. You must remember what the Institute did so we can protect the public. I mean, look at what they've *done to you*. I will fix up a few new plans to help jog your memory. You must write as much as you can even when it hurts."

So, to fill my prescription for knowledge and memory, he talks to me about the last few weeks, talks to me about his days, talks about anything, hoping it'll jog my memory. It soothes my "paranoia," loosens and lubricates the rusty gears cranking in my head.

I do get upset when he says that. I'm not paranoid, doctor. I am the perfect amount of 'noid. *They're coming.* You even told me that I'm the one who told you about the bad people in the Institute in the first place, but we never thought it was this bad. Is that why you're keeping me down here? To protect me? Are you lying to me just like everyone else?

What must I do to make him believe me, little rat journal? Why do you hold so many secrets? Tell me!

Okay fine, you're right, maybe you will tell me, but only if I remember more.

One time the doctor told me that in the past few days he'd been looking for a new job, since he'd been "unjustly fired from *The Post*" early last week, and he "didn't have time to lose."

He said he had had an interview for a "dead-end tech writing gig" for a petroleum company this week. "PR," my friend, Doctor Andrews, said and scoffed, wiping his hands on his knees. "Should I just sell my soul to the Devil?"

He told me that while he was driving back from the interview in his gray Subaru, he checked his phone, which sat in the middle-console cupholder. When I asked him if he was texting and driving since that's a very naughty thing to do, he assured me, "No sweet professor. Don't fret. The light was red."

Then he smiled at me and patted me on the head.

Always treating me like a child! Probably serves me right, little rat journal, yes, probably serves me just right for my paranoid ramblings.

He told me that while his gray Subaru sat at the light, his pixel-lit iPhone 32b.2 popped up a message from his wife: "I know things are tough. I'm sorry we've been at each other's throats. It's because of the selfish things I did. You know I'm so sorry. Please remember how much I love you. I made your favorite. Catfish! ♥."

I know why things are tough. I'm why things are tough.

Yes, you are, but Andrea's appetites weren't helping much either, he tells me. I think it's a little strange that my chubby doctor would have a problem with appetites, though.

My doctor told me that after reading the message while sitting at the red light, he had smiled and sighed; he had forgiven Andrea, even though any time he imagined her with another man, he became self-conscious.

He said he didn't have much time to reply before the light turned green because "a mad-eyed, punk kid driving his mother's mini-van shouted inane nonsense about saving someone from danger," and beeped and beeped, howling at my doctor all the while. My doctor said he'd been craving fried catfish all week, and was not about to let "some angsty, rambling kid" ruin it for him. Slowly he licked his lips in anticipation and "flipped the damn punk the bird and waited for the next green light before budging at all. You know, to teach the punk a lesson," the doctor had said, his lips forming a wry smile.

He kept talking for a while after that, said the past few weeks hadn't been going so well; he was afraid of what might happen since he was out of work. Andrea sells her paintings for income, but he can't convince her to take a day job, no matter how hard he tries.

"We have three mouths to feed, now," he had said. "Four if you count this bowling ball!" He jiggled his belly. I laughed.

The doctor told me that he'd been feeling depressed and anxious since he was fired from *The Post*. Mostly because he wasn't sure why he was fired and that bothered him. Apparently, I'd given him some dirt so good on the Institute, on that Deputy Secretary and what she might be hiding from Sherman, that we'd finally "get those government junkies! No more tricking the public! We were about to bring journalism back!"

That's why he needed me to remember so bad, so I could fill in more details, be a testimony to prove the nasty rumors true. Maybe he was fired since he didn't have a lot of proof, or maybe since I didn't have a lot of proof, just what I thought I knew about the Deputy, but not what actually happened. I'm not sure though. Regardless, he said he couldn't publish anything on the government with less than a "B+" accuracy rating and get anyone to believe him.

Still, it irked him, he told me. Not one soul had gotten eyes on his manuscript or knew what I'd told him, so, "why the hell" was he fired? It wasn't like his editor had said he needed more sources. He was going to help the cause, help journalism regain some public trust—it just didn't make any sense. He told me he didn't dare pitch the article to another paper even after he'd been fired since "they're all Institute termites, munching away at the pulp of truth that's left, filling the public with lies. All afraid of getting lower than a 'B-' rating in their accuracy reports, afraid they'll lose readers. *The Post* was the last beacon I knew of. Seems unlikely, anymore." He frowned. I don't like it when the doctor frowns.

He talks about his last day at work a lot. He must have told me the story six or seven or eight times. He always mulls it over, always ruminates and replays the day "like a terrible montage," in his brain-mind, "a rolling tide of spew and muck and shit." He often yells at himself (I can hear him upstairs), "Enough! Too much! It's over. Done," and I know that's what he's thinking about. I always tell him he can talk to me about it.

"Yes. We will always have each other, my good friend," he says to me when I say that.

It's not a surprise to me that Dr. Andrews gets so worked up. He's always had a keen, yet malleable mind, prone to self-shaming. His deep inner monologues steal the reigns, hungry for self-doubt, shunning confidence. Poor doctor. Who does a doctor see when he's sick? I don't know.

Maybe he can treat himself. He *is a good* doctor. He tells me every day how much better I'm getting at remembering who I am and that if I remember I can help him take down the Institute. We even have a new treatment plan, little rat journal!

It's a sort of a memory test. Earlier today, my doctor came down and told me in more detail about the day he was fired from *The Washington Post*. He asked me to "write down as many details" that I can remember about the story he told me. He let me take notes as he was talking so I can try to write in as "sophisticated language" as I can (and to keep at it even if it hurts my head). He said he'll evaluate it later. So, I have to get to work.

Here goes. I must make my friend proud:

You, Dr. Drew Andrews, sat up in bed, wearing heart-stitched boxers that your wife, Andrea, had given you last Christmas. You thought them childish and a "sartorial cliché," but, then chided yourself, "what do I know anyway, using a phrase like 'sartorial cliché?'" You told me that you then shifted your weight with some effort, pulled your legs around the side of the bed to fit your swollen, chubby feet inside slippers. On account of morning grog, you had missed a slipper and barely caught yourself with your left arm on the oak bedside table. The table "didn't seem very happy about this," you said to me and laughed. I laughed, too.

With an exasperated sigh, you told me that you had meandered into the bathroom to "rinse of filth," before heading to work. You jostled the unyielding bathroom doorknob, pulling at it hard before it opened. I asked you one time (I can't remember when) if the doorknob had been fixed, but then you looked down and looked sad. I won't ask anymore.

You had heard a slight rustling in the sheets, and glanced back over at Ms. Andrews "tossing about" in bed. You always say and have said that "Andrea could be quite the devil" in the mornings if roused prematurely, so naturally you did your best to be a "dutiful husband," even though you always tell her that she shouldn't be "coming home so late from getting drinks with the girls." (And you later admitted that she wasn't getting drinks with the girls.)

After the stroke of "good luck" in not stirring your wife awake, you entered the master bath, clicked the light switch and stared "mouth agape" at your reflection. You wondered aloud how the once "cherubic complexion" had "transmogrified" into the "grotesquerie" before you. Then you let out a shrill, involuntarily laugh. You were *very surprised*.

"Aging is quite the irony. The mind learns, recalibrates, but the body withers away," you said to yourself, "another thought, another wrinkle."

Splashing water on your face, you remembered anticipating the day: "It was going to be *big*. A day to change everything." To give yourself some confidence, as you do every morning, you sniffed Andrea's perfume which sat behind her bathroom sink. "I always did love lilacs and honeysuckle; gets me every time."

You were nervous since you had missed the past two deadlines on the Institute exposé. You needed to talk to me about it a few more times than you originally thought to even come close to a "B+" rating. The first time you said that, I didn't remember telling you anything about the Institute, but you comforted me, "No problem, my old friend. Just listen, then. Maybe you will."

I hope so. I think I am now. I hope I get close to a "B+" rating on this new treatment plan. How am I doing, doctor?

You told me that you said aloud to the mirror, "This piece is my redemption. Yes, today, *today* I will polish what was tarnished. Yes, today I'll clear the blemishes from my name."

And why? Well, your columns had been getting a lot of negative attention the last few weeks. They'd been making people "very angry," since you didn't agree "with the mindless followers of that *damn* Institute." Sooner rather than later, an inquiry for an Official (Non-Institute) Journalist Accuracy Report would arrive at the door. Then any chances of publishing an exposé would "be toast."

Your readers had to see, to understand—"damn it"—what was happening to the free press from this "godforsaken government ploy to control the people." You'd been given an opportunity when I told you I needed to talk about the Deputy and her schemes, that I'd be able to give you "the scoop to bring the bastards down."

Like you said, the piece was supposed to be your "redemption," a piece truly to be remembered by. It was "BIG NEWS," since I'd mentioned in our phone call that there was some "hidden chamber underground," one that the "people's man, Sherman, was oblivious to." But then the phone cut out before we could finish our call. There was no time left for another missed deadline though, not with "that damn accuracy report on the way," since the public would never trust a word you said after that. You had to run to work with the piece "as it was" to show your editor, and to tell her that "the plot was thickening," and you planned to call me back later. And I think you've told me you planned to call more than once. Do you want me to feel like you haven't abandoned me?

Don't worry, doctor, I don't think you've abandoned me. Even though I think you don't want me upstairs since you believe that *they're coming* or may be watching your house, you're my very good friend and I love you. But back to my assignment, good doctor:

The drive to work "hadn't been abnormal" unless I count "the extra three minutes in the car," as abnormal. I replied that I wouldn't count it abnormal. You patted my head after that and said, "I never thought you would."

After parking your gray Subaru in your "designated spot," you "waddled into the office." That made me laugh, especially when you got up and waddled around the basement to show me. After we had a good laugh, you continued, telling me about the "profound and emotive" speech prepared for your editor, a speech where you'd say, "Listen, chief, I know I've been a little *off* because of all this negative feedback, but let me tell you, this story is gonna knock those argyle socks right off your damn feet. It'll be the first in a series. The Doctor is back!"

Naturally, the boss would be intrigued and say something like, "Oh yeah, Drew? I have to be honest—we were worried whether you'd make a comeback. Thought you might be a goner. The Institute's up our ass and we're losing readers since we've had so many failing Media Accuracy Reports."

You couldn't stop imagining how the meeting might go (honestly, it's a little annoying how much you talk about it). While your boss might give "a bit of sass for being so damn lazy on account of missing the deadlines," maybe even call you an "uninspired buffoon," you had tried to console your doubts:

"No, they will be happy, grateful even" for such a heavy-hitting story, and for the scoop I'd given you about the Deputy going behind Sherman's back.

After pacing around *The Post's* lobby for "nearly ten minutes," you had said to yourself, "Enough is enough. Time to go. You're the *doctor*, for Christ's sake! They *need you*," and then waddled on up to the opinion editor's office.

Huffing up the stairs, you thought about me, and how we'd work as a team to "take those Institute bastards down and reclaim our freedom!" Then, with "as much gusto as you could muster," you burst open the editor's door without knocking, "so animated and wild and crazy to share your big scoop."

You blurted out as you entered the office, "I know. I know I've been off," but then a stranger cut you off, and said, "You're fired, Drew. Executive orders."

You didn't even have time to question the Institute cog who sat at your editor's desk, since they immediately had security escort you out. You were confused and livid, suspicious that "there was something deeper going on in the Deputy's underground, something grotesque and deadly happening behind the scenes in that *damn* Institute."

When I showed up at your house a few days later you were convinced of it. You wish I'd get better soon, that if I get better soon, I could help you finish your story.

I hope I get better soon, too. I think I am.

But my head's starting to hurt now...I think I need to go to sl—

Chapter 15: The Furtive Frog
Starts to Remember

Halls of the Institute for Information Dissemination
August 10, 2035—the day of the escape
Around 1:30 p.m.

After he returned to the Intern Office from dabbing some water on his shirt to clean the coffee spittle, I see him slurp brown-bean juice and pretend to talk with the blubbering, intern-office secretary, Donna. I see our friend Danny jumping around the room with a metaphorical fire underneath his behind. He's yelling "Out. Out! Gotta get out."

"It appears that someone in the room was forgotten. I slinked like a snake back in, and Dee will like that. Eeeek!" the man thought as he quietly sipped his vanishing fourth cup of joe and left the office, hopping down the hallway. But, Earl, aren't you worried about what might happen to the interns?

Danny and Dina's conversation mandated Earl to report a likely "rat on the run" to the Emergency Breach Department (likely threats were only Grade 2, but employees in Dee's department were still required to report threats of any grade). And yet, as he trotted to report the interns, Earl found he couldn't fight his building empathy towards Danny's plight, and the fact that he'd have to report Dina as a potential accomplice. No stone unturned.

Despite his throbbing eyeballs, Earl empathized with Danny about how stressful it was to be recruited into the Information Gathering Initiative directly by Dee. Institute employees could no longer be shielded by distance as citizens could. Workers were in the belly of the beast with nowhere to hide. And it never ended well for Institute employees who were personally asked to join the Deputy Secretary's Information Gathering Initiative. They were molded into soldiers, working tirelessly for the department that Dee had the most control over: The Capital T Truth Division. Some envied those in the Division, some feared them. It was nearly as prestigious a position as working for Sherman himself, at least in the eyes of a handful of envious colleagues.

To calm his wandering mind, Earl tried to remind himself that he was grateful for the job, grateful for knowledge, grateful to have such a nurturing, strong-willed boss. He said aloud to no one in particular, "G-g-gods, I'm th-thankful for Dee. I p-p-promised her that I-I-I would n-nuh-nuh-never let my conscious get the better of me again."

At least his job had prestige, and that prestige came with a swelled paycheck built for a bullfrog's fat, bubbling croaker— no more worrying about how to afford his sick salamander's medicine! The money was well-earned, though. As the Lead Assistant to the Deputy Secretary of the Institute for Information Dissemination, he had some very special duties. He was given permission by Dee herself to know about the near-omniscient cloud, but that he "mustn't tell a soul, no not a soul at all, else Momma Dee will be forced to call him a bad little frog and punish him." He did not want to be a bad little frog. He wanted to be her sweet, good little frog. And a handsome frog, at that, so she would keep looking at him with her sanguine eyes and touch his hand to make him feel so very good. There certainly was no reason to be upset about reporting Danny and Dina: what did a tadpole know? Only to swim with the current that feels good.

Desperate to reject bad, untrue thoughts that pulsed through his frog-noggin about those pesky interns, Earl kept thinking loudly: "What's so great about my job is that I got the chance to work with my darling Dee. Everyone is envious of such a lucky frog." And he was well aware that he would not be a lucky frog if he got distracted and slipped up; Dee's protocol for potential information breaches had to be followed to a T. She had told him: "Whenever there's even a sniff of a nasty little breach, my sugar frog must go to the Emergency Breach Department *before* you tell momma, else they will all get suspicious of us. Yes, they will. And never, *ever* tell Shermie. He doesn't need to know. They are all jealous of our underground initiative, envious of our power to protect the people, our power to know. Envious of you and me. They would try so very hard to steal you away. My sweet little frog wouldn't want that, would he?"

Earl couldn't tell his darling Dee immediately even if that was what he wanted: she was so far away in the underground, unable to be disturbed when working with a new client. Perhaps her distance contributed to his wandering mind.

For as Earl came closer and closer to the Emergency Breach Department, his mind unsettled and continued to race, worrying about Danny and Dina's fate. He shook his frog-face aggressively, so aggressively that his wide, full lips flapped on each other. It did little to pacify his flighting mind. His gut still screamed of duplicity woven into Institute practices, feared Danny and Dina might meet an unwelcome fate.

Disloyalty and doubt built in his chest, triggering a memory fraught with holes, blurred by blips of fog and confusion. His freewheeling mind refused to quit. Earl couldn't help but associate and empathize with Danny, so his froggy subconscious took hold, digging deep to the day of his unlikely "promotion."

A woman, who would become his boss, had incessantly tapped her fingertips on her desk, ever impatient. He had been tardy by two minutes, since he was preoccupied with sopping up the sweat soaking his frog face after Institute officials had taxied him from Ms. Dipper's office. He couldn't remember why he was so nervous. As he had walked in, the woman behind the desk said:

"Oh, we have a little croaking peeper on our hands. My, my, aren't you just delicious! Oh! Where are my manners? Please do sit. Earl, is it?"

He sat and wiped his hands on his knees.

"Ye-yes, ma'am, th-th-that's me."

The stutter was odd; he couldn't ever remember that happening before.

Dee tilted her head to the left and reached out her hand to his, smiling.

"Well, Earl, I do wish you'd stop grinding your gills and relax. I know why you're here, but you are not in trouble, dear," she had said.

"F-frogs don't have g-gills, ma'am, but they can go on land and water," Earl croaked.

"Is that so? Well, I must be mistaken then, yes! Was quite sure they did, the slippery hoppers. Gills or not, our little frog-gy sitting right here is about to jump, hop, and leap into a much bigger lake. From what I know, he's clearly outgrown the last one."

The memory of his interview pestered him as he walked toward the Emergency Breach Department. He could distinct-ly remember how scared he'd been at the beginning, and was unsure why he'd ever accepted in the first place. Maybe it was because he felt pressed to live up to his name: any animal so bold as to spend much of their lives near predatory waters was worthy of praise; he admired frogs for their courage. During the interview, Earl hadn't liked that the Deputy was making assumptions about him and about his favorite animal. He re-gained his composure.

"A bigger lake? What? I don't know what you're talking about, ma'am. With all due respect, of course."

"Oh fine, let's get straight to it then. Yes, we should not waste any more of our little croaking peeper's valuable time. We are on the clock! And I had to squeeze our unexpected meeting in."

"Sorry about that, ma'am. I didn't mean to cause you trou-ble. I can just take the consequences of my actions with dignity and be on my way. You won't ever have to hear from me again," Earl said.

What the Deputy did next had never been fully sensible to Earl. *Shouldn't he have been punished?*

"Oh, you misperceive! You are not causing me trouble. This is a very important meeting. But speaking of consequences, not all consequences are bad!" the Deputy said, and poked at a pile of papers with sprawling black text. "My sweet, please read and understand the terms of this contract. We strongly discourage signing if your little jeeper's peepers haven't run up and down the contract."

She had yet to hand him the contract.

"Left to right, you mean."

"What?"

"Never mind, ma'am, just a m-manner of thinking, I guess," he said, still intimidated enough that he masked his annoyance.

"Earl, would you do me the teensiest, tiniest, most itty-bitty favor?"

"An-an-anything, ma'am, you name it," he said, wanting this to go as smoothly and quickly as possible. He mustn't rock the boat; he had heard the Deputy Secretary was quick-to-anger, prone to intense mood swings, and had little patience for incompetence.

"Stop calling me fucking ma'am. It's unbecoming," she said and licked her lips.

"Ok. I g-guess, Miss, then?"

"Ah, much better. It preserves my glowing youth. Oh, and Earlie, here at Capital T we don't ever guess. We *know*, yes! We know!"

"I don't mean to sound curt, Miss, but if you haven't fired me yet, why am I here? What's this about, uh, a contract?"

Dee then had frowned and shook her head with gusto as if she were shooing a petulant little fly, before perking her lips into a smile. Unnaturally white teeth!

"The Capital T Truth Division, my personal department, is why you're here, silly man! You have shown you're *quite interested* in what happens behind the scenes, here. So much in fact, that it is imperative to expedite your promotion. You see, I want you to be my special assistant," Dee said, pressing and petting the contract smooth, crinkle-free. "Cleanliness is next to godliness!" she had commented to no one in particular.

After she slid the promotion contract over to him, he saw the document was very long, daunting, and confusing with sprawling fine print—maybe he *should* try to read it up and down. Not that it would do much good; Dee still had her hand tightly clasped to the document's end closest to her. Earl tried to tug it gently to be able to read it. No such luck.

"Oh, no need to be frightened Señor Frog, it's all very simple," she said, ripping the contract out of Earl's hand so she could read it aloud.

"Take clause 34.23abz, which says: 'I, Mr. Earl Eunice Frog, indubitably and undeniably, without any doubt, doubtlessly, hereby grant access, to the U.S. Institute for Information Dissemination's Deputy Secretary, of: past, present, future, present progressive, past progressive, future progressive, perfect, past perfect, future perfect, present perfect progressive, past perfect progressive, future perfect progressive, conditional subjunctive, and future past thoughts; feelings, ideas, light-bulb moments, inquiries, ruminations, broodings, dirty secretive desires (fetishes), and regular desires; ponderances, reflections, inner deliberations, considerations, contemplations, and musings; memories, recollections, imaginations, beliefs, doubts, fancies, reckonings, and comprehensions; presumptions, assumptions, skepticisms, judgements, realizations (sober or otherwise), suspicions, and the like, indefinitely and permanently in order to maintain the integrity of information consumption by the public of the United States...' pretty simple, yes? Yes!"

Earl sat silently, confused, looking at the dragon trinkets lining the Deputy's cabinet, barely able to listen to the long-winded legalese. He didn't even notice the contract had incorrectly stated his middle name.

"Here. Right, here. Look in my eyes. Thank you. But wait! Aside from working with me, Miss Dee, the information trade is not at no benefit to you, no! We're not asking you to sell your *soul* or anything like that."

"Uhhh...."

She had talked so fast it was impossible to get a word i—

"Quite right, Earl, yes, quite right. 'Uh'. And you haven't even heard the best part! If you agree to the terms listed in item 34.23abz, then the U.S. Institute for Information Dissemination agrees in return, under item 456.768zax: 'to grant Mr. Earl Eustace Frog limited access to the U.S. Intelligence Information Cloud housed within the Institute for Information Dissemination.' You know I had to get them to add that clause special just for you, yes! Just for you, just for my special little assistant. No one else is allowed down there, no one else but me and the Director of the National Security Agency, and that's because we must work closely together. But shhh! Don't tell anyone," she said and winked.

"B-but what ab-about—" Earl said, trying to interrupt.

"Nope. Not even his *honorable* Secretary Shermie. He would be oh so very mad to know about the cloud. He was a red-faced, tantrum-throwing toddler when I got the President to sign my specialized contract...of course, he only signed after we had a very, *very* long meeting, but I digress my sweet frog."

Dee was unforgiving with her uncomfortable eye contact. Earl didn't give in, instead fixating on the pastel colors of the dragon trinkets.

"Oh. Poo. What have I done? Why so glum?"

Earl couldn't stomach the Deputy Secretary's hypocrisy any longer. Not one minute longer. He didn't care about the consequences or her short temper or impatience.

"I think the public would be pretty upset if they knew anything at the Institute was done behind Sherman's back. He and President Bosterton promised they'd be a unified front. No secrets."

"Very, *very* good. You've always been quite the thinker, Earl, a frogman who thinks his own thoughts. That's why the Institute wants *you* to be in a much more important role to aid in in our mission to provide the very best and most accurate information to the good citizens of the United States," Dee said and beamed a smile flaunting those unnaturally white teeth. "Any other questions?"

"Well, I haven't even read the damn contract. Out-of-the-blue, you bring me here for a job offer. You must understand why I'm skeptical," Earl had said, becoming impatient and terse.

"Of course, *of course*, I understand, Mr. Frog. I know you didn't like your job at Dipper and Co., but you're just too good of an employee to let skip away. Think of it as a counteroffer so you don't leave us, leave me."

Fine. The least he could do was think about it if it were a good opportunity, he remembered thinking. But it was still a mystery why he was there in the first place.

"I'm st-still not sure I understand th-the terms, here, so I'll need to see myself."

He reached for the contract, wanting to read it himself, and not hear the clauses through some surrogate amplifier. Dee did not soften her grip; Earl had enough with her games.

"If you'd let me see what's in the contact, then *maybe* I can make an informed decision. It's hard to agree to something you're only *told* about," he said, regaining composure and again focusing on the dragons' pastel colors and scaled textures.

"Oh, yes, but trust me, the terms are right here, spelled out, right here on paper with ink! Very formal, very real once it's been written you know. So, what do you say? Work with me? Your job becoming something bigger than your little froggy self?" Dee said as she caressed his hand and leaned over the table, revealing her cleavage.

Earl remembered he had felt his eyes (and something else) bulge when she leaned over. It did sound tempting to work with her, but he was skeptical: he'd never having any luck with redheads, never really liking girls in the first place. Or guys for that matter. He had always preferred to be alone. So why was there this mystical, alluring quality to Dee, emanating mainly from her sanguine eyes? He shook his head, as if trying to escape a trance. He wasn't at a first date; this was a damn job interview!

"Oh, we are a naughty frog," Dee said, gently tugging her V-neck shirt farther down and winking.

"Uh. So-so-sorry about that," he said, embarrassed of his newly wandering eyes. For some reason, he couldn't look away from her, started to feel an ambitious urge to work as her assistant despite his reservations about Institute practices. No! He couldn't give in, right? That's when the day truly began to blur for Earl, had moments he could never reconcile or recognize— why he chose to work for the Institute.

"C-ca-c-can you maybe give m-m-me an example or something? I d-don't know h-how th-this is g-g-g-gonna work."

"Why, I've just *told* you the terms of the contract! What else is there? You've got it all, all of it, every last little piece. Right here, right on paper, yes. Very formal! Fine. Let me explain: as my lead assistant, there will be times when I grant you access, times when you will need access to special-secret knowledge housed in the Institute's underground cloud for special, secret projects. No one else, my little frog, has access unless we let them."

"Yeah, I've heard. Not even Sherman."

"Yes!"

The puzzle started to piece together, however foggy he might had felt in the Deputy's presence. Was this underground cloud, whatever it was, how Ms. Dipper added information so quickly to the citizen accuracy reports? He needed to tell someone, and now. His suspicions on Institute foul play had been right; he'd been right to walk out on Dipper and Co! Then why, or what, had inspired him to contemplate a contract with the orchestrator of deceit, herself? And almost…feel thrilled by it? The guilt began to overtake him, and so the memory became blurrier, just like always, as Earl dug into his subconscious feelings about that day.

"Quite right, Earlie, the cloud is how Ms. Dipper added the information with such lightning speed to the citizen accuracy reports," Dee said, looking at him longingly and bopping her legs underneath her desk.

"Excuse me?" Earl said, surprised.

"You're excused. Now, back to the contract. You are certainly just as perfect a little frog as I thought you'd be!" she said, unable to contain her excitement.

"I don't mean to be rude, Madame Deputy, but this doesn't seem like a contract I'd be interested in. Now, if you'd be so kind, I need to get home to give my salamander his medicine," he hoped he said, but he wasn't sure.

"I don't think so," Dee said and snapped her fingers.

Earl sat back down impulsively.

"I-I d-d-don't think I wanna sign this. You can just f-f-f-fire me," Earl said, foggily, barely able to speak.

"Fire you? Oh no, little frog, that simply would not do. Will you humor me, pretty please?" Dee said, batting her eyelashes at him.

"F-fine," Earl had said, his annoyance bubbling into ire, but still unable to look away from her eyes.

"Oh, my sweet, sweet little froggy, I know you thought Ms. Dipper's methods were old-fashioned, teeming with spineless inefficiency. If Dipper had even a lick of industry knowledge on how to run a business, your recruitment rate could have been as high as 90%. Don't worry, Momma Dee knows. As my lead assistant, *you'll* get to write the protocols yourself for all the Liaisons for Institute Escort Offices. You'll be in charge of all the L.I.E.S!"

"Ye-yes, of course, to e-erase mis-misinformation from the world entirely," Earl said, his consciousness failing.

"Oh! Quite the bullfrog bollocks on you. We can only try our very best! You are quite right: The Capital T Truth Division certainly does help sift through all the bad thoughts and all the untrue thoughts and all the misleading qualms and... poof! Makes them go away..." she said.

"Fo-for-forever?"

"Oh, not entirely, but we will learn of that once we sign the contract! We are going to be just the best of friends, you and I. Yes, we will. My little amphibian man, you will be perfect my little frog, a perfect companion for Momma Dee," she said, now gently caressing the back of Earl's neck, puckering a kiss on his cheek.

Earl then remembered that before he could ask her to stop, Dee slid the contract across the table and handed him a red pen. He heard her fingers snap. Then he saw his name sprawled sloppily in dark red ink.

I don't think that Earl remembers this day as well as I do. And that's saying something. My mind must truly be inside his brain but his brain isn't truly in control of his mind, since as he walked slowly to the Emergency Breach Department, Earl still couldn't fully understand why he'd signed the contract, and quickly forgot why he wanted to remember in the first place.

He then continued down the marble hallway to the Emergency Breach Department, and felt devastating love for his darling Momma Dee. He would do anything for her, couldn't wait to tell her about the interns. She would surely think he was her perfect little frog, then. Maybe she'd even let him help her strap them down in the underground. To hear their screams.

Chapter 16: My Old Friend Saved Me
A Professor's Diary #2

A Basement

Date unknown, sometime in mid-August 2035

To a professor who's in more trouble than he's worth:

I try so hard to remember that day—my last day as me—try so hard to remember what happened, what they did to me. I really do try. I think it's important. I think it's important to know who I am, to know who I'm not. It's important so that the doctor will know, will believe me that *they're coming*. And important so that we can take those government junkies down. But I wish Earl wasn't one of those government junkies. I like Earl. No! He's with *her*. Back to my remembering, little rat journal, yes!

My good doctor, you said I remembered your story so well, but why can I barely remember my own? Let me begin with what I know you've told me about the day I showed up:

Before I came to your doorstep, you "embarrassingly failed" the interview with the P.R. agency since your mind was "horrifically preoccupied" with why you were fired from *The Post*. And that you hadn't been able to follow-up with your editor. She wasn't returning your calls.

After you pulled your gray Subaru into the driveway, you huffed up the stairs to the front door. While it wasn't uncommon for you "to be out-of-breath from the 23-foot walk" from the driveway and up the stoop's three cement steps, that on this day, the "melancholy enveloping" your heart "may have had, and still have, some adverse health effects."

In response, I said that doughnuts and 13 cups of coffee per day probably aren't helping; you smiled because I remembered, smiled and said: "Oh, what do you know? I am a doctor, after all." I laughed and you laughed. It felt good.

While standing in the doorway, you hesitated, didn't know how to face Andrea, how to tell her that you hadn't gotten the P.R. job, how to ease her concern on the overdue bills— never mind keep the mortgage afloat—how to convince her they could keep paying for the dog, Strawberry Shortcake's, monthly diabetes pills. And what was she going to say when she found out that you wouldn't be able to afford that weekender to Virginia Beach now? Damn it, you both needed a vacation. How were you two going to fix the busted tile in the downstairs bathroom? (Well, I always think you'd be silly to bring that up, my doctor, since you'd have to remind Andrea of the time she slipped after she had a little too much tequila. No, it doesn't matter that you *always* tell her that "three should be the limit for anyone.")

You were very upset, rambling even. I told you that it was going to be okay, that I didn't know if I had any money, but that if I did, then my good friend the doctor could certainly have some. You sighed and admitted, "You always did have a leg up on me financially. Didn't you my old friend?" I told you "I guess so," but you wouldn't let up, trying to help me remember. "I mean it, little professor, you usually doubled my savings every year with your book deals and speaking fees." I told you Ms. Andrews shouldn't spend so much money on the dog. Then you laughed and laughed.

It was then I found my sense of humor again. That moment was important for me: I remembered your laugh, the cackling rise giving way to deep intermittent booms from your gullet. I can even hear it now.

Still afraid of facing your wife, you stood before the doorway, "shaking nervously, grasping for any semblance of confidence" to bring with you to tell Andrea the sour news of your failed interview.

But you're never one to quit, and got a little "muster." You'd just have to go right in there, right up to her and say, "Andrea, I've got some sour news." And then she'd get concerned, naturally, because she always "gets a little too concerned," which would make her do that "weird thing with her lips and her eyebrows," and oh how you hate that, hate it when she does that weird thing with her lips and with her eyebrows, and then of course, with that weird concerned look on her face, she'd say something like: "What the hell did you do?" rather than a more loving, "what's wrong, honey?"

You got sad after you told me that, looked down at the concrete floor and admitted she almost never called you honey anymore, even though she used to more times than your "feeble mind can count..." I took your hand and said that I could be your honey now and you replied, "In your dreams, bub," and you cackled again. You told me that you probably "fabricated a few more scenes" while standing at your doorstep, before remembering your 7th cup of coffee sitting idly in the car. You might not be one to quit, but there's nothing wrong with mulling over a cup of joe.

As good an excuse as any to procrastinate a bit more, I'm sure.

So, you "moseyed back down the steps." Though you still hadn't quite caught your breath, you opened the driver's side door of the gray Subaru to retrieve the brown, jumpy liquid. You told me that you sat in the driveway, leaning on the car, in a "caffeinated daze" which "probably didn't help the rushing anxiety," and rocked back and forth and forth and back.

You were riled up when you told me this, all right; I could see it in your face.

Amidst your downward spiral sitting in the driveway, you told me that something caught the corner of your eye. I yelled out, "Me!" like a little child. That made you smile but you chastised me, told me to keep quiet and listen.

Your "manic mind" just couldn't be stopped: "Jesus, Mary, and Joseph, I've done screwed myself with my damnable ambition...but I don't even know what happened. I had *insider information*, from the Head Researcher himself, people have killed for less! Government corruption at its most dastardly!"

Insider information, you had said to me. Yes. I was on the inside. But more than just as a fly on the wall... I headed the Research Department, carved out protocol for verifying information and how it was to be presented to the public so they'd believe it to be true. There was so much work to be done in order to correct the public doubt in mass media. Of course, I had access to the ins and outs of Institute corruption. But I didn't quite remember that far when you first told me the story.

I asked you if I was the Head Researcher, if that was my position at the Institute after I left my teaching job. You looked at me hard and said, "Yes, my good friend. That's who you were."

I still know, Doctor. My memory is coming back.

You were happy and upset at the same time after I remembered. Your fists clenched; your teeth grinded; you looked angry. I told you it was okay, but you rebuked me and told me it wasn't. You hated seeing me in pain. There was no forgiveness for the government junkies who did this to me. I got afraid again but you consoled me: "No. The doctor has you now. They won't hurt you anymore, my old friend. I'll make damn sure of it. We just need you to remember what happened on the day you escaped."

But what did happen to me on that day? I know you said this was when I made my entrance, so I will go off what I have:

You cocked your head to the left, cued from a potential, impending danger; a stranger approached. You said something weird about how your monkey brain tried to "protect you from harm," to be careful since "you never know when someone might be after you."

You never know when they might be coming, Doc. But you'll never listen. Try to do us all a favor and take your own damn advice.

You said you saw a man "looking and walking like the undead," that this man limped toward you, but with "an animated ferocity of fear propelling each step." The man had a torn sport coat in a "dilapidated state," and ripped khaki slacks, but you were most disgusted by the zombie-man's "swollen, unnaturally hot-pink feet."

They looked like they'd been in a vice, and one was bleeding, you said.

So that's why I have a bandage on my little pink foot-claw.

As I limped toward you in my zombie-state, you said you thought, "No way he's headed this way, the damn sewer tramp better not come this way." But then you stopped because you could tell that I was really sad that you said that.

I still am, now that I reflect on it. How could you fail to recognize your best friend? How's this for remembering, Doc?

You did try to console me—I'll give you that. Said something like, "no, no, sweet professor, my old friend. You see, I didn't know it was you! You looked terrible, and that's why I took you down here to patch you up."

I wandered across the street and approached the driveway, and "madly barked and squeaked out whatever insanity penetrated" my mind, a "rambling ruckus trickling off" my tongue. You were afraid. I was coming, coming closer, and it was too damn late for you to run into the house. I remember you shouting to me:

"Ge-get the hell off my lawn! I don't want to have to say it again! I'll-I'll call the police you blathering fool. I swear I will. They'll be down here in a minute. I'll start counting...one...two..."

Ouch! Damn it. My head. Not now. I'm finally remembering. I must stay here. I won't give in. Must remember so I can tell him that they're coming.

I approached your lawn, trembling and blathering, standing only ten feet away, ready to pounce for the kill. I had leaned forward and blurted, "The hospitality of your hall has lessened as of late, Theoden King! Tut-tut-tut, donotworrymylad, they have yet to take my staff! I shall *release you!*"

I guess I was mimicking a wizard holding a staff, and bopped you square on the head. I was unrelenting. Bop. Bop. Bop. What normally would have been a happy reunion, was quickly turning into an old-fashioned brawl.

I kept screaming and shouting. I said: "Oh, don't you see, can't you see, they're making an enemy of me. Tired but true, a fleeting squeaker, Kalamazoo. A spoiled rotten, ungrateful little rat! Amenities she said, amenities they gave me, yes! No. Why is this? What say you? It's me, of course, and look, there's you! But everyone else is here, too! Look around, you'll see! Tut-tut-tut, yes, but what's in a name? A rose by any name would smell as sweet. But no! Grown in depraved, shit-riddled fields, could we ever still call it a rose? A crop of inextinguishable regrets! Regrets and poor little feet claws! Ouch! It hurts, please. Do you think I look pretty? Tell me I'm pretty, doc. I don't feel pretty. Aha, better yet, give these tired eyes an exam!"

It was odd we'd meet like that. But what's truly odd is that you had talked to me just a few days before on the phone. No semblance of insanity then.

You shouted back, fists in the air. You looked almost cartoonish in your suit that fits too tight, scowling like a champion boxer at the start of a fight. You shouldn't have shouted that I was a "mad man" since all it did was animate me all the more. I replied, "Perhaps mad, yes, but a mad man, no! Only once I discover who I am will I be free. Yes! No net ensnares me. With an independent will, I will be free! But not right now.

I can't be free now. I'm a caged little rat. Yes! She snatched me up for being a sweet little rat. No. Please. Help. You must help, Doctor! *They're coming!"*

When I called you doctor, that's when you knew.

We embraced.

You cried. I cried.

I even knew then, Doc. And once I get these dreams in order, I'll know more. You'll believe me then. Else we're fucked.

Chapter 17: Naughty, Naughty Intern

Intern Office of the Institute for Information Dissemination
August 9, 2035—The day before Danny meets Dee
About 4:30 p.m.

My friend Danny is slumped in his folding, makeshift office chair, pretending to scribble on some paperwork. He's not with Dina, and not freaking out about Dee, so I don't know when I am.

He seems to be waiting for something, or for someone. He checks his watch, and the time reads: 4:37 p.m., August 9, a time when most of the unpaid interns have been released from their shackles, a time when their boss, Dennis, would be at least 45 minutes into his daily schmoozing session with Madame Deputy Secretary, Dee.

Now it is time to watch, and do my best to remember:

Something had been bothering the hell out of our boy Danny. One of his favorite papers, *The Washington Post*, hadn't published any news articles other than syndicated *Associated Press* repeats, never mind the abrupt stoppage to their normally prolific opinion section. Had their low Institute accuracy report ratings finally caused them to shutter their doors? No. That seemed too out-of-sync with the paper's typical resiliency and resistance to the Institute. Of papers, *The Post* was the cranky old man shouting at teenagers to get the hell off his lawn. The only thing that'd make the crank-pot stop shouting would be his death. Perhaps the Institute's malignancy had infected the paper's internal organs to crippling effect, and the old man was dead.

"What the hell's going on? There's gotta be some shady shit going on if a paper with such a long history of investigative journalism is gonna go under without so much as a squeak to the public on who shot them dead. Their slogan is 'Democracy Dies in Darkness' for God's sake! Maybe the rumors are true," Danny thought as he continued to scribble, a fake performance for a nearly empty office.

He triple-checked that no one but the office administrator, blubbering Donna, remained, and waited for his opportunity. *The Post's* distinct silence, combined with his professor's unexplained absence, were too much to accept. Danny couldn't go on pretending that the Institute wasn't up to something, something vile, and Danny had a plan to find out what it was. Donna was the last hurdle to overcome on his way to the finish line.

"God damn it, Donna. Hurry the hell up and take your fat ass to the can," Danny thought while forgetting his manners: don't stare.

"Bl'uh...can I help bl'ou, Señor Umberto?" Donna said from across the office, jokingly.

Oops. Now he'd have to improvise.

"Was just admiring your necklace," he blurted, "Is that blue topaz?" Danny bit his tongue at Donna's racism. He was American, damn it. So what if he spoke English and Spanish at home? Donna could barely speak English, and it didn't help that she always shoved snack-cakes and cookies down her gullet. Nevertheless, Donna seemed to genuinely like Danny, even if she didn't know what the hell microaggressions were. He planned to use that affection to his advantage.

"Bluh…it's sapphire, bl'ut… thank you," she blubbered, her raspy breath heaving in between every other word.

"My mistake, Donna. I'll have to remember that. Wait—now that you mention it—you might be able to help me."

"What?" Donna asked sincerely.

"You see," Danny said, walking over to the front desk, "this sheet doesn't have the office number for the Data and Inquiry Department, and I've never been there."

"Bl'ugh…interns…" she said, struggling. "Bl'uh…haven't you been…bl'uh…here for four months?" she said, shaking her head. Then she laughed, but the force of compressed air in her gullet was too much, and so she emitted a rough-cut, mucous cough fit for the three-pack-a-day smoker. After she composed herself, she smiled at Danny through her wheezes, and took out a purple pen with sparkling ink and wrote down the office number located on the second floor.

"Bl'uh…they're closed though. Close…bl'uh…at 4 p.m. today since the floor…bl'uh…has a reception," she noted.

"Damn. Oh, shit—sorry—then I can't go down there? It's just I'm going to get in so much trouble," Danny lied, trying to look as sullen and innocent as possible, hitting her with a puppy-dog stare. "Fuck. My parents will kill me if I lose this internship…I can't lose it…I'm so screwed…"

"Bl'uh…What's the trouble? Bring…bl'uh…it tomorrow," she said, shrugging her shoulders and rasping and coughing again.

"Well...I got caught up with paperwork. You know how Dennis treats me like crap, makes me do all the grunt work?"

"He...bl'uh...sure does."

Danny knew Donna didn't like Dennis, thought he was "a bumbling people-pleaser," and spent too much time with the Deputy. Then again, Donna hated anyone who flattered the Madame Deputy, felt as if they betrayed Secretary Sherman. Donna liked Sherman since he made the time to stop by and talk to her every few weeks. He'd always ask her to do him little favors, like personally deliver his outgoing correspondence to the mailroom or organize his desk. *Such a naughty Secretary, flirting with a married woman!*

"It's fucking...sorry..."

"It's okay," she said and smirked.

"It's annoying. So, like today, he gives me this mountain of papers to work through, piled on more throughout the day. And, of course, *of course*, before I could even get halfway through it, he told me to deliver this file to the Data and Inquiry Office Supervisor before they close. He said it was urgent but wouldn't let me get up before I finished the pile. You saw him! He didn't even leave until 4:15 p.m. It's like he wants me to fail. And *of course*, he didn't even tell me they were going to close early today!" Danny said, wallowing, welling tears in his eyes.

What a performance! Bravo Danny! 4.5 stars for the little intern.

Donna looked to Danny, sighed, reached for the hook underneath her desk, and pulled out a keyring, a hulking, heaving mass fit for maintenance. She dangled it, the keys jingling loudly under their sheer weight.

"Bl'uh…don't tell anyone. Sherman's given me…bl'uh… some extras…bl'uh…to keep an eye on things," she blubbered in a whisper, smitten by Sherman's trust in her.

"Really?"

"Really. But make sure…bl'uh…you bring them back tomorrow."

Danny couldn't believe his act had worked, but then again, he could. He *was* good, even did a little improv comedy on campus last year. Sure, he'd charmed Donna since the beginning of the summer—he had that effect on older women, even seemed to exploit it—but he didn't realize his charm would reap such a benefit.

He took the comically large keyring with gratitude, nodded to Donna, and walked toward the Data Inquiry Department. "Now I'll be able to see for myself what the hell they're up to," Danny thought.

Lucky for Danny, as Donna so kindly told him, there was a second-floor reception that day. A "monthly celebration of good Institute work," the supervisors said, but Danny thought it was more likely a cheap sham to maintain employee morale despite low wages and long hours.

"Fucking capitalism coming through for once," Danny joked silently.

He exited the intern office, walked through the marble hallway, passing the statues of Sulzberger and Hearst, and down the right-wing staircase. He made sure to jam the keyring so it fit snugly in his jean's back pocket; if any INFO Guard noticed a grunt-intern possessing such access, they'd certainly get suspicious, and would give Danny some major heat. That would take far too much time. He needed to investigate unhindered. At least some of them got drunk at the monthly receptions. That would help, but there was no time for a scolding nor an elongated conversation where he would have to fake remorse or conjure a bunch of shoddy excuses to get the guard off his back.

He moved swiftly passed the second-floor office party—and quite the decadent affair it was, with filet mignon and chicken parmesan and $50 bottles of wine and fine cheese. An excellent use of taxpayer dollars! All those vendors served. He had to move quickly; it would lessen the chance somebody he knew would call to him. They might get suspicious as it was unlike Danny to pass up free meals. It appears he didn't move fast enough, though.

"Kid! D. Hey kid. Get over here!"

He ignored the voice and walked faster, but heard boots padding, getting louder, catching up to him. "Ugh, damn it. I gotta be covert. Who the hell needs me, *right now*? Can't it fucking wait?" Danny thought.

"Danny! Where the heck are you off to in such a rush? Come by the party!" the man with broad shoulders and a casual black polo, said.

"Sorry, Daryl. You know how it is. Dennis has me working late," he said in a half-lie.

"Ah that dog. What a bitch. Well, if that D-bag Dennis has got you working, there's no reason you can't have a bit of fun while you grind after hours," Daryl, the Head of Shipping and Receiving, said.

Daryl chuckled, urging Danny to take the last glug of his vodka soda.

"Ugh," Danny winced, tasting more vodka than soda.

"Bold and strong, eh? Makes it worth your while. Gotta get our wages from somewhere. Here. Take this nip too. I know ya college kids run a bit dry when you're home for the summer," he said, with a knowing grin. "I'll see you out back soon to talk girls, yeah?"

"Yeah," Danny said, relieved he could now be on his way. "I'll come by the party in a little while."

"Good enough," Daryl said as Danny turned to continue his mission.

But not more than ten steps from the reception, he heard a young woman shout:

"Danny!"

It was a voice he couldn't ignore. Reluctantly, he turned and waited while she jogged up to him.

"Hey, Dina. Sorry, I'm kind of in a rush."

"In too much of a rush for free food? They have chicken parm. You can't say no to that," she kidded and scooped up a healthy bite, dangling cheese strands. "I see you stayed to get a lowkey drink from Daryl, anyway. You two pretty close now?"

"Yeah, we shoot the shit over cigarettes. Asks me about girls," Danny said, pretending Dina wasn't the girl always on his mind, and consequently, always the subject of their conversations. He saw Daryl back at the cheese-and-crackers table, winking.

"Oh, girls, eh?" Dina said, jostling Danny's shoulder in jest.

"Yeah, he's cool. Has some batty advice, but still cool. Listen, Dina. I really can't talk right now. I have to deliver this stack to the Data and Inquiry Department or Dennis will be more on my ass than he already is. I'll come back after."

Danny found it tough to leave Dina, especially when her face looked so disappointed. Maybe she *did* like him, maybe the two of them together wasn't such a farfetched idea after all. No. It wouldn't ever work. She was way too smart and pretty and talented and cool to like him. Plus, they'd been friends forever; she probably just saw him as a brother. He only could hope he wasn't sitting rosy-eyed, waiting perpetually in the dreaded, devastating and disappointing place all young romantics feared: the friend-zone.

"Snap out of it, man," Danny thought to himself, picking up the pace toward the Data Inquiry Department.

Arriving at the department entrance, he scanned the corridor before trying the keys. Danny couldn't believe his luck: no INFO Guards on patrol right now, probably on account of the reception. It was true: they needed morale boosts, too.

Quickly fumbling through the keys, Danny inserted the one Donna had identified for him and turned the lock. Success!

The room was dim, the only light peeking through the slits of closed blinds.

I think Danny debated for a minute on whether he should flick on the light to aid in his investigations, but if crime movies had taught him anything, it was better to stay in the shadows when flying so close to the sun.

"I'm no Icarus," Danny thought.

He placed the envelope on the front desk and wrote a sticky note that he positioned on the front page:

"Sorry for the delay! Hope tomorrow morning works for your deadline. Damn intern's fault. Surprised?" - Dennis

At least by signing Dennis' name, Danny could reasonably deny that he'd ever been to the Data Inquiry Department. Proud of his subterfuge, Danny raced over to the file cabinet which housed confidential documents. The system was archaic, but cunning. He had recently learned the Institute only kept single, paper copies of its Grade 4 and 5 Security Clearance Assignments in order to prevent hacking. Though the Institute did have some of the most advanced cyber security protocols and firewalls, even Secretary Sherman's pomposity couldn't convince him to trust such sensitive information in the internet cloud, ripe for picking. Danny hoped Sherman and Donna had the rapport Donna claimed they had, or that Donna was some secret asset to Institute investigations. It was his only chance.

"Whew. Can't believe I'm actually doing this. You're in it now. Now for the hard part," Danny said quietly to himself, beginning to rustle through the keyring, hoping one would unlock the cabinet.

After about three minutes of scrabbling for the correct key, he heard a glorious sound: a metal latch unclicked.

Pulling open the drawer, he searched for his professor's file, to see if Institute malevolence accounted for his old mentor's continued absence the past week. Danny found the file. In it, there was a manila envelope sealed delicately with red tape, which had "HIGHLY CONFIDENTIAL" stamped in bold letters on the top.

Probably best to not rip open the tape, he thought. Too obvious. Scrounging for anything else, he came across an unsealed document in a laminate binding, labelled, "RELATED PAR-TIES." He plucked out the laminate folder, which read:

INSTITUTE FOR INFORMATION DISSEMINATION
WASHINGTON D.C.
CONFIDENTIAL, POTENTIAL GRADE 4 BREACH

BREACH REPORT SUBJECT DETAILS:

    Name: Drew Andrews
    Alias: The Doctor
    Occupation: ex-reporter/columnist for *The
    Washington Post*
    Height: 5' 11"
    Weight: 247.45 pounds
    Race: Black
    Location: Unknown; believed to still be in
    Washington D.C. area
    Vehicle: Unknown; changed recently.
    Threat Level: Grade 4—CAPTURE; DO NOT KILL
    Other Notes:
    Presumed to be unarmed
    Close friends with Grade 5 Threat—The Rat
    Washington Post editor in custody

ITINERARY FOR CORRECTION OF BREACH:

    1. Interrogate Supervisors at *Washington Post*
    2. Hire skilled hitmen to capture and frighten the
       subject.
    3. Deliver the subject to the Deputy Secretary.
    4. Extract knowledge and upload to cloud
       database.
    5. If subject knows too much, increase to Grade
       5 Threat.
    6. If item 5 proves correct: Exterminate
       subject.

It turned out looking for information about his professor had answered Danny's other question about *The Washington Post.*

"Fuck. I knew they were up to some sketchy shit. Killing reporters for doing their job? Keeping editors 'in custody'? Sick. No wonder *The Post* hasn't published an opinion column lately. And what the fuck do they mean 'Extract knowledge and upload to cloud database'?" Danny said quietly to himself.

Understanding he shouldn't push his luck, Danny snapped a quick photo of the document and then slid the confidential file back into its original home. He closed the drawer to the file cabinet and jostled the key to lock it, like no one was ever there. As he stood up, light abruptly entered the room, spilling in from the department entrance. The door quickly shut, ensconcing his new officemate.

"Just what the fuck are you doing? Someone's very naughty!" a woman's voice said, pointedly.

"Uhh, oh—uhh," Danny said, still unable to discern the shadowed figure standing by the door, but preparing for the worst. "I was looking for...my boss, Dennis, sent me..."

"You're in for it, now. You are certainly aware that little interns aren't allowed in the Data and Inquiry Department, unsupervised. No, certainly not," the woman said, stepping towards him.

"Fuck."

As the woman got closer, her visage slowly came into focus, but was too veiled to determine. Danny began to tremble, scared that the rumors of Institute torture were true. He bolted up from his knee-crouch, his mind in a fight-or-flight conflict.

"Please. I didn't mean anything by it. I was only curious. Please. I won't tell a soul, not one!"

A pause. Danny heard the woman begin to laugh.

"Okay—I can't anymore. Don't pee your damn pants, Danny!" the woman said.

"D-D-Dina?"

"Daryl tossed me his keys to make sure you weren't getting into any trouble," Dina told him. "He really likes you."

"Fucking hell. You got me good."

"What were you doing, anyway?"

"Nothing. Just snooping in places I shouldn't. Let's get the hell out of here before someone actually shows up."

"All right, but hey, listen—watch your back. This place would be a drag without you. You're lucky you have Daryl and me looking out for you. I hope you didn't do anything stupid."

"Me? Do anything stupid? Nah. I'm fine. Let's go get some of that chicken parm. But first…a little of this," Danny said and glugged half the nip Daryl gave him before handing the rest to Dina.

"Like I said. Very naughty," she said and smiled.

Chapter 18: Solitude and Rapture
A Professor's Diary #3

A Basement
Date unknown, sometime in mid-August 2035

To a holed-up man who fixates too much on dreams:

"Paranoia," the doctor keeps saying to me, "just a bout of paranoia, old friend. No need to worry. They are not here.

I can't hear my own thoughts very well today and I know my head's pounding and spinning. I can barely think. You don't have to *remind me*, little rat journal. Your sass doesn't help.

Stop laughing. I know I stumbled in the dark when I woke up, unsure of the time, but I know it was dark, and I smashed my foot into the cement wall. I squeaked and squealed in pain. My little foot-claw was throbbing so I couldn't help it, and I know, I *know*, I need to be a quiet little professor.

It was pandemonium packed into a foot-sized package.

My doctor and Andrea sprinted down the stairs like the house was on fire. They were both worried but still scolded me. Told me to hush like I didn't already know. Andrea quickly replaced my bandage. I tried to gain some points by complimenting her lilac-and-honeysuckle perfume, but she wasn't having it and told me to be quiet.

What's worse, little rat journal, my "incident" ruined any hope I might have had to get the doctor to believe me about my dreams, about how I saw Danny look at the secret Institute report that said they were after my doctor. It was all right there, very formal, since it was written in ink! Or is Danny not real either? Wake up, Doc.

He tells me I've never met any of these people, so they aren't even real, but he can't see and I can see the hawk and his clam and the devil-woman coming for us.

I've realized that until I fully come back, there's just no way he'll believe me, no, no way at all. I wrote down all the details from the Institute's confidential document, the document *on you*, doctor. But instead of believing me, you punish me instead! No dinner for little rat-men who "prefer fiction over fact," little rat-men who are "silly enough to believe dreams." He gets mad when I call myself a rat-man, though, so I guess I should try to call myself the professor.

HUSH!

What was that sound? It's them. It *has to be them.*

No. Nonono, those couldn't have been gun shots. Just the noisy washer, the noisy washer roosting and banging and keeping me up all night.

I've tried to keep count of them, the voices, the people I see without seeing them. I really try but there are too many inside me to keep count. Some are young and some are old and some are fraught and some are bold. But it's so dark in here. There's no way to tell if I'm sleeping or if I am awake, a desperate victim, a mal-conceived bastard of sleep and torture and vivid dreams.

And we know that dreams are not real and that real people can be in dreams but not be doing real things even if they seem like the things they do are real. I need my mind to *slow down*. My subconscious is on fire. I'm hungry for dreamless sleep and thirsty for memory. Please. *They're coming!* I don't care what my doctor says. You believe, don't you me, don't you little rat journal?

It's so hard to think, so hard to think down here, with mania oppressing the recessed forefront of my mind. Even when I think that I can think, my own volatile stench stings my eyes with ferocity, but that's not the worst part of my tenure as a sweet, little caged rat.

It's funny, no, not funny, but yes, funny, how your mind plays tricks when its main purpose is the opposite: to help us learn safety from danger, to help us sift through peril, damn it, to help us survive. Maybe my mind's hallucinatory tricks, the kaleidoscopic travels, are telling me that I am in danger. A defense mechanism. Survival. Maybe my mind isn't playing tricks. Maybe it's trying to help.

How's that for a psychological self-assessment, Doc?

No equilibrium, no, none at all. When there's too much darkness, it feeds on all your light, engorged and fat, too insatiable to quit. The grotesqueness makes me giggle. No, hush! This is no laughing matter. The enveloping dark then becomes the light and then there has to be darkness for there to be light. No dark without the light, but what if I can turn the darkness into the light? What if I can? I think I can. Then the light couldn't be without the dark. Light would be the absence of dark. I must appear in my dreams. Be the light in the dark.

It's going dark dark dark again to see the light but light to see the dark...

PART IV:
WHAT WILL HAPPEN
TO US?

Chapter 19: Dance, Dina, Dance

Intern Office of the Institute for Information Dissemination
August 10, 2035—the day of the escape
A little before 1:30PM

I see a girl with skinny legs looking at the slick-with-sweat neck of a young man. They are in an office building, and very nervous.

"SHHH!" Dina said, trying as subtly as possible to eye the frogman who had reentered the office. "He's back."

It's Earl! Earl, please don't hurt the interns; they're nice! Danny, Dina, get the hell out of there!

"Fuck. Fuck. Fuck," Danny said, adding little to the conversation.

They waited a few moments and watched Earl leave the room. The two interns sighed in relief, for now.

"Wait. I *know*. I know why you're freaking out. This has something to do with what you did yesterday in the Data and Inquiry Office, doesn't it? You almost shit your pants when I snuck up on you. What did you do?"

Silence.

"Danny. What the hell did you do? I'm involved now, whether you fucking like it or not. Sometimes knowing is worse than doing."

Danny didn't like the indisputable ring of truth in Dina's words, but she was right, and now they'd have to figure out what to do.

"I needed some answers. Got some answers. Now it sounds like she wants some, too. She asked me to join the Information Gathering Initiative. Kept talking about how I would be, 'just of the most help, yes' to my old professor, the Head of Research."

"Did she say anything about yesterday? You should have known better to snoop. I hope it was worth it," Dina said, still upset at Danny's brashness, ignoring him.

"No time to tell you about it now, but let's just say the media isn't folding because they don't have readers," he said, and pantomimed slitting his own throat with his index finger.

"And what are you, an intern, going to do about it? You really think she doesn't know of what's going on under her own roof? God, how can you be so damn stupid?"

"I don't know what to think anymore, Dina. I gotta get out—*now*," Danny panted, now pacing about the office again. Good thing Donna was on the phone, or she would have told him to sit his ass down.

"*Sit the fuck down*," Dina commanded before looking toward blubbering Donna through the open door of the intern office. "You'll get us both in trouble."

"Don't tell me what the fuck to do, Dina. Just leave me alone. I've made my bed, no reason for you get in it with me."

Dina was disgruntled by Danny's fierce snap, but pushed it down, knowing she'd want a friend if she were in Danny's shoes.

"Hush. Keep it down, all right? Listen. *Listen.* I have an idea."

Dina tried to tell him her idea, quiet as a scampering mouse on the hunt for a melting pot of Port Salut cheese, but Danny's mind was singular and fried; he'd already gotten up from the chair so he could jam and pack items into his backpack. Among the contraband, Dina saw him stow a manila envelope sealed delicately with red tape, stolen from Dennis's desk.

"Wait, what're you doing? Taking stuff from the office is just going to make it worse."

"What if I need evidence? And don't think I don't know how fucked I am. She told me how special I was, how she was impressed with my mind, how she wanted me to join her department. But it gave me this eerie feeling. It was like a game of cat and mouse. Fuck that. It's a summons not a negotiation. *That's* why I'm hauling ass," Danny said, agitated and afraid.

"What? An intern in The Capital T Truth Division? That's Grade 5 Security. You can count on one hand how many officials have access. They keep a tight ship."

"I don't fucking know why."

"Yes, you certainly fucking know why, Danny, but you won't spit it out."

"Because she'll hear me!"

"Danny. If the rumors are true, she'll observe your every move until you accept, making sure you don't rat anything confidential from the Institute. That means she'll know you'd been talking to me, so you might as well come clean. It's not like once you say it aloud she'll learn something she doesn't know. What the hell did you see yesterday?"

"Fuck...FUCK!"

"Chances are she's already sending out a search brigade after me."

"Not funny, Dina. You know how terrible I'd feel if that happened. I didn't even want to tell you because of this. Just leave me alone."

"I know. I know. I'm sorry," Dina said, and then thought hard, weighing her options. They needed to have at least one stable head in this shit-storm.

If the Deputy truly had the surveillance capability that the rumors suggested, then Dina would be considered an accessory. Not only had she listened to Danny recapitulate his meeting (partially), but she also snuck into the Data and Inquiry Department to check on Danny. Dina doubted the Deputy would care much that Daryl had given her the keys willingly in order to make sure Danny wasn't getting into trouble (a whole lot of good that did). And it's not as if rogue, rule-bending behavior was new to Danny, or to Dina for that matter. She'd always needed to check on Danny from the time they were in elementary school, since he was always getting into *something*. It was like the kid thrived on reverse-psychology; he had an insatiable curiosity that could only be satisfied if he figured out why he *shouldn't* be doing something, by actually doing it. Still, they rarely got caught though, except when they split up to fend for themselves. She trusted Danny, regardless of the fact that he pushed his luck a bit too often.

Dina applied for the Institute internship for its prestige, but she had to admit she was happy when Danny texted her about it. His presence by her side this summer certainly didn't hurt. She liked him since they were kids, and always wondered why the hell he was too scared to make a move. But there was little time for that now. How would she live with the guilt if Danny met some sour end since he made a different bold move? Worse yet, what lie would she have to make up when the Deputy and her cronies came for her next? The best option for both of them was to stick together.

"Dina. You're freaking me out. I don't like it when you have that look on your face," Danny said.

"It's just a little ironic, no, serendipitous even, that we're finding a way out of trouble again. Kind of like when we were kids."

"Dina. Don't. Don't even think about it."

"I'm already an accessory...mine as well be an accomplice to your escape, then, eh?" she offered, ignoring him, more comfortable with the idea than she anticipated.

"What? No. You can't do that," Danny commanded. "This is my problem. You stay away from it. Far away."

"Oh. I didn't realize you had authority to determine what I can and can't do," Dina said, her words cutting and final. She had decided.

Danny knew Dina well enough. There wasn't much to do once she had decided something; she had iron-clad convictions, so he had no choice but to let her help.

"Okay, fine."

"What do you say?"

"Really?"

She waited.

"Help me."

"Was that so hard?" Dina said, half-joking. "Listen. There's an Institute Info Conference for the Good Citizens starting in a few minutes," Dina said, checking her watch. "We might be able to slink into the masses, unnoticed. And—"

"And then when the cattle herds out of the front doors—"

"We moo like good cattle and hoof on out before the INFO Guards are any wiser," Dina said, smiling.

Danny always admired Dina's intelligence, how quick she was under pressure. "If we ever get outta here, I swear I'll marry this girl," Danny thought.

"Worth a shot, Dina, worth a fucking shot. I mean, what do we have to lose? It's either moo with the mediocri-cattle or be arrested by the INFO Guards where your only right is to *not* remain silent," he said.

"Worth a fucking shot, right!"

They glanced around the room and waited for the clock to strike 1:30 p.m., the time the Good Citizen meetings were "held for the convenience of our vigilant, informed patriots," in the front hall of the Institute for Information Dissemination.

Dina had never understood why the meetings were held at 1:30 p.m., in the middle of the workday, never understood how the meetings were always packed to the brim with "informed patriots." Every day the INFO Guards had to turn some of the Good Citizens away, pointing them to the "viewing room" on the left side of the Main Hall. At least a packed hall would make it easy to blend in.

The simplest part of their escape still made Dina nervous. How would they pass the admin, Donna, at the front desk? Whatever the plan, it needed to be executed fast. Dina knew "word travels fast but truth travels faster at the Institute." All it took was one phone call to Donna's desk unveiling their plan, and they'd be trapped before getting the chance to leave the intern office.

An idea struck Dina. Donna loves munching on cookies throughout the day, and interns could often could hear Donna chewing and chomping. So loud was the slobbering sound that it often weaseled its way into Dina's dreams.

Her brain was travelling fast, working through potential scenarios. That's it! Dina might be able to bribe Donna with the double-chocolate-chunk cookie that she had brought for an afternoon snack, but even if the distraction worked, it was the winding, entropic, networked halls of the Central Hub that scared her most. She knew the Central Hub boasted at least one tributary to each major sub-department within the Institute, so, if they were forced to abandon their planned route to the front hall, the remaining egresses would likely be manned by INFO Guards, dispatched directly from the Capital T Truth Division, revered and feared by their formal name, the Federal Information Battalion, or, the FiBs, for short.

These were no average security guards. They were like the green berets of the Institute for Information Dissemination, but with a singular mission: to vigilantly serve the Deputy Secretary. Dina knew that all FiBs must undergo an intense training regimen: months upon months of physically and psychologically demanding trials. The FiBs wore the same uniforms as regular INFO Guards to blend in, except had a patch identifying their loyalty was to the Capital T Truth Division.

Suddenly fear smacked Dina. They needed to leave.

She snapped into action, grabbing Danny's sweaty wrist so the two could pad out of the outer-office doorway.

Sam Sarkisian

"First stop, Donna. Decadent Donna," Dina said quietly to Danny. She reached into her backpack's zippered pouch to retrieve her chocolate artillery: two rich, fat-charged disks of flour and chocolate and sugar.

Cookied ammunition in hand, Dina extended her other arm to halt Danny, overhearing Donna's blubbering "bl'uhs" which whished out of her mouth-hole as she rasped for breath.

"Now bl'uh…listen here, bl'ub. I…bl'uh…don't get paid… bl'uh…nearly enough for bl'uh…your sass. Policy…bl'uh… clearly states that…bl'uh…you must come prepared…bl'uh… with all…bl'uh…the required documents," Donna said, huffing and wheezing.

"No, sir. I said…bl'uh…no sir. I will need you…bl'uh…to cool it, sir."

She was mad. That was good news.

"Lucky for us. She stays on the phone when she's mad. Wants to get the better of the argument, I guess. Or until the caller gets too damn tired of trying to figure what the hell she's trying to say," Dina whispered to Danny. He snickered.

Understanding their opportunity window had now opened, the two interns whipped through the office about to pass Donna's desk, and feigned casual conversation with one another. Donna looked up for a moment, was about to say something to them, but Dina gestured that there was no need, and laid the cookie down on the desk. Donna smiled, shoved the entire cookie in her cavernous mouth, and returned to the phone call. In part a symptom of their anxiety, and in part because of their disgust, the two interns' steps became swift, scampering out of the intern office.

Now walking through the congested webbing of the Institute, Dina said:

"We just gotta act natural. Act like we're taking a half day. Good thing Dennis is out to lunch."

She looked over to Danny, worried about his glazing eyeballs and fountaining sweat.

"Natural, right. Organic. Authentic. Just a regular ol' half day. We're diligent interns," Danny said, desperate to compose himself.

As they wisped through the long marble hall of the third floor of the Institute, a hall decorated with gold-foil letters stating "Veritas" and other dead-language verbiages, our two friends stopped, hearing a bubbling commotion from inside the Deputy's office:

"I-is sh-sh-she back? Sh-she must know!" A little man with bulging, bulbous eyeballs said, hopping along the marble hall into the Deputy's office.

"She's down there with her most important client, Earl. It'll have to wait. Just follow protocol. Have you already told the Emergency Breach Department? Nothing else to do. She said she'd be a few hours," one of the FiBs said to the anxious frogman.

"Wh-what! No! Sh-sh-she won't know if sh-she's down there! There isn't m-muh-muh-much time."

"Cool it, Earl."

"Eh-eh-eh-excuse me? And-and who are *you,* telling me what to do? I-I-I'm yo-yo-your boss!"

The two FiBs around him laughed.

"Sh-She'll huh-huh-hear about this, FiBs 48 and 72, guh-guh-got it," he said and walked deep into the office.

They stopped laughing and called out to him, realizing they'd get reprimanded for not working diligently while Dee was in the underground. "What should we do, Earl?"

"I-i-if D-Dee doesn't know, th-then you have to t-t-t-tell Sherman, and t-t-take orders f-f-f-from him," Earl shouted back, displeased.

The FiBs then slammed the door, in a huff.

"That's the Deputy he's talking about. Quick, we've got to go now while they're distracted," Danny said, looking to Dina. "Looks like she's onto us, or at least her toady is. Won't be long before the whole place is on our heels."

They busted out of the Central Hub and into the foyer before the main hall, witnessing a sea of Institute Good Citizens in a fish-school, eagerly waiting to hear the divine words of Secretary Sherman. The front hall balcony was packed, too. The two interns threaded their way into the center of the packed crowd. Now all they had to do was wait for Sherman to speak, wait for the crowd to roar, to roar and command attention.

Their budding escape plan was about to bear fruit, and must have sprung insurmountable relief from the fear which enveloped them moments ago. It was there, near the rear entrance to the balcony of the main hall, dancing in a warm glow of angelic light, that Dina felt a gripping tightening in her chest. She was certain that it must have been a symptom of the adrenaline-induced, skin-of-her-teeth style getaway, until she looked down by her waist and realized that her hand was laced with Danny's.

"Finally, he grew some balls," Dina thought.

Their insecurities waned, and for a brief moment the two were distracted from impending danger, its volume softening to the decibel of a sewing-pin drop. She moved to meet Danny's lips. And again. And again. So, they went along in their lip-locked dance, nearly forgetting the thunder of the Institute roaring and booming at their heels.

Then it got light again.

Chapter 20: I Tell the Doctor of My Ramblings
A Professor's Diary #4

A Basement
Date unknown

To a professor who has suffered, but now just might be able to see the light:

With some reflection, I remember much more from the day I arrived at my doctor's house. Journaling and my dream-mind friends have surely helped me, though I do wish I had a bit more control of when and how and what I see and have seen and will see.

On the day I arrived at my old friend's house, though I still don't know how the hell I managed to navigate away from the Institute to his house in my manic state, I was agitated, in pain, and terribly confused. I still struggle to hold onto any memories from that day, but I promised my doctor I'd try. After we recognized each other and embraced, my good doctor, here's what happened:

"Hurry, we're not safe here, doctor, I need medical assistance, please!" I said, only a hair away from my zombified state.

"Stop shouting, hush. Hush. Keep your voice down, damn it," you replied, trying to placate me in your yellowing front yard.

"Take it out, take it out of me, *please!* She's here, I know she's here. Please! Take it out! There's too much too much."

"Listen, I can only help you if you come on inside."

"But *they'll know.* They surely will; she'll come to find me, yes! No," I screeched.

I've been saying it since day one. See doctor? Later on, reflecting on the inane nature of my entrance, the doctor told me that he felt as if he were coaxing a reluctant toddler to bed.

"Hush now, it's all going to be all right. Come with the doctor, huh? Come along with your old friend," you cooed. "Oh, Andrea's not going to be happy about this. Andrea won't be happy *one bit*," you said under your breath.

Again, you stood on the front stoop, idling by the front door, your hands reaching and then retreating, reaching and then retreating from the doorknob. Shocked at how unnaturally, uncharacteristically unkempt I appeared with the tears and slashes to my clothes, the cloudy myopia in my eyes, the rusty-jaundice of my skin, you dismissed Andrea's inevitable apprehension.

"What the hell happened to you?" you mumbled, looking into my vacant and swollen, gray eyes. Sensing that I could not answer you, you declared your intention to "find out." And get me "a morsel of food, or two..."

I was still afraid, but you weren't. With sympathy and pity in your heart, you no longer had time for inconsequential concerns like failing your P.R. interview. I now know you had a burning desire to help me. Yes, camaraderie and compassion overwhelmed you.

I saw you, at last, whip the door open, call inside to Andrea that you were home, and tell her not to bother asking about the interview, that it was pointless now, and that you'd brought a guest, an old friend, whom Andrea would indeed be happy to see again.

"Coming, coming, Drew. I'm coming!" she shouted down from the bedroom upstairs. "Just finishing up one of my stories. Give me a minute. Who's here?"

"You'll just have to come down and see," you said.

Now, I must say that I am embarrassed about my behavior once I'd arrived in my good friend's house. Normally, I'm a respectful house guest. I have profusely apologized, but he "won't hear it, damn it." My doctor says that he's just glad I sound like my old self again, and glad that I'm (hopefully) inches away from remembering what the hell happened at that cursed Institute.

I want to say that I was a good little boy, innocently staying put at the heels of my protector, but people want to say a lot of things that they just can't say. And I'll tell you what, I can't say I was a "good boy."

"Professor put that down! What are you doing? Professor!" you shouted, concerned.

"Tiny little bits for the tiny little bits, mmm, yes."

"Put that back. Not off the floor. Get up, get up and show a bit of decency, damn it. Oh Lord, oh sweet Mary, what's happened to him," you said.

It was during my lamentable floor-sniffing, scampering stint that Andrea entered the kitchen.

"What the *fuck*, Andrew? What the hell did you bring into this house?" she said, alarmed at the dirty little beast nibbling up doughnut crumbs off her floor, not recognizing me.

She still hasn't apologized for that, good doctor. I even swept up your dirty kitchen floor.

"Is that? No, that couldn't be—"

"It's the Professor, honey. It's him."

"Why...what's wrong with him? Stop that!" she said, and pulled on my torn shirt collar, preventing me from continuing to lick scraps off the floor.

"I know, *I know*. He just kind of appeared out of nowhere while I was sipping coffee in the driveway a few minutes ago," you replied.

"Wh-wait. Sipping coffee in the driveway? What's going on?"

"I'm as confused as you are," you told her.

"Oh, Andrew, I cannot *believe* it! I cannot believe you'd bring him in here. I expect you'll want him to stay too. How are we going to take care of him with no income? You know I care about him, but with the Institute at our heels, and you being out of work...we're fucked!"

"He's babbling in fits and that's what you're worried about? Let's hold on a minute, let's just hold on *one* minute. We need to decide what to do with him. He hasn't stopped rambling and bumbling since he found me. That Institute must have—must have done some pretty terrible things."

"Oh, no, oh, no! I see right through this. I see it right to the end, Andrew, and it doesn't end pretty. Don't you think that *they're* out looking for him? Look at him! He looks like a goddamn mess; I don't think he just slipped out of the office early, do you? Something happened to him obviously. Did you even think about that? Hell, they called us not too long ago when we had *nothing* to do with the damn Institute. Remember when those cronies wanted me to join their public initiative? The poor caller was scared shitless himself! Even their workers are kept in the dark! Don't you believe what you wrote in your own exposé? The professor, here, eating crumbs off of our floor is living proof of *much worse than that.*"

She was shouting so loudly it hurt both of our ears.

You should believe your wife, Doctor, believe me that they're coming.

"Oh…I-I but-but I didn't think it was as real as this—not that they were destroying people! Just that they were coercing people to share sensitive information. Look at him! He's sniffing the floor, emaciated, and ranting like a fool. What am I supposed to do? This was one of the sharpest minds around, if you remember. We can't just leave him for the dogs. I won't do it. He's staying with us."

Andrea paced around the kitchen, desperate for some divine intervention, desperate for *something* to help.

"Wait," she said, still pacing.

"He's staying with us," Andrews said, stalwart.

"Fine. Fine. You're right. He needs someone to take care of him. But who knows who's watching the house? The Institute will look here first. You know they will."

You then sat heavily at the kitchen table, your head in your hands.

"I have an idea," Andrea said, and left the room. "Give me a minute."

"Wh-wait—where are you going?"

"A minute, Drew!"

You rubbed my head as I nuzzled at your feet, and we waited for I don't know how long.

"Okay. I have a plan, but you're not going to like it. Just hear me out."

"Okay."

"I think we should stay at Daryl's. He's got the room and—"

"You've absolutely got to be kidding me, Andrea. Do you realize how *humiliating* that would be for me? There's no way I could sleep in that house, knowing—knowing what you two have done under that roof!"

"It's not ideal. I know."

"Not ideal? It's madness is what it is!"

"Listen. You want to help your friend. I want to help him, too. Calm down and *actually* listen to what I'm saying," she said, her eyes locked with yours. "Daryl's got an extra room for us, and a basement that the Professor can stay in until he recovers, where we can keep an eye on him, and keep him safe."

"Madness...madness...my wife asking me to stay with—with *that* man. In his house!"

"No. *That* is madness," Andrea said, pointing to me. "Just calm down. Think about it logically for a second, Drew. The last place the Institute would think to look for us would be at Daryl's. They'll think you'd stay anywhere but there."

You sighed at the table, and looked down at me with sorrow in your eyes.

Your wife did have a good point. Dee would never think you'd be so brash as to stay with the man who screwed your wife. Maybe that's why they haven't found us yet. But they're looking, good doctor, they're coming.

"Please, Drew. It's a good idea. Daryl's on the inside and can update us on anything he hears. Obviously, it's only temporary. He's a good guy, Drew. I'm the one who fucked up, not him. He said he wants to help us, and that he's suspicious of foul play, too. No one at the Institute would suspect him helping us, either. He's just the happy-go-lucky Head of Shipping and Receiving. His lips are sealed. I trust him. Anyone we stay with is putting themselves in danger. Please."

"He works there! That's exactly why we shouldn't go. He could so easily let it slip, pass someone information that he's got three very strange guests."

"No! He's not one of those people, Andrew. He's simple, but he's a good person. He always used to tell me—" Andrews winced. Andrea started again, "Sorry. He told me what he thinks about the Institute. It's just a job to him. I think he'd protect us when it came to work."

After a long pause, you looked intently at Andrea, your eyes full of both love and spite, but mostly love.

"Damn it. I guess you're right. Good enough. Let's get him down there, and pack our bags. Only bring what's absolutely necessarily; I'm going to grab a few things I think will help him remember who he is, too."

"Good idea. Who knows when we'll ever be back..." Andrea said, nostalgically looking at her home, frowning. "Well, we've got to hurry. But we can't bring him to Daryl's like this; he'll cause a scene."

"Right...pop a Benadryl in him. I'm sure he hasn't slept much...maybe a bit of shut eye will get him back to some semblance of normal..." you said, delivering your initial diagnosis.

"Professor. Professor! Up. Get up, damn it," Andrea commanded, surprising herself with a domineering demeanor.

"Go easy on him, Andrea."

I know Andrea loves me. We'd been friends for years. She was just scared, and rightfully so.

I sprouted to my feet at her behest.

"That's a good boy," you said. "Would you like something to eat?"

"Food, yes! Very hungry."

"Well, we'll make you a real meal in a little while, but for now, eat this," Andrea said, handing me a protein bar. "And once you finish, we'll give you nice little piece of candy as a treat."

I grabbed the protein bar, suspicious.

It's not something I admit easily, but I then sniffed and held the wrapped bar near my mouth...and bit into it, foil and all.

"No, no, honey," Andrea said as she wrested the bar out of my hands. "You have to unwrap it first. Here, let me help you."

After I ate it, I said:

"Candy? Time for treats?" I said, holding out cupped hands.

"Yes, professor, it certainly *is* time for treats," you said, embarrassed and looking increasingly sullen.

Quite the clever and dirty trick, Doc. But who could blame you? I'd have done the same if there were a chirping lunatic in my kitchen. It was best for me to be asleep and hidden during my transport to Daryl's.

You then unpeeled a Benadryl from the child-proof casing and stretched out your palm. After a quick sniff, I lopped up the pill and swallowed.

"Not very sweet, not very tasty," I complained.

"No, but it will be soon," Andrea said, gingerly grabbing my hand to lead me to the basement until I fell asleep. "Now, it's going to get dark in a minute, professor, but I just want you to close your sleepy little eyes," she said as if cooing a baby.

Chapter 21: The Frog Makes a Leap

Neighborhood of the Lead Assistant to the Deputy Secretary
August 10, 2035—the day of the escape
Around 5:30 p.m.

I see a man hop through an industrial parking lot and take a seat in a powder-blue Toyota Prius.

The man drove toward his home after tattling on my friends Danny and Dina, but as he continued to distance himself from the Institute for Information Dissemination, he couldn't shake the teeming apprehension from the workday. Earl had tried to tell Dee about the interns after he submitted his Rat Report to the Emergency Breach Department, but he couldn't get ahold of her since she was in the underground. And he was *not* to disturb her when she was working with a client for the underground cloud. His inability to perform a vital function of his job caused his froggy brain to leap and bound, itching to swamp-spiral out of control. He was anxious because she didn't yet know about the interns—but she would want to know of the interns: a potential breach was urgent. There was tremendous inefficiency in his Momma Dee's methods, but he wasn't about to be the tadpole to tell her.

After Dee's interview with Danny, Earl had (uncharacteristically) pleaded with Dee not to attend the rat in the underground, to be patient, to wait and see how the intern might react. His pleading failed, for when Dee's fixates on her prey, she's mono-maniacal; she stalks, hidden, through the underground brush until she has the chance to sink her claws deep inside them. She was drunk on a game of cat-and-mouse, her confidence climbing dangerously to the tallest peaks of obsession, becoming dumb and blind to more pressing threats nipping at her heels.

You see, Dee couldn't stop herself from interrogating the Head of Research in the underground; she needed to confirm her suspicions that he'd been in cahoots with a certain *Washington Post* reporter. Without the Head of Research's compliance, Dee would have no way to justify sending out her hit on his fat-cat reporter friend. And she wanted to do that as soon as possible, regardless of if she'd confirmed the intel or not.

Earl thought her overconfidence and bloated ego would be the death of the Capital T Truth Division, Earl conjectured as he drove home. No! He shouldn't think that, was afraid to think that.

But still, why, why does she harbor so many secrets? It was strange that his job description even bothered mentioning "limited access" to the ominous cloud when, usually, he was forbidden entry. Their relationship was imbalanced—she knew so much about her sweet little frog, he so little about his darling Dee. This might be typical for Dee's working relation-ships: coworkers were happy to remain ignorant about how she operated, but her sweet frog wasn't. Perhaps this was how she trudged through so much distaste from her coworkers, yet still commandeered the Institute in her own vision, uncompromis-ing to any other ranking official?

Now as he drove back to his modest, colonial lily pad, though, no one was here to nip his budding distaste for the Deputy Secretary and her methods, no one was here to beat his disconcerting and doubtful thoughts into submission. They'd been nagging him all week. Earl's disgust began when Dee became obsessed with squeezing information out of the Head of Research. But why? Was Dee nervous for the first time? So jealous of her own power that she might blunder?

Earl first sniffed Dee's anxiety just a few days ago, on the day of quite a peculiar meeting with the press where Sherman folded, publicly, to Dee.

Outside the Deputy Secretary's Office
Institute for Information Dissemination
August 4, 2035—the day before Andrews was fired

Earl slowly approached the Deputy Secretary's office door with a memo bearing bad news: an unknown Institute employee had recently leaked confidential Institute tactics to the local press. He stood concentrated at the door, trembling. His hesitation must have sprung from Dee's leaps and dips and blips of melancholia and mania and madness these past few days: she hadn't been sleeping well. Dee had been harboring, and consequently investigating, a sneaking suspicion that their "snide little head researcher" was about to "do something very, very bad."

Dee had been frustrated that her titillating powers of persuasion failed her in the professor's contract renegotiation last week, and her failure steeped a perfect brew for disloyal(tea). Too, she was irritated, but not surprised, that Sherman, in their bimonthly personnel meeting, refused to acknowledge her concerns on a freewheeling, contractually unbound Head of Research. Dee had never wanted to hire the haughty Head of Research in the first place, but unless she were hiring for the Capital T Truth Division, Sherman regrettably had the final word. Although she prodded Sherman during the personnel meeting, harping that he was only inclined to rehire the professor on account of bureaucratic laziness, Sherman scoffed, and told Dee to remember who appointed the staff, that she better be careful. This did not go over well with Dee. Dee had been so angry the day Sherman slighted her that when she returned to her office, she screeched a bleeding-eardrum-shriek and pounded her desk with such astounding force that the poor desk now wears a lightning-bolt crack as a badge of remembrance. Her eyes glowed a deep, crimson-sanguine as she fumed and paced around her office, calculating a brooding, budding vengeance.

Dee was so adamant about wanting to renegotiate the Head Researcher's contract because, somehow, when the professor was hired at the beginning of 2035, he had managed to join the Institute on his own conditions in the first place. He had been rigid, refusing to sign away his soul on "a covertly loaded government contract written with subtext to discredit and take advantage of [him] and [his] work." Dee didn't like the "pompous self-righteousness" of such a "little beady-eyed professor" but she knew that the Institute needed him in their good graces, since his studies would expedite Dee's cosmic and catastrophic hunger to become the public's puppeteer. So, she relented, choosing not to put up a fight with Sherman about it.

The few-and-far-between prospects who had denied Dee's contract negotiation tended to meet underground ends, all of whom consequently realized their "grave mistake" in defying a call for "admirable public service." All past prospects now worked for the Institute in the Capital T Truth Division, emanating a dazzling joy from their eyeballs, resonating in their whimsical whistles that chirped from circled mouth-holes, all of which scared the bejeebers out of Earl. The Head of Research was one of the few who slipped away from Dee's grasp.

As Earl had stood outside Dee's office door and reflected on his boss's increasingly frequent and volatile sour moods, the thought of bearing bad news, especially news with potential to endanger Dee's cloud project—her Information Gathering Initiative— provoked Earl to gulp.

Scared or not, Earl had to open his boss's door sometime. He'd be in more trouble if he didn't deliver the news. But he was nervous on how Dee would react to hearing about a treasonous Institute employee who allied with the local press. The envelope in his hands contained a summons to an official, Institute meeting about it. Dee was convinced it was the Head Research who was responsible for the leak, and she did have a point since he had shown insubordination in negotiating his contract. Once Dee could confirm the Head Researcher had leaked information, she had a pretty good idea on whom was writing the exposé.

"E-enough," Earl had said aloud, before taking a large sigh and banging his knuckles on Dee's office door, aware that any more delay would infuriate his mercurial boss:

Knock, knock

"I'm busy in here. Send it in a damn email. Yes, the super-highway, send it to me there! I don't have time for your quibbling administrative crap!" she shouted from behind the door.

"It-it's m-me," he croaked back, his knees about to buckle.

"Who? What? Email, I said. Send it in an email," she snarled.

"It's impo-portant. Info Risk Grade 4, boss. Could be a Grade 5, very soon. Eeek!" Earl said.

"Ah, my sweet bullfrog, yes, well I could never mind seeing your slimy skin, could I? Especially in a matter of such dire importance. Come in, come in, come *in*," Dee said as she pressed the button buzzer to unlatch the door.

Earl hopped into the room and closed the door behind him. He slid the document over to Dee, and said, "I-I think that your spec-speculations about the Head Researcher might be t-t-true, boss. S-s-says here an Institute employee leaked c-c-c-confidential information."

"Ah, has Shermie called a meeting? Finally, the bimbo has gained some common sense. But is it that any surprise, my dear froggy friend? Of course, I'm right. And since I'm right, he likely told his fat-cat reporter friend from *The Post*. Don't worry, I shall confront our ratty Head Researcher soon, and the fat cat's bosses from *The Post*. But first, I must attend this meeting, to make sure the press doesn't get ahead of themselves. We wouldn't want another poor accuracy rating to crumble their feeble foundations, now would we?

INSTITUTE FOR INFORMATION DISSEMINATION
WASHINGTON D.C.

Fact Sheet #12743
August 4, 2035
8:42 a.m.

To All Officials Above Rank 5.437:

There has been a GRADE 4 SECURITY BREACH
confirmed by Institute surveyors and intelligence. As you know, a leak of this caliber
has potential to decimate public confidence in
the Institute's goals to provide sanctified,
streamlined, and above all *true* information to
the American Public.

For those of you working in the CAPITAL T TRUTH
DIVISION, the EMERGENCY BREACH DEPARTMENT, or in
the MEDIA AND PUBLIC RELATIONS DEPARTMENT, this
will require your utmost attention. Officials
above grade 5.437a must be prepared to remedy the breach. Please extend deadlines on all
pending and in-progress projects and agendas.

A MANDATORY MEETING for the departments listed above will take place promptly at 9:30
a.m., today, August 4th, in ROOM 234. All
editors-in-chief of the media will be present
to help us navigate this trying time. Please
delay or reschedule any other engagements or
appointments you may have.

We appreciate your cooperation and your dedication in achieving the Institute's goals.
Your efforts have not gone unnoticed by the
American people. We will ensure inaccuracy and
rumors don't reach them.

Sincerely,

Dexter Sherman
His Honorable Secretary for Information
United States Institute for Information
Dissemination

Dee then slapped the document down with both hands, and sighed, "Time to get to work, my sweet."

Later that morning, at about 9:28 a.m., Earl was waiting for the Institute Press Meeting to start—since as Dee's Lead Assistant, early was on-time, and on-time was late.

Attendees arrived and walked around the long, rectangular table to find nameplates designating their seats. Earl received several "hellos," and "howdys" and "how are ya, damn its" and "gosh it's sure been a whiles," but noticed that Dee received none, except from one naïve, good-humored "what's up?" from Daryl, Head of Shipping and Receiving.

"Ah Daryl! Come here and shake my hand," Dee said, and subtly sniffed the Head of Shipping and Receiving. "Oh, what *is* that delicious smell? Lilacs and honeysuckle?"

"Uhm."

"Naughty boy, Daryl. You do know she's *married*," Dee whispered.

Daryl winced and sunk deep in his chair after sitting down. Those around him recoiled at his retreat. They all knew that "devil of a woman" was always up to no good.

At approximately 9:32 a.m., Secretary Sherman and his entourage entered the room.

"You're late, Mr. Secretary," Dee said, to Sherman's surprise. "I thought we cared about accuracy at this Institute, but I guess you could say that I'm wrong based on the empirical evidence, here."

"I suppose an apology wouldn't go very far on deaf ears," the Secretary retorted, straightening the collar of his oxford shirt.

Eyes darted back and forth from the Secretary to his Deputy and back to the Secretary, all trying to wager why Dee was in attendance. They knew that even for the most urgent breach meetings, Dee would get her notes from her Lead Assistant and chime in accordingly via email in the hours following the meeting. They knew the Madame Deputy usually was the one who found out the intel which mandated the breach meetings, so attending would be a waste of her time. They knew her attendance meant this breach was serious.

"Though I detest unseemly commentary, I will admit that I *am* a minute late, and for that, I apologize," the Secretary muttered after scanning the baffled faces of his subordinates.

"Two minutes," Dee said and smiled.

The room remained silent, the tension drowning out any desire to speak.

"Now, to business. As I'm sure you're all aware—"

"Sorry, sorry. So, so sorry I'm late!" the Associate Director of the Data and Inquiry Department blurted as she burst through the threshold of room 234.

"It's fine. Just sit down quietly next time," Sherman said, a little annoyed.

"As I was saying, I'm sure—"

"Here. I'm here! Please don't start without me. I apologize," the Assistant Supervisor of the Emergency Breach Department said, rushing to his seat.

"Uh-fine, it's okay. We were just beginning. You didn't miss anything. Please be quiet. This is important. So, as I was saying, I'm sure you're all aware that we're experiencing a Grade Fou—"

"Mr. Secretary, I'm terribly sorry! I got held up by those dastardly interns of mine. A swamp of rot, the lot of 'em," the Lead Supervisor of the Institute's Intern Office, Dennis, called out as he bumbled into the room.

"Damn it, *damn it*! Lock the damn door! This is *important*. No more interruptions! INFO Guard #549, if you would please post yourself outside and tell any other tardy employee that they may acquire meeting notes for updates," the Secretary snipped.

"Would you like me to start typing meeting notes, sir? I wasn't sure if I was to record the meeting since it's a classified 5.437, sir," his assistant, a little man in a little gray suit with little gray suspenders, and a little gray hat to cover his little gray hair, said.

"Type the notes? Yes," Sherman said. "God, we won't get anything done like this."

"Yes, sir, yes, yes! They're a bunch of bumbling bimbos, aren't they? Bimbos and fools. No. God, we won't get anything done like this," Dee agreed, mimicking Sherman's cadence.

The little gray scribe began typing.

"No, not *that*. Start when I start," the Secretary said.

"Yes. When *he* starts, you buffoon," Dee echoed.

"Okay," the little gray man in his little gray suit with little gray suspenders with the little gray clips clasped to his little gray pants said.

"So, as I'm sure you're all aware, we've had a confidential information breach by an undetermined Institute employee," the Secretary began. "Why aren't you typing?"

"Oh," the little gray man in his little gray suit with little gray suspenders said.

The Secretary sighed.

"Let me just get to the point, here—"

"Finally. We all, desperately, oh so desperately, want to know about the breach leaked by our Head of Research, don't we?" Dee gambled, looking into Secretary Sherman's eyes.

The room gasped.

"Now, we don't know if the Head of Research is responsible. It is only allege—"

"Oh, sweet Shermie. We do know. We talked about it just last night. Why would you hide this essential data from the respected officials in this room?" she retorted, a partial lie in order to incense the officials in the room and solidify her plans to interrogate the Head of Research. She reveled in their shocked faces, looked to Sherman, and then snapped her fingers.

"I—I have blundered by forgoing this information from our respected Institute workers. eeek!" he said with suddenly inflating eyes, swollen in their sockets.

"Such a pity. Such a serious folly from our respected Head of Research, hired and recommended by our own leader. Wouldn't you agree, Mr. Secretary?" Dee continued and snapped her fingers.

"Well, erm, yes, quite a serious folly, eek!" the Secretary said mechanically, his eyelids wide. "Our culpable Head of Research has leaked false information about our Institute to an unknown reporter, presumably one from one of D.C.'s local papers, but we don't yet know which for sure."

The members of the press looked to one another, their survival instincts beckoning them to throw a member of the competition underneath the metaphorical bus. They rarely were calm at Institute meetings, especially one called so suddenly. And so, they simultaneously barked in a chorus of flattery and supplication:

"Not us, Mr. Secretary" / "You know we have always given any and all information required of us, Mr. Secretary" / "We have consistently and unwaveringly been content ambassadors of the Institute mandates" / "We would never betray your trust like this, Mr. Secretary," and the like.

There was one editor notoriously silent, the editor of *The Washington Post*.

"Well, it certainly looks like we are all loyal liaisons to the Institute for Information Dissemination. So, then, my sweet Secretary Shermie-Wermie, what are we, the humble servants of the Institute, to do? Well they've *said* it wasn't any of them," Dee asked and giggled and snapped.

Sherman's bulging eyeballs looked to his staff and the summoned editors-in-chief as he replied:

"We have no choice but to institute emergency provision 76.93dq of the INFO Act, in order to place all our efforts in halting the budding breach," Sherman said, now looking to the editors with his bulbous eyeballs. "As you well know, we don't enact this measure lightly, but your compliance is essential in maintaining the integrity of information disseminated to the public. Every story or opinion piece must be sent to the Institute's Press Accuracy Department for review before publication. Eeeek!" the Secretary said.

Most of the room nodded, compliant, having heard the rumors of what happens to squeaky-wheel media, and knowing they'd get a poor accuracy-report rating if they resisted. But the crotchety old man, *The Washington Post*, could be silent no longer.

"This is absurd. Ridiculous!" *The Post's* editor-in-chief shouted. "Working with the Institute is one thing, but commanding us to ignore the First Amendment, no, worse, threatening and forbidding us to publish wrongdoing is unconstitutional and not written into the government mandate. I will not have it. You can talk with our lawyers," she said and stood up. It was high time to leave.

"No, please stay for one moment," Sherman said, before gesturing to the other editors-in-chief. "You all may go. The Institute appreciates your cooperation in our mission to supply the public with flawlessly accurate information."

After the other editors had left, the room was tense and quiet, but the silence was eerily loud.

"Oh, Mr. Secretary, it looks like our lovely *Post* editor doesn't think you have the legal power to mandate Institute review. What are we to do?" Dee said and snapped.

"We understand your distaste. And we understand that the majority of your readership is built upon your opinion section. So, in exchange for your cooperation, the Institute will formally offer your paper compensation for the temporary dip in expected readership. $20,000 dollars for your cooperation in the pursuit of truth," the Secretary said as his face became red and tense before yelping, "Eeek!"

"Is that a bribe, Mr. Secretary? I had thought you better than that," *The Post* editor said, before hitting "stop audio recording" on her phone.

"Oh, enough of this. It's high time for her to learn *The Post's* rightful place in the food chain, Mr. Secretary," Dee said and snapped.

"Y-Yes, indeed. Detain her. Dee will negotiate a fair offer for both sides in my stead, eeeek!"

The Post editor sat aghast, confused and concerned, unprepared for the INFO Guards who detained her as she squirmed and screamed.

Chapter 22: A Professor's Diary # 5

Daryl's Basement
Date unknown, sometime in mid-August 2035

I've been dreaming for too long. If I dream too much, how will I remember all I see and know and hear?

Ouch! No...the doctor...me...Danny...we are in danger...unless...Earl...?

Chapter 23: **A Froggy Diary**

Inside of Earl's House
August 10, 2035—the day of the escape
About 5:30 p.m.

A Bullfrog's Diary: What's Happening with My Darling Dee?

8/10/35

Entry #2438:

"She barely had to say <u>anything</u>, and Sherman caved like a puppy with his tail between his legs. Sherman is not one to cave to anyone, even her; he's a strong-willed man, one of the only folks at the Institute willing to directly defy Dee. His hatred of her is rampant and well-known to Institute personnel. I know Sherman has suspicions as to what villainous and contemptable acts she gleefully commits in the underground. He might not have details but knows that her methods are not up to code, not right. Sometimes I think he looks the other way, since Dee gathers intel as if she were a supercomputer hacking the public. I'm not sure why he hired her in the first place, but Dee did have a brilliant track record as a private investigator. But she was a nobody; in fact, it was an asset to her success as a private investigator that she had maintained a low public profile. And yet,

Sherman couldn't have predicted her insatiable desire for power and executive overreach.

Sherman certainly would have preferred Dee not attend the press meeting at all, but knew she would. Any information breach that Dee hadn't detected herself, mandated her participation. Sherman didn't like that he needed her there, wasn't happy about it, and I don't blame him: Dee is known to be fiery-tongued. Her words are lined with corrosive acid.

No. You shouldn't say things like that. You're her sweet little frog. Right? Still, sweet darling frog or not, I just can't rid myself of this abhorrent disinclination to her after I leave the office. And yet, why must I always feel so drawn to her whenever she's around? It's almost as if she summons and subsequently coerces me and my mind through some sort of voodoo dark magic! No. That can't be true. She's _human_ after all. Right?

At least I can think when I write freely about her, far away from her. I can't deny that I experience moments of foggy daze whenever Dee needs something from me. It's almost as if my tongue muscles respond to some outside force, some greater reckoning, cajoling my mouth to spit out words I never thought to think. Never thought I would think. I must bring it up to her. Get some answers. If Momma truly knows best...

My disbelief tends to subside after a few moments of rumination. I always end up justifying my own aberrant behavior with some shoddy conclusion along the lines of: "well, if that's what I said, then that's what I think, all right. Momma Dee knows what's best. She wants to root out the bad and untrue and misleading thoughts, just like I do." I always feel so very _good_ around her, euphoric even.

And, as much as I hate to say this, I feel oddly attracted to her. I've never been attracted to girls much, and I'm not sure that's what the feeling is, but I am bound to her. Bewitched. I've never known the Secretary for Information to fall victim to that unexplainable urge, and he certainly has no desire of intimacy with his deputy. He'd never stoop to such a scandal; it might tarnish his reputation. So why listen to her now? How has Dee bent him to her will? How has Dee bent <u>me</u> to her will?

What bothers me most is that I can't recall what happened the evening after I signed the contract to become her Lead Assistant, regardless of how hard I try. The closest I can get is my oddly elated feeling after Dee handed me the red pen to sign, and my initial aversion to signing. I've always been bothered by this lapse. My memory is too strong to have such a significant day be blurred and tainted. I almost feel as if I've always worked for the Institute, always worked for her. Frogwash!

I must have given more to this wretched Institute than I had originally planned. No, I mustn't call it wretched. Oh, no. Mustn't call it that...I want to be a good little frog...

There was <u>something</u> about having access to memories, desires, inclinations, and the like...they go to the cloud...but then what? And how? How would she know? It's not like I've had a sit down where I told her every thought I've ever had. There's got to be a damn good reason why she won't let anyone down there in the underground, down into the depths—some shady business with her beloved "information cloud."

Darn it all! Why can't I have any clarity when I'm with her? I must find out. I need to know. Maybe after she finishes with the professor, or at least feels confident about the reporter, I'll bring it up—catch her in a good mood.

Damn contract—"What constitutes 'past'?" Can she very well know what I'm thinking right now? What I just thought is in the past. No. Earl, now you're just getting paranoid. Damn the fine print. Damn those convoluted semantics!

While I'd never tell her, I sure hope that those interns didn't do anything they will regret. They don't have any idea whom they're dealing with. I barely do. Better to run. Safer that way.

More soon—

E

I then saw him stand up from his writing desk, pacing around the room, before abruptly stopping and glancing to his bedside table. He heard a vibrating buzz, and so picked up his phone. The phone screen illuminated the caller, "Momma Dee." Concern and guilt and fear washed over his face.

"Oh n-n-n-no, I haven't told Dee about the interns! She was d-d-d-down in the underground," he said aloud. He still had yet to tell her what they did, what they said. He would have to tell her that he got so worked up about the information breach that he'd forgotten his primary assignment, that the only reason he didn't tell her was because of protocol, because she was down in the underground. He was only listening to his darling Dee's orders.

"H-h-hello? I-I-I was j-j-j-just about to call," Earl said into the phone.

"Oh! My little froggy friend, I was so desperately hoping that you would call. I just got to it first! We are so very in sync, you and me," Earl heard through the receiver, followed by a muffled clicking sound.

"I hope you weren't waiting long. You always know what's best, are always helping this poor little frog. Eeek!" His eyes started to hurt again, and his fluttering heart lifted, to his own subconscious dismay.

"Why yes, yes, of course, my sweet amphibian. You know I am here for you always, forever, yes. You are mine, and Momma will always help. You're my number one frog. You wouldn't let the Institute down! Would you?"

"No. Nuh-never."

"Yes, that's right. Nuh-never. Now, tell me your toady tales. Be a good frog and hop that info into the superhighway. Tell Momma Dee about those dirty, nasty little mites!"

Earl heard a snapping sound through the receiver.

Earl told her what those "dirty, nasty little mites" did, what those "dirty, nasty little mites" said. He told her that mite number one had burst through the door to the intern office after meeting with her, paced around the room, and worked himself up into a fit. He told her that the intern mite seemed afraid. He told her that mite number one had said what Dee said didn't matter, since it didn't look like the mite wanted to do what she asked anyway. Told her that's when he knew to go immediately to the Emergency Breach Department.

"Oh, Earlie, you certainly have become such a great listener! You really are my special little frog," she said.

He told her that mite number two seemed very concerned about mite number one and that mite number two tried to calm mite number one down. He told her that mite number one rushed around the office squawking like a chicken without a head.

"Oh, my sweet Earlie pearlie, this is quite the spicy story. But there's something remiss, here. He took something that wasn't his, too, didn't he, that nasty little mite?" she said, interrupting Earl's telling. Earl heard a clicking sound in the receiver.

He paced around the room and felt his eyes widen, bulging and bulbous and dazed.

Earl told her that he didn't see anything like that, but then Dee told him that mite number one had in fact taken a manila envelope sealed delicately with red tape that didn't belong to him, since you see, Dennis had told her when she came up from the underground.

He agreed that mite number one had to be punished for stealing government property, stealing it with no regard for property rights. Stolen it. He told her that mite number two probably came up with the idea for their escape.

"Oh yes, very juicy indeed! Yes, you're quite right, the little chicken-legged intern mite most certainly *did* come up with the idea for their escape. But Earlie, we have a little problem here."

"A p-p-p-problem?"

Earl was confused: he went directly to the Emergency Breach Department in order to follow protocol. He told her that he looked for her and the FiBs told him she was still in the underground. Then he sent the FiBs on lockdown so the

interns couldn't escape. He'd done everything right, waited diligently in the office, preparing an action plan on how to plug
The Post reporter's leak, and started the paperwork for when
Dee inevitably hired a hit. When she was still down in the
underground at the end of the workday, he was sorry, but had
to go home and feed Salvatore, his salamander. Sally needed
him. He told Dee that he was a very sorry tadpole.

"It's okay my sweet frog, my head FiB Lieutenant told me.
Soon, we won't have to worry about the two little interns anymore, yes!"

"We-we won't?"

"Well, not for long, no. In fact, that is precisely why Momma must ask her favorite frog a favor. You would do a teeny-ti-
ny favor for your darling Dee, wouldn't you, Earlie?" she asked.
Earl heard a clicking sound in the receiver.

"Of course. You're my darling Momma Dee," he found
himself saying.

"Very good, sweetie. Yes. Very good. It's a very special favor.
Momma needs you to come back to the office—after you feed
your salamander, of course. She knows how important a baby
amphibian must be to a little amphibian man—yes, Momma
needs you to come back, needs you to come into the underground. We have some guests. A very special favor, yes!"

Earl tried not to think that he was scared of the underground,
scared of what might happen and what had happened in the
basement of the Institute. Instead, he found himself starting the
engine in his powder-blue Toyota Prius and driving down the road
back to the Institute for Information Dissemination. He couldn't
remember whether he ended up feeding Salvatore, his salamander.

During the drive, he tried to quell his incessant fear of the underground, his fear of what might happen to Danny and Dina, especially if they were already there.

PART V:
THEY'RE COMING

Chapter 24: The Clam Tries to Swoop

Streets of Washington D.C.
August 15, 2035—the last day
2:22 p.m.

The rusting Chevy's tires screeched and smoked from a surprise turn. Inside the car, I can hear them say:

"Jesus, you damn near got us killed with that fucking move!" Corporal Davis roared to his intervening passenger. "What the fuck are you on? Get your damn hands off the fucking wheel. Just fucking great. We're already late to the meeting at O'Hoolihan's. I make the turns, damn it."

As Davis reluctantly inched further away from the coffee shop, where the Deputy Secretary and her Lead Assistant impatiently waited, searching for a street that isn't a "fucking one-way" to turn back around, his anger subsided a little, and his head cleared, but he still couldn't shake his rising anxiety about missing the meeting at the coffee shop. It was almost as if a force called to him, gaining traction, a near-silent whisper that beckoned, seeking his compliance and ardor like a Siren-call, a magnetic, indistinguishable murmur echoing through his psyche.

"What the fuck am I on? A hunt," Dahlia replied. "That bitch Deputy gave us the wrong address last time, and I'm about to fix it. Who cares about this new job with a little rat? So much for not being P.Is. Keep going straight."

"What?"

"I'm on a hunt. Found him."

They're coming.

"Oh, don't give me any of that cryptic bull. Not in the mood. There better be a good fucking reason for that wrong turn. She's waiting for us," he said as the rusting Chevy's engine coughed and revved from overwork, now on the scenic route to the coffee shop.

"Well, my swooping hawk, I think your little clam has the best of reasons. Just stay on this road. Let's just say I got us our get-out-of-jail-free cards. See? Your little clam's always thinking of her big bird," she said.

Davis tried to look over, but his neck muscles tensed. He let out a grunt, barbaric and involuntary.

"Oh, it's okay, baby," she said, rubbing his neck. "I know you're nervous. She'll let it slide if we're a bit late and we come back with a fat-cat whistle-blower. Coming to a meeting with a job done is just good business. I asked around last night before you got back from meeting with her. That's his new car. Andrews'," Dahlia said, pointing ahead to a beat up, gray Subaru.

"Then take his license plate down and we'll put it in the Institute's system. That ship has sailed now. She cares more about the researcher rat," Davis said, intractable.

"Who cares what *she* cares about? What the fuck is wrong with you? We take the reporter out, now, and grab the quarter million. We don't work *for her*, Davis. At least I don't. A job is right in front of us. The money is literally sitting in that damn gray Subaru. Why risk it?" asked, before continuing: "What happened to getting the money and quitting this line of work?"

For a moment, I think Davis was on the cusp of agreeing with Dahlia. As usual, she had a point: they could just take this one job and scram, say "fuck it" to the next job on the researcher rat. The fat-cat-reporter job certainly paid well enough, and then they'd get to be together, free from money worries. Despite his rage, Davis reflected on how much he loved Dahlia, how much he loved that "feisty little clam," but then his thoughts came to a screeching halt. He got mad, felt confused, and then felt even angrier.

He knew what Dahlia was trying to do: divert his attention from pleasing the Deputy Secretary. His anger suddenly reignited because Dahlia was ignoring what Dee wanted in this moment. Dahlia was jealous.

"If we don't get this rat job done, I'll tell her it's your fucking fault for distracting me," Davis said coldly.

"Seriously, Davey, what the fuck? I'm not trying to distract you. I'm trying to get us *paid*. You know, money? The point of all this? Tell me what's going on, and tell me what the fuck is going on, right now."

Davis swerved the car into an illegal U-turn back toward the coffee shop.

"Gotta get to the meeting. Already twenty-two minutes late," he said, mechanically.

"Jesus. Prideful bastard! What the fuck is your thick skull thinking? We get hired since we get jobs done. We're not lackeys at anyone's beck and call. Especially not hers."

Davis sat silent, his foot a steel-brick on the gas pedal.

"Why won't you look at me? I swear to god if I find out she fucked you, if that's where you were last night, I'll kill that hateful bitch," Dahlia said, slamming her hands on the dashboard.

I don't think that sat very well with Corporal Davis, no, I don't think that sat very well, at all.

With spiteful fire in his eyes, he looked to Dahlia; she'd sparked a smoldering ember to conflagration, flames raging and hungry to combust objects to dust. Davis almost winced, stopping himself from doing something stupid, but some force compelled him to act and not think.

He slammed the still-lit end of his hand-rolled cigarette into Dahlia's bare leg.

I can hear it sizzle.

"You motherfucker! God damn it. damnitdamnit damn you—you—fuck that hurts! Cocky, mommy-issue sack of shit!"

Davis ignored her, breezing on his way to the coffee shop with his hand out the open window, flowing with the passing air.

"Oh? Oh! You're fucking happy with yourself, are you? Oh, look! Just look! Your partner tries to figure out what hell is going on, your partner who's getting more and more fucking worried about you by the second, and we're going to use our piss-poor manners to show her respect by sticking her with a lit cig? That's it," Dahila said, gritting her teeth and breathing heavily. "You did fuck her, didn't you? Well, you sure put on a show yesterday pounding away at me and sobbing. You're such a fucking dick."

Her attempts failed to hold back the tears welling in her eyes.

Davis must have looked at her smugly, and after a few seconds, his lips parted in an automatic smile.

"Oh, fuck you, then," Dahlia said, her anger boiling. Refusing to coddle Davis any longer, she unsheathed a baby blade, a three-inch pocket dagger that she kept bound to her left thigh, and promptly plunged it through Davis' worn cargo pants.

The rusting Chevy struggled to stay on the road, swerving violently.

Chapter 25: A Professor's Diary #6

Daryl's Basement
Date unknown, sometime in mid-August 2035

To a frustrated professor with graying hair:

I don't think I have much time before my astral-dream-coerced visits (sorry that's the best I can describe them), come to snatch me from my basement reality again. I must piece together what these voices and visions have been trying to tell me, been trying to warn me of. I don't believe in a higher power nor fatalism, but it's hard for me to deny these visions as arbitrary or irrelevant. I am learning more about myself each day, in great part thanks to these involuntary, but still conscious, dream-states. There are just so many, and I can't remember them all.

Earl's been struggling, Dee's grip ever tightening on his fragile psyche. It seems as if he's an ally, but he continues to play the villain. Is he doing it on purpose? Or has the devil woman truly wrapped him 'round her finger and I should abandon all hope? He did want to be a hero all his life, if what I heard him think was true and not just some fabrication of my own mind.

I want to believe he won't buckle under pressure. I have a sneaking suspicion, an ill-feeling wanting to burst from my gut, that Danny and Dina are in grave danger, a fatal danger.

I try to shout to them, but they can't ever hear me, so I've stopped trying. Maybe I should try more.

No...wait...I must stay...control your mind...silence the voices...silence the dream-states...focus...write...

I must remember to tell the doctor that his editor did not want to fire him, that she tried to stick up for him, that it wasn't his fault, but Dee's, the Inst...

Chapter 26: The Birds Try and Take Flight

Institute for Information Dissemination, Main Hall
August 10, 2035—the day of the escape
A little after 1:30 p.m.

The last time I saw my two adolescent friends they were emerging from their steamy, PG-13 mouth-hole embrace. But what was it that Earl said about their fate? Why was he afraid of what might happen to them? This does not sound good. I need to wake up. I need to find them and tell them.

Danny and Dina awoke from their hormone-induced trance, and not a moment later fear overtook them. They looked around them, out into the sea of Good Citizens who were all dressed in their Sunday best, eager to listen to hear Secretary Sherman's weekly speech. The two love-birdies could practically hear the sheer anticipation enveloping the room, rising with rabbled cadences, shooting up to the stars!

"Here he comes," Danny said quietly to Dina. "We'll have to make a break for it soon."

A vociferous silence fissured through the crowd as a little man in a little gray suit with a little gray tie and little gray suspenders holding up his little gray pants walked with purpose to the Main Hall's mahogany podium. He leaned in and opened his gray lips:

"If you could all take your sea-, erm, ensure that you have some elbow room. Yes, that's it. Give one another some space—it behooves the process. It grants me great pleasure to introduce His Honorable Secretary for Information Dissemination, Dexter Sherman."

Danny thought the little gray emcee tried—and failed—to hide his distaste for the vulgar pulp riddling the shining marble floor below as a growing shadow lurched slowly forward from the left side of the curtained proscenium.

The room erupted in uproarious applause and bacchanalian conviviality when they saw their beloved Secretary. If there weren't INFO Guards and FiBs lining the perimeter of the Main Hall, with a particularly greater force stationed toward the front of the stage, the room very well could have transmogrified into a locust swarm, eager to ingest whatever had the misfortune of being in their path.

Sherman gripped the sides of the podium, glanced down at his notes, took a sigh, and then addressed the fan-girling crowd.

"Please, please. Ladies and gentlemen, please. Thank you. Yes, thank you. I'm overjoyed that you could all attend today's meeting. It's quite special, this one, as I'm sure you'll see," the swelling Secretary said to his enamored audience. This was his show. Danny and Dina saw Sherman wave to his supplicants, but he was interrupted:

"Mr. Secretary! Mr. Secretary! What are the Institute's thoughts on the rapid decrease in available news outlets for the American public? *The Post* hasn't published a new article in five days! You must keep us informed; it's what the Institute is for!"

The Secretary did not wince, but contrary to his professional disposition, he did become frazzled and annoyed, crinkling his brow.

"Sir, if you please. This is not a press conference. I will happily have you escorted to the Media Relations Department if you have an inquiry."

"Isn't the point of the Institute to keep us *all* informed? Why won't you be honest?"

There were several boos from the audience as the reporter was jostled and sneered at. They clearly did not like him questioning the integrity of their divine Secretary.

Soon after, the Secretary sighed and gestured to the FiBs camped at the perimeter, prompting the Institute soldiers to thrust through the crowd—encroaching the constituents' elbow room, mind you—motoring to part a fleshy wake. Though the all-too-daring reporter was snatched from the crowd, wailing and flailing in the arms of the Institute guards, the Secretary responded to the inquiry over the reporter's kicks and screams.

"My Good Citizens, please pay him no mind. You know that we at the Institute for Information Dissemination have always done our best to try and work with the media, but they don't always make it easy, harping on with their vigilante disavowals of the Institute's mission to provide the public with accurate information, resenting our pleas for peaceful coexistence."

The supplicant crowd booed with disapproval toward the ignorant press.

Pleasure lined the Secretary's bulbous eyes, content with his followers.

"We couldn't be here without your committed support. Thank you for your diligence in our fight for TRUTH!" the Secretary boomed. He had gleaned kernels of confidence from each conference, and now sowed a flourishing field of pomposity. The Secretary's rabble did love to be roused and riled.

Fighting the sonic boom of the crowd bouncing off the chamber walls, Danny said to Dina:

"Jesus, that dude looks fucking high."

"Yeah, his eyes are practically popping out of his head," Dina replied.

"Did he always look like that?"

"I'm not sure. I haven't watched this shit since we got the internships."

"Well, no time to start now. We gotta go," Dina said, peering around anxiously. She tried pulling at his hand, but he pulled back, intent on listening to the Secretary.

"Hold on. Just another minute."

Danny wanted to gather as much data before he left as possible, regardless of the danger creeping and crawling at his heels. The two heard Secretary Sherman continue:

"I want to begin, of course, by thanking the valiant defense of our truth stronghold, by none other than the FiBs and INFO Guards. Raise your veri-rifles!"

The rise turned heads. It was as if the crowd morphed into a flamboyance of flamingos, squawking their bird-brained heads in a chirping symphony of adoration. Sherman then gestured with both arms out, both palms open, to the animated crowd:

"The efforts of your citizen task force cannot be understated, either; you are all truly the pinnacle of our battalion of info warriors," he commented as the crowd at last began to quiet down. "I hope you all don't think this praise goes unmerited or unheard by the leaders of our nation—we are truly, truly blessed by your commitment to our cause," Secretary Sherman said as he scratched his neck and adjusted his collar back to factory-press standards.

"Now, knowing that all here are vigilant vanguards of truth, the Good Citizens—"

Another roaring interruption vented from the Good Crowd.

"Yes, yes, knowing that all here share a relentless commitment to our mission to dispel perpetuated lies, I'm sure you're aware of the proclamations that our elections were manipulated this last term by none other than our respected Institute," he said, feigning remorse.

A boisterous "BOOOOOO" echoed through the crowd.

"Fucking cattle," Danny whispered to Dina.

"This claim of election fraud is nothing more than a shoddy denouncement from the press. They are a jealous and spiteful bunch, afraid of losing power. It was the Institute who prevented another atrocity like the North Korean Double-Election Fiasco of 2026!

Be wary, Good Citizens, as the slime of untruth oozes into every corridor, aiming to dismantle the Institute. We even saw the oppressive spread of misinformation here today at the opening of our meeting! Accusations only. Dirty, unfounded accusations. We've sent you all the documents, all the research, all the reports from our Institute concluding that there hasn't been and will not be any media manipulation. How much more does the press need? Is no evidence sufficient? Eeeek!"

Another "BOOOOOO" erupted from the crowd. Then, the Secretary stopped for a moment, looking dazedly around before regaining composure.

"Now, I want to be terribly clear," he said, smoothing his auburn beard and peering at the stanchion-partitioned press section ensconced in the back-right corner of the hall, "it has not, is not, and never will be a goal of the Institute to bash or disintegrate the free press of our great nation. The Institute is an appendage of The Constitution, whose aim is only to bolster our democratic processes. We work with you, work for you. How can we truly be the world's greatest democracy without access to the truth? Eeeek!"

He paused to let the power of his rhetoric seep and stick in the flamingo-crowd. The Secretary must have felt good, really good, intoxicated even.

"Now, as we all well know, free speech inherently feeds into the formation of the laws of our nation, no? A misinformed public will, unfortunately, vote for misinformed and malicious policy—unknowingly and innocently, of course."

"YES. YES!" the crowd cheered, bursting into applause.

Danny scoffed at the gullibility of the crowd, refusing to believe that he'd ever been one of them. "Christ, these simpletons will believe any crap spouting from that garbage-mouthed secretary. They don't even know that he's not really in charge. Hell, he doesn't even know," he said quietly to Dina.

"Danny...Danny!" she yell-whispered. "People are looking at us funny. We've *got to go*. NOW!"

As she pulled Danny through the crowd away from the stage, Sherman continued:

"We ask you humbly, to keep this mission in your mind: confer with your neighbors, speak with your friends, call up your relatives and tell them to get out and vote for Bill 17.76! Let's finalize permanent representation in the President's Cabinet. Like a Supreme Court Justice, the Secretaries for Information Dissemination serve for life! I personally recommend our good Deputy Secretary to be the point-person in the Cabinet so I can better attend my duties, but that is neither here nor there. Eeek!"

Dina had heard enough, didn't care if Danny wanted to keep judging the rabble, only cared that the two of them hightail it out of the Institute as fast as possible. She yanked at Danny's hand with great force as she wove their way through the crowd.

"Ouch, Dina. You're gonna rip my shoulder out of its socket."

"I don't fucking care. We've got to keep walking while everyone's distracted, or else we'll never get out of here. Sherman sounds like he's getting to the end of his speech."

As they walked toward the balcony's bannister leading to the staircase that segued directly from the third-floor to the Main Hall to the first floor, the two could still hear Sherman:

"Our extensive search for credibility and truth will only serve to improve the intelligence of the Executive Branch. The laws of our land must not be bent. The laws of our land must be reinforced by, and only by—"

Before the Secretary could finish, the little gray man in his little gray suit with his little gray tie just touching his little gray belt that had little gray clips for his little gray suspenders scurried on to the stage and whispered into the Secretary's ear.

Sherman's eyes widened, prompting his inflated eyeballs to dart toward the balcony that overlooked the second floor. He glared, the blaze in his eyes set upon two young audience members peering down; however ignited his fury, the Secretary—true to the disposition of successful government officials—maintained composure.

"Excuse me for a moment please, Good Citizens. I trust you understand that the duties of the Institute are paramount."

The rabble nodded to each other, impressed by the dedication of their Honorable Secretary for Information.

The Secretary took a step back, retrieved his walkie talkie, and whispered. Several FiBs (not INFO Guards) could be seen pressuring their earpieces, and, after which, those FiBs thudded their thick combat boots to briskly spread through the hall, breaking original formation.

Dina poked Danny in the shoulder, interrupting his disgust at the rabble beside them, her face washed with worry. "Why did he stop? Why the *fuck* did he stop? We've got to move faster."

"Wh-what's up? Oh shit. Let's keep on," Danny said, as they came nearer to the staircase that would taxi them to the first-floor exit.

"Looks like the Deputy's toady already ratted us out. Those FiBs are on the move," Danny replied.

"We gotta go. We gotta go!"

Danny scrutinized the floor below, weighing the severity of their latent danger. At first, nothing seemed out of the ordinary: the same cattle folk who didn't make it in to the main-conference herd, nothing extraordinary. Surveying more intently though, he saw FiBs breaking their perimeter, freshly hustling in response to command.

Run, Danny, run! *They're coming.*

Our two love-birdies realized they would need to abandon their original plan of walking out with the rabble. Danny felt intense pressure on his wrist from Dina's grip. Underneath her grappled fingers, his bronze skin turned white. She pulled him away from the balcony's marble bannisters. She looked desperately into his pewter eyes, her fear palpable.

Danny had never wanted to comfort her more than in that moment. With all his heart, all his empathy, all his budding adolescent love, he wanted nothing more than to tell her, "Don't worry, it'll be all right." But he knew that'd be a lie.

The FiBs militant stomping clacked through the chamber hall, coming ever closer; they were hunting. Danny and Dina didn't have much time. Even if the Institute's soldiers were, in fact, not aiming to capture our two birds, Danny wasn't about to take that chance. They looked down to the entrance of the Institute and saw two beefy FiBs posted by the door, stiff, vigilantly observing as patient predators stalking their favorite haunt. It would only take one careless misstep from our lover-birdies for the FiBs sink in their teeth.

"O.K.," Danny thought aloud. "The front door's a bust, Dene. Sherman demands the Deputy dispatch 57% of on-duty Federal Information Battalion officers to attend the Good Citizen conference each week. We gotta find a way out from the balcony floor."

"Right, O.K., before they close in on us from above and below," Dina said. "In a security breach, they're told to guard all exits. Shit. Shit. What do we do?"

"We gotta get outta sight, first. Wait. I think I have an idea. Follow me," Danny said, tugging her wrist to follow him.

"Don't run," Dina cautioned. "We don't want more eyes on us than we already have."

So, the two slowly padded through the center hallway on the second-floor balcony, trying their best to divert from the two main staircases in the Institute. Danny planned to hole up in an executive bathroom, one that FiBs and INFO Guards didn't have access to. It was just three doors down when he heard a shout.

"There! You two. Stop!"

"No. Don't look," Dina said. "Pretend we're out of earshot."

They booked it to the door. Now nearly running, Danny retrieved the keys from his pocket, fumbling for the correct key. Donna only had a few labelled, but did have one that said "EXECUTIVE PISSER, BAL." It was probably the only key she ever used.

"Halt! By order of the Institute and of the United States, halt!" the FiB Lieutenant shouted again before howling into her walkie that she had eyes on the fleeing interns.

Too bad for her, Danny and Dina had no intention of halting by order of "fucking anyone." Ignoring the bathroom's signage detailing "Official Use Only," Danny unlocked the door and the two intern doves hurriedly flocked inside. After slamming the door shut, he secured the interior lock, hoping the Lieutenant wouldn't have a key; he'd never seen anyone but high-level officials and blubbering Donna go into this bathroom, but knew not to trust his eyes, not here.

"Danny—Danny—what do we do? We're fucking trapped!"

"Shh—shh. Remember when Brenda gave us that tour on the first day?"

Dina remembered the day as if it were branded into her psyche. And how could she not? Her entire family was so "goddamn proud" of her for getting such a prestigious internship. Her dad even said, "You're gonna do great things, kid. I just know it. Show those hacks who's boss." Her mom had said "my little girl is a government professional now," as Dina left the house. She hadn't slept a wink the night before, her anticipation and excitement refusing drowsiness from melatonin release.

No, Dina, the tour! Please...we're running out of time...

"No, Dina, *the tour*," Danny said. "Dina. Dina! Where did you go in there? Come on. Listen. Remember when Denise asked about the basement and Brenda gave us that shoddy answer?"

"Uhhh."

"Blabber told us that the basement was for maintenance only."

"So?"

"And...she said it's where they store the heat and ventilation systems, so don't get freaked out if the elevator won't take us there. We'd need a special key."

"What's your point?"

"Look," Danny said as he pointed to the A/C vent in the back-right corner of the room.

"Danny, this isn't some damn spy movie. Get real."

"You're right. It's not. But we're fucking going down there anyway. There has to be a fire exit at least," he said as he kicked in the vent. "Plus, if you need a key to access the basement, we're less likely to be found."

After maneuvering and squeezing their bodies to fit inside, Danny and Dina were crawling through the vent pipes, with their phones serving as flashlights, the two seeking any path with a decline. The only positive Danny gleaned was that since he went in after Dina, he had a nice view. *Gross! Smut!*

After what felt like hours, the newly ex-interns were pretty sure they were in between the first and basement floors. Through the intermittent illuminations thanks to the air-vent grates, the two birdies no longer saw marble floors, but instead a coarse, gritty cement. Danny couldn't see much, but he thought the basement rooms looked like prison cells, or surgical quarters. No windows. Cinderblock walls. The two stopped, hearing obsessive, psychotic rambling from holding cell up ahead.

"Dead, dead, very dead, yes, the press is dead. Nothing more to post, not for me, not for this sullen chief. Dead, the Washington press is dead, very dead. And they'll come after you next, that's what this sullen chief says," a ragged woman in torn clothes said, over and over again in a rhythmic trance.

"Danny. What. The Fuck. What the fuck?"

"This Deputy's got problems."

"So do we if we don't get outta here."

"Let's keep moving. Try to find a hallway or something. "

They moved cautiously, conscious of every patch of groaning metal and echo of their tormented breath.

"Shhhhh!" Dina said, though Danny wasn't saying anything. "I can hear someone. Sounds like two."

"I wasn't saying—"

"SHHHHH!" Dina commanded. She shoved her hand on Danny's chest, stopping him, in order to hear the voices resonating through the vents, eavesdropping:

"Now, professor. Can I call you professor? Surely, since that's what you are, yes! Or were, I suppose I should say. You know, I wouldn't like it very much if I have to ask you again. What did you tell your fat-cat reporter friend?"

"Nothing. He's a reporter; he has his sources. You think he'd need to rely on me? Are you losing your touch?"

"Oh, you're not the first I've had down here. But the others have shown surprising resilience and loyalty. Oh, he's a feisty little rat, forgetting where he is and who he's talking to!"

"This is ridiculous. You haven't a shred of evidence. I'm being held here against my will! Why would I betray the Institute's trust?"

"I don't verily know, professor. Why *would* you betray the Institute's trust? You sneaky, sneaky little rat, you. After all the access and amenities we've so generously given...a shame, really...you had so much promise, so much promise tinkering with those little words, mixing and matching their orders and their syntax and their impact...no more promise now, no!"

Overhearing, Danny thought the voices sounded oddly familiar. Danny and Dina did not dare to move amidst the muffled conversation. Then they heard the man whimper:

"Now, wait—wait. No. No. It doesn't need to come to that. You don't need to do that. I'll be good. Please. Not again. Put it down. Please. Put it down. I told yo—"

They heard a scream. And again. And again.

Then it got light.

Chapter 27: A Professor's Diary #7

Daryl's Basement
Date unknown, sometime in mid-August 2035

To a scared, sick, but slowly enlightened little professor:

I woke up screaming this morning. There's so much to record, but too much to remember, especially for an addled mind.

I don't think I've slept for days.

Still. I'm coming back. I can feel it. At least I have more cognitive awareness within my dream states. More lucid, no longer just a passenger. The pain in my feet-claws is beginning to subside, too. No, not feet-claws. Just feet. Humans don't have claws (most of them anyway).

It's becoming difficult for me to sustain any semblance of hope.

Chapter 28: The Waiting Continues

O'Hoolihan's Bean Brew and Draught
August 15, 2035—the last day
2:45 p.m.

I can still hear her tapping her fingers on the diner tabletop, intent as a crouching cougar stalking an unwary prey.

Earl noticed his boss's anxiety, and that his head felt a little clearer with her distracted. She still glared out the window with purpose, again murmuring something about "the corporal" and "love for his darling Dee," while rhythmically tapping her fingers. Earl's rendition of the first day they met didn't help her calm down. He felt sad she was so upset but kept reminding himself what he had written in his diary just a few days ago, his struggling yet budding rationale that Dee was subliminally manipulating him and Secretary Sherman. He did not want to forget, needed to investigate these irregularities, else his conscience be damned, and his spine permanently turned to jelly.

Oh, she is vile, Earl! Why can't you remember? I've seen it!

And yet, his animosity still hopped away as his froggy eyes drowned in hers whenever she stole a look over to him. But the only looks she stole now were out the window. He didn't like seeing his darling Dee so upset; he reached over to grab her hand. As he halted her incessant tapping, he said, encouragingly:

"Dee, they will come. I kn-kn-know that they w-will. N-n-nobody ever t-t-turns you down."

She recoiled her hand ferociously, fire glowing in her sanguine eyes.

"Don't fucking touch me, you slimy frog! What the fuck do you know anyway?" Dee snarled.

Earl sat, worried, ripping another paper napkin and letting the contents float down to the floor. Dee had been stressed with so many underground clients lately.

"Oh. I'm sorry, my sweet amphibian. You're just trying to help like a good little frog should. I do need to relax," she said and got up, heading towards the bathroom. "Could my sugar tadpole order me another hibiscus tea while I wash up?"

"Sh-sure," Earl said.

After Dee exited, before Earl could get Sheila's attention, the comely waitress was already on her way to the table.

"An-another hibiscus, Sh-Sheila."

"Fine," Sheila said, peering at him suspiciously and filling up his coffee. "But I have to ask, Earl. What's happened to you?"

"Wuh-what?"

"Don't 'what' me, honey. My favorite regular hasn't come in for more than half-a-year, and now he comes in with some high-class hussy and stammers each and every word like some common, blabbering fool. Somethin' ain't right."

"Shhh! Y-yuh-you shouldn't t-t-t-talk about her like th-that," he whispered.

"I don't remember you ever acting so scared before, or coming in with anyone like *that*," Sheila said, curt, before witnessing the fear in Earl's eyes. "Listen, honey, I'm sorry. I didn't mean to get you upset. I'm just worried about you. It doesn't seem like that lady's any good for ya. Be careful. People care about you."

As Sheila finished, the ladies' room door opened. She sighed, but winked at Earl to pacify any of his doubt she'd confront Dee. "Hibiscus, you said? On the double, Earlie."

He was grateful to Sheila, but Earl didn't know what to say, didn't know what to do. He felt himself getting angry at Dee, getting angry at her snapping, getting truly angry at her for how she'd changed him, how she took advantage of him. With her scaffold beginning to be torn down, Earl grappled with his brief moment of rising clarity and consternation, aiming to confront his boss about his recent suspicions.

Sick her, Earl!

"Oh, what's the sourpuss face for?" Dee said as she smoothed the bottom of her dress and sat down.

"Now listen, D-dee. I try m-m-m-my best for you an-an-and you don't give me any re-respect," Earl said, gaining confidence. "I'm sick of not knowing."

"Oh, we are feeling quite belligerent today, aren't we? I'm sorry. Have I grinded those sensitive gills of yours?" she said, mustering faux sincerity.

"N-n-n-no. You're not sorry. And f-f-frogs don't have g-gills, ma'am," Earl said and glugged a mouthful of coffee for confidence. "I always l-l-l-look out for you. Always! No re-respect."

"No re-respect? Well how can I respect a stuttering little miscreant? Or did we forget our recent betrayal with the interns?"

"No-n-no-now you're mocking my stutter? Classy," Earl said, ignoring her, his voice rising.

"Oh, yes, poor widdle Earl, no wun wants to wisten to him," she said.

"D-d-d-dee, I've be-been doing some thinkin—"

"You have, have you? That must be a difficult change for you. When you *do* think, I'm the one who has to clean the damn mess. We wouldn't even *be here* if it weren't for your incompetence with the professor-rat and with the interns. Not an original thought in all your head worth pursuing."

"N-now, th-that's just unfai—"

"If you don't snap that croaker shut, I might just be inclined to shut it for you. Your insolence is really rubbing me wrong. Must I do everything myself?" she said as she raised her hand to snap.

In moment of brash, caffeinated and clairvoyant confidence, Earl snatched both her hands and slammed them down on the table, a pounding slam which disturbed their mugs and roused clinks on the tabletop. He made sure to clamp her fingers. Coffee shop patrons gawked and gasped at the sudden burst, and looked to Sheila who raised her index finger to her lips. Shhh!

"What? Just what do you think you're—how dare you touch me without permission. Get your slimy fingers off me! NOW!"

"N-n-no. It's m-my turn to talk now. I kn-know you've been manipulating me. I-If no-nothing changes, I'm going to quit. I don't care. I kn-know you tricked me wh-when I signed the contract and-and who knows how many other times. You make me commit vile acts and then make me forget. Admit it!" Earl shouted, realizing he was beginning to cause a scene.

Dee subtly tried to jar her hands free from Earl's grip, coaxing her lips into a wry smile.

"Admit it," Earl whispered, turning his attention back to Dee. "Admit you've manipulated me. Fixed my memories. Overheard my conversation with Ms. Andrews at Dipper and Co. then spun me up in your web."

"Earl, can you name even one time I've 'fixed' your poor froggy mind? Am I some witch bubbling, toiling, and troubling? This is madness, my sweet frog," she said, menacingly. "And madness means we have to visit the underground again."

"No, what's m-madness is that I can't name one time. And that's what's so fr-frustrating. But I know. I want you to know that I know," Earl said.

"See what you've done to Momma? She's upset and you're hurting her fragile fingers. Listen to your frantic croaking. We must have evidence if we're going to make such consequential and dangerous accusations. I'm hurt you'd say such a nasty thing. Momma Dee only wants to help her sweet little frog. And she is very disappointed he'd fall victim to the nasty rumors about us."

She's a demon. Stick it to her!

Dee looked at him, her eyes now flashing with waltzing embers. She tried to break her hands free, but, despite his sweaty palms, Earl restrained her folded hands, steadfast and steel-fisted. Dee sighed and tried a different tactic.

"Oh, but my sweet little frog, you know Momma always listens, always thinks about her perfect little man," Dee said, leaning over to expose her chest. Earl refrained—it certainly wasn't the time for nasty, lewd thoughts. Deep in his body, Earl vaguely remembered that Dee often used her seduction as a manipulative strategy against him. He fought against it.

"Th-that's not gonna work. Put 'em away. I need you to listen. I'm not a-attracted to you like that," Earl said. I felt his sense of relief at his own bold tenacity.

"Suit yourself, but what is a salacious little lady to do...it's just so hard to contain myself with your man-hands gripping me tight. Yes, so tight," she said and moaned, much to the delight of the enthralled male patrons. *Smut! Dirty, vile smut!*

"Be quiet."

"So domineering! Unfortunate, you know, tonight I was thinking...maybe...if you can ever forgive me...that you might want to see what Momma Dee can do for little pent up angsty frogs. She'll make you feel better, promise, then we can talk all you want," she said as she drifted her ankle up, up, and up Earl's leg, rubbing his upper thigh.

"St-st-stop," Earl said, but when Dee gazed into his eyes, he had to fight the urge to not submit to his darling Dee. He felt like a cornered and rabid dog, punished to the point of biting the hand that feeds.

"There's my little frog man! I know the tadpole between your legs doesn't work, has never felt tense urging, except in the presence of Momma Dee. Oh! Not so little anymore. He's my big frog and Momma can't wait any longer," she said and giggled. "You said you could never deny your darling Dee a thing. But, did you mean it? Come, now. Come back over to Momma."

Earl tried to look away, but his eyes magnetized to Dee's hypnotic stare and seductive cadence. Earl must have felt himself hesitate, might have felt his grip loosen on her hands, might have felt the sweat bead on his forehead, must have felt a repressed desire begging to be released. *Shame!*

"That's it, Earlie. No need to be mad at Momma Dee. Yes, that's it. She always looks out for you. Now I need you to finish, finish up whatever little qualms you have," Dee said, pressing harder against him with her foot.

"D-Dee. Pl-p-p-please. If you'd only j-j-j-just listen," Earl begged, now distracted from his questioning, and struggling to maintain his grip. Spellbound, he felt helpless to her advances—something about those fiery, sanguine eyes! With his brain having migrated into his other, typically defunct, downstairs head, Earl slackened his grip just enough: Dee broke free.

"D-Dee, I just w-want to talk. I-I'll be good. I p-p-promise. I-I d-d-didn't mean it," Earl said, his voice trembling.

"Oh, shut up, ignorant frog. You're mine," she said and snapped her fingers. "And you always will be. You'd be inclined to never forget that again."

Earl acquiesced, feeling grand, euphoric even, at his abrupt reconciliation with his darling.

"Yes, Momma Dee. I'm always yours, eeek!" Earl found himself saying.

"Good. Now shut that frogmouth up and never croak like that to me again," Dee commanded. "You won't like what happens if you do."

"Yes, ma'am," Earl said and then winced. He knew he shouldn't have called her ma'am. "L-l-look," Earl said, noticing the Chevy's whipping past O'Hoolihan's, roaring through the streets. Dee turned to look out the window with Earl.

"Damn! Unreliable savages! I wanted to keep this clean and simple. I didn't want to do this—always so messy. No choice now, Earlie. What do I always say? 'Contracts are cleaner.' But we can't have them running wild." Dee pulled her phone out of her snakeskin purse. "So messy, so *very messy*," she repeated, furious. "It's going to take me days to cover this up. Those miserable creatures are going to wish they'd never been born."

She yelled into the phone for her head FiB Lieutenant to get his ass to the coffee shop in the next five minutes, and to send out a battalion to hunt down the hawk and the clam. The two assassins had bent one rule too many.

I think I kept dreaming and feeling and knowing after that. Why can't I wake up?!

Chapter 29: Underground Hallucinogens

Location unknown
Date unknown

The room is bright. I assume, to save energy, LEDs. But the whole room has that old, orange glow of tungsten, so I can't be certain. I'm sitting in a soft, black chair that cushions my bottom. I like the chair. This doesn't feel like a dream.

Across from me, behind a maple desk with a green-shaded office lamp and meticulously stacked papers on top, a woman is sitting, staring at me.

Why is she staring? Is she leering, peering, or eyeing me like candy? I can't tell, but her sanguine eyes bewitch me.

"Professor, what a pleasure it is to meet you, finally. Where have you been hiding all week? I just want to say, we're so happy you decided to join us the Institute, yes! I hope you've found everything to your liking—your office, your subordinates. Some of them are brash, but if you ever have a problem, you just send them over to me, yes!" she must have said with a big, porcelain smile.

Why is she saying it like that? Why the added affirmation? How can someone be that happy? No. They certainly can't be—they certainly can't. Not like this. She can't be that happy hurting people. You don't know that I know, but I do; I'm onto your plots. You can't stave me off forever, devil!

"Of course, I'm happy you're here! Yes!" she must have said. I think that's what she said.

I know her. She's the one who's mean to the frog, makes him do things he doesn't want to do. The voice from the vents, the voice Danny and Dina heard torturing the helpless man. It's her, the Demon Deputy.

"It's an honor to be thought of so highly that the Institute even considered hiring me," I said. "I can't believe it's actually happened."

I keep hearing the words, then realize I've said them. No. What am I saying? Get out.

"Yes, we've been watching you, little professor, yes, watching. And, I must say, we have been utterly, yes, *utterly*, impressed with the work you've done," she said while crossing her legs and swiveling gently in her chair.

I see her chair is bigger than mine. The desk is bigger than mine. I want a bigger desk and I want a gentle swivel chair and I want a pretty lady twirling her hair to sit in it. Do I have that? No. But I do have a doctor who waddles in and sits with me.

"Well, while it seems to be a happy accident, you've been a crucial force in our mission to get Congress to pass our bill and open the Institute. That article you wrote back in 2032...just divine, simply divine. And now, your work on the effects of sentence construction has struck quite the chord with our staff. How you assessed the public's response to syntax, measured their perception of credibility," she shivered pleasurably.

"Secretary Sherman told me it was the academic fodder that won over the necessary votes for the Institute," I said.

"Oh yes, surely it did, yes! You might even say that we couldn't have done it without you, yes! And now, so very lucky for us, Sherman has decided that we must have your talents all to ourselves," she continued.

This is all just an act! She doesn't want me here, never wanted me here except on her own terms. If I could go back... but I am back?

"Well, to be honest, I didn't mean my article to have such a profound impact," I hear myself saying.

"Oh, sweet professor," she began, gazing with her sanguine eyes and a wry smile showing unnaturally white teeth, "do we ever, truly, *mean* to do anything profound? No! But we at the Institute are grateful, nonetheless. I mean it when I say: We couldn't have done it without you," she said.

No, certainly they could have done it without me. Couldn't have done it? Who needs a little rat scampering through the basement halls leaving little droplets of digested and stolen morsels? Not me, that's who. No, certainly not. Maybe she does though.

Ouch...my head...where am I? Take me back, back to the basement.

"I'm just happy to be of help. Plus, the research was fun," I'm saying, wanting so desperately to make a good impression. "The pay is good, and the potential for change is better. I'm honored to be here."

I feel myself smile, yes, a big smile, with the pearly whites people always say to show. I feel like I need to her to like me, want her to like me.

"We here at the Institute are *certainly* glad that you're having fun. There's always more fun to be had, and now you get to direct it, yes! If all goes well, I'll have to show you where I do my research," she said, "yes."

No. I certainly don't want to go down to where you do your research. Never again...ouch! Be careful, that's my tail. What? Where is my mind going?

I'm lying down now. The surface is very cold and very hard. The lights are so bright. I can't see any windows.

"Um—"

"Oh, no, no, no, no, sweet boy, I certainly do understand your confusion, but we might not even be here if you hadn't been such a brat with your contract renegotiation! But no, our esteemed, little professor-rat was much, much too prestigious to sign on with the government's terms. Some good that did you. And yet..." she said, pointing up to a fixture on the ceiling, a spider's web of blue and black wires with a chrome sheen, all of which surrounded a glowing red nexus. "No one's too good for the cloud! Just a little more convincing and all those thoughts will be mine! We must know what you told your fat-cat reporter friend, so Momma can send her hawk after him. We *do have rules,*" she said, now walking over to a wall of fierce-looking instruments of torture.

Moments later, I feel my leather restraints tighten, sending throbbing pulses to my hands and feet. She twirled a bladed tool, which looked like absurdly large hedge clippers, above my head.

"It seems the sweet little boy has turned his back! Now he's a gross, disgusting little rat! Momma has a very special tool for dirty little rats," she says, petting the giant clippers.

I was sweating, am sweating, barely able to speak.

"This is illegal. Please. Let me out, now!"

"You see, your confusion is curious, considering you *are* the head researcher, after all. It's not *quite illegal,* you know. We've a special clause in the Institute bill that allows 'enhanced interrogation' under extenuating circumstances. All in good faith, only to protect the integrity of information, of course. We must remember that, yes? Hmm. A Head Researcher who knows so much, yet so little!" she said and sighed. "If only you'd kept your yapper shut, understood that we at the Institute don't take kindly to traitors…He's been very naughty, now, yes!"

"Sherman will hear about this! There's no way he'd sign off on such medieval methods!" I'm shouting.

"Oh, Sherman and I have a *very close* relationship. In fact, he was down here just a few days ago! It only took a little coaxing, and then, well, let's say, he was very impressed," she said, laughing at her plan coming to fruition. She came closer and closer to the table, armed with those clippers!

It's cold underneath my back. I see the hedge clippers open and begin to shred and snip my feet. Slowly they open, slowly they close, starting with my toenails, and inching through the skin of my feet. Blood sputters, spits, and spurts, staining my skin.

Ouch. Please! Please, it hurts, no stop, not those. You're hurting my pink little feet-claws! No!

It went on and on and on and on and on and on. But I don't think I told her a damn thing. In and out of consciousness for hours, I still protected my doctor. At least I think I did, lying that

I had no reason to betray the Institute, desperate for a way out. She said, almost responding to my thoughts:

"...I don't verily know, Professor. Why *would* you betray the Institute's trust?"

I heard myself scream. And again. And again.

Chapter 30: Back at Dina's

Dina's Parents' House
August 10, 2035—the day of the escape
Around 4:00 p.m.

"Jeez, that was a blur," Danny exhaled as he shut and locked the door to Dina's childhood home. He walked past the foyer, which donned a flotilla of candid and portrait style family photos, into the living room. Dina followed.

"Yeah. I—I just don't know what the hell we're going to do now," Dina said as her face warped in concerned consternation.

With a sigh of relief, the whims of Danny's heartstrings could now see their desire come to fruition. "It's going to be all right," he said, "honestly."

The mounting rush of adrenaline had yet to subside, intermingling with the bubbling and frothing adolescent hormones of our two birdies. There was a certain, erm, inflation, so to speak, blooming between Danny's legs, unintentionally, of course. *Smut! Crass, smut-garbage!*

Quick to action by the rising entropy of teen chemicals and adrenaline bounding and bouncing throughout their bodies, my friends' prefrontal pleasure centers were hijacked as swiftly as a seasoned car thief would pilfer his goods before racing down the highway to pawn his pillages to the local, shifty, used car lot. Danny's body gravitated to Dina's, and the two embraced. Their ribcages squeezed tightly together; tears from worry and stress coursed down their faces. The two's hormone-cortisol cocktail catalyzed their second mouth-hole tango.

Danny and Dina fell back on the couch, desperate and afraid: desperate to concoct a plan, and afraid their eventual plan would fail to be cunning enough to deceive an institution bloated with resources, teeming with knowledge.

"Seriously Danny, what can we do? There's no way they're not gonna catch us. And then we're screwed. Did you *see* what they were doing to that guy? I almost threw up," Dina said.

"Ripping off toenails..." Danny said and shuddered.

"Not to mention the psychotic rambling of the woman in the holding cell. 'Press is dead, very dead, the Washington press is dead,' she kept saying over and over, like a lunatic. Hell, I knew the Institute was probably into some shifty, underbelly stuff, but torture? Pretty sure we had that outlawed after Iraq."

"Well, it sure as hell looks like we have some vigilantes running that basement," Danny said. "I'm almost positive that was Dee's voice, the Deputy."

"The rumors aren't really rumors then, are they?" Dina replied, rubbing her face and tugging at her hair.

"I guess not. No. I'm positive that was definitely the Deputy's voice. Who else's could it be? But that other voice—the guy. It's so familiar."

"I'm scared, Danny. What if we're next?"

"I'm scared, too. But I can't shake the feeling that I knew the dude's voice. It's been bothering me ever since we left."

Ignoring the fear pummeling his chest with boxer-ring-style precision, Danny wracked his brain about the torturer and her torturee.

"If the Deputy was torturing him, then the guy must have some influence," Danny said, thinking aloud.

"She did call him a rat. It sounded like he worked for the Institute," Dina said, absently staring at the wall.

"Right. How else could he betray the Institute's trust? Damn. Who the hell *was he*?"

"Do you think your professor knows about this? Didn't she call him professor?" Dina said.

The thought struck Danny with heaving force. His racing mind had muddled his memory. How could he have not made that connection earlier?

"Fuck. Dina. Fuck," Danny panted.

"Oh, shit. You think?"

"Fuckfuckfuck. Yeah that was him. He's the Head Research-er. And I hadn't seen him for five days! It was why I snooped in the Data and Inquiry Department in the first place. I had a bad feeling. I knew it," Danny said and shot up from the couch.

"Danny. Danny! Don't do anything stupid. We're safe now. All the doors are locked. My parents will be home soon. Have your mom do something about it. She's a lawyer. She can help him."

Dina's attempt did little to assuage Danny's determination.

"Do you know how long it will take for my mom to file a case against the Institute? Even *with* the picture I took of the planned assassination of a journalist. I could send it to a reporter to be published, but what's the point? The Institute'll just issue a Media Accuracy Report, and it'll be Fake News, with no chance the public will ever believe it. You can stay here. But every second that passes, she tortures him more. I wouldn't be able to live with myself. Give me your keys."

"No."

"Dina. Give me your keys."

"No," she repeated, stalwart.

"Fine. Tell your parents I borrowed their car," Danny said, already removing the keys from the key ring in the foyer, before walking out the door without looking back.

Before Dina fully processed Danny's exit, she heard the car engine start, and her mom's van peel out into the street. Dina sat stunned, in shock at what had happened and terrified of what might happen. She put her head in her palms, feeling like she was about to cry, but then noticed Danny's backpack leaning against the arm of the living room couch. Unzipping the main pouch, she pulled out a manila envelope sealed delicately with red tape, which had the words, "HIGHLY CON-FIDENTIAL," stamped in big, bold letters. Figuring she didn't have anything to lose, she broke the red tape, and opened the document.

```
INSTITUTE FOR INFORMATION DISSEMINATION
WASHINGTON D.C.
CONFIDENTIAL, GRADE 1 THREAT
Date: August 9, 2035


BREACH REPORT SUBJECT DETAILS:


     Name:           Daniel Umberto Hernández
     Alias:          Danny
     Occupation:     Intern at the Institute for
                     Information Dissemination.
     Height:         5' 8"
     Weight:         160 lbs.
     Race:           Latino/Latinx
     Location:       721 Diamond Avenue,
                     Alexandria, VA 22301
     Vehicle:        N/A.
     Threat Level:   Grade 1—INVITE TO JOIN
                     INFORMATION GATHERING INITIATIVE
     Other Notes:
     Keep close to Deputy
     Overly suspicious of Institute foul play
     Likely will investigate and leak confidential
     information
     If invitation is rejected, upgrade to Grade 3
     Threat—BRING TO UNDERGROUND
```

Dina gasped and bolted to her car. She knew she had no choice but to follow Danny into the lion's den.

Chapter 31: The Hawk and the Clam in Love

Streets of Washington D.C.
August 14, 2035—Davis Meets Dee, the penultimate day
Mid-morning

The tires of the rusted Chevy screeched through the streets of D.C. Like the people inside, it had one or two fewer scratches than I remember. A woman's voice could be heard, shouting:

"You were supposed to take a left, damn it! The directions are pretty clear," Dahlia said.

"Oh, hush that salty tongue of yours. I'm trying to fucking find the right street to get to the back. This place is a maze. Damn it!" Davis said as he took another wrong turn, trying to find the driveway to the Institute's back entrance. "Ugh. Sorry I'm yelling, babe. It's just, Dahl, we need that cash, need it bad if we want to really kiss this kind of work good-bye," he continued as he intermittently licked the adhesive strip of his rolled cigarette.

"Need the cash so you can take this little clam out to a nice meal and primp her with pearls?" Dahlia asked, fluttering her eyelashes in jest.

"A primp for her, a pump or two for me," Davis said, laughing.

"You're sick! Sick! I would never let a dirty hawk swoop into this sweet little mollusk," she said, spreading her legs.

"You must have a short memory, then," Davis said as he leaned over for a kiss on the cheek.

"Fine, but only because you asked so nicely," she said as she kissed his scruffy cheek and ruffled his feathered head. Davis nuzzled into her caress.

"Ah yes, you sure do like it when clammy baby does that. But! Just a taste for now, just a raw-bar appetizer. We've got to get more details on this *Post* reporter first, and we're about to be late. She knows what she signed up for," Dahlia said, winking at him.

"It didn't help much that the Institute gave us a bum address. We searched the place up and down, not a lick of him!"

"And now we're in big trouble, called down to the principal's office. What's with her? Is she afraid of texting? That someone will be watching?" Dahlia jested.

Davis laughed.

"But really, Davey, promise me this will be the last run. Promise me!"

"I promise it will and I promise we'll find him fast," Davis said, and playfully scratched behind Dahlia's hair.

"I wanna be rich! Yes, filthy rich, by the time this job is done."

"I want you to be waddling by the time this job is done," Davis said as he corrected the Chevy's course toward their meeting with Institute officials.

"You're such a naughty, dirty bird," she replied.

Davis then saw her retrieve the meeting prep notes the Deputy sent after their bum luck in taking out the reporter. "Okay, let's review what we know before your libido costs us a cool quarter million," Dahlia said.

"Okay, fine, but only because you're all right, Dahlia," Davis replied, stroking her leg. "Read off the details again for me, so those Institute loons don't think the hawk and his clam are a sham. We mean fucking business."

"Say please."

"Please," he said, complying, thinking that he could never deny her anything.

Dahlia looked through the notes and said, "Most of it looks the same. No known address, no known vehicle, for now. Wait. Here's something. It says that the reporter we're supposed to take out is harboring someone else wanted by the Institute. That if we catch and kill them both, the Institute will double our payout," she said, salivating at the prospect of 500 grand. "Maybe that's what she wants to talk to us about."

"Damn, Dahl. We better hurry," Davis said as he squeaked the brakes to park.

Then it went light again.

Chapter 32: A Frog Waits by the Pond for a Clam and Her Hawk

Outside the Institute for Information Dissemination
August 14, 2035—Davis meets Earl, the penultimate day. Late Morning

I couldn't really see very well in my surrogate dream-mind, but I think he's standing outside on the steps of a big gray building, looking down and rubbing his shirt on something in his hands. Then I could see. Oh! It's my good friend, Earl.

Earl sighed heavily as he adjusted his glasses, feeling a bit nervous about the forthcoming meeting with Dee and the two hitmen. He knew Dee had hired them last week to try and capture *The Washington Post* reporter, but he'd never met them in person. As he waited, Earl thought about the rumors that had been spread throughout D.C. about the notorious, assassin pair, the hawk and the clam. Earl remembered that he had tried in desperation to dissuade Dee from hiring the two on account of their tendency to bend contracts to their own whims, but she balked at his concern: "Oh, my little sweet tadpole, don't you worry your slimy little gills. You will always be Momma's favorite. We need these two. Well, we need the corporal, but they come as a package deal."

Still, it was odd, Dee never had her Lead Assistant meet with any of her hired hitmen, since she preferred to stay elusive and unknown, even to her favorite tadpole. He suspected Dee was beginning to distrust Davis and Dahlia on account of their flakiness these past few days. She was getting nervous; Earl could feel it.

The sweat drip-dropped on his neck from his forehead, speckling his glasses and deepening the hue of his powder-blue shirt collar as he waited. As he glanced down the long, sprawling, back-entrance driveway to the Institute, looking out for a red and rusting Chevy taxiing the two assassins-for-hire, he couldn't refrain from obsessing over those rampant rumors about the hawk and the clam.

He had heard that Davis and Dahlia had been partners for a few years. Well, they had at least been partners since Davis returned from his North Korean tour with the Marines, during the short war after 2026 North Korean election hack. Davis had started out as a grunt private slinking through the dense countryside before being promoted (with the utmost expedience) after superiors recognized his superb talent for killing. It was said that Davis could paint lush, verdant fields red, all while grinning a ghoulish smile each time he splashed lifeblood on the budding leaves of spring. Meticulous and cunning as a prowling lioness, few of his prey would become aware of the ambush just before propelled brass pierced through their soft flesh. Earl winced when he heard the grimmest of these rumors: Davis would then whisper, "Good night, my sweet," to his victims as the deep, crimson liquid stained the nearby shrubbery.

Comrades and officers alike believed Davis to be as good a marksman as they come, but all the greats come with an

Achilles' Heel, of course: Davis thought killing with a scope was the coward's way. As sound of a shot as he may be, his preferred tool was not a rifle, but a sleek, eight-inch hunting blade stored in a smooth leather sheath on his lower back. Perhaps it was Davis's stubbornness that prevented him from gaining a position of command. His squad-mates would whisper that Davis polished and sharpened his blade for up to three hours a day. They used to joke they could hear the metallic whisk of Davis sharpening his blade even when he was in the shitter: "I swear man, he must love that knife more than his schlong, and he seems to really like his schlong," they would chide. Naturally, they had avoided saying this in front of Davis, especially after the soldiers heard where three-finger Kevin got his nickname. Perhaps the most curious of the rumors was that before Davis met Dahlia, he'd never had much luck nor interest in women, preferring the company of his knife.

Dee had Davis's dedication to weaponry in mind when she advocated to Sherman for his hire; she made it a point to harp on it, in fact. Earl was nervous about Davis's knife, nervous there was little a frogman could do to disarm him.

As for Dahlia, she apparently had been a member of an elite hitman federation, a select organization where she garnered a gruesome and grisly reputation as an assassin with such remarkable martial arts' prowess that she quickly worked her way up to the third-ranking member. As such, she was trusted with assigning missions to the appropriate lower-rank members in her club, according to their skill. While she was nearly equal in skill with a .9mm, Dahlia's choice tactic for mid-range combat were her lethal, 3" throwing knives which she kept strapped to her upper thighs, right bicep, and ankles. Earl heard that while Dahlia usually favored a fatal blow—a steel-tipped puncture to her assignments' necks—sometimes, if Dahlia needed information or was just in a sour mood, she would instead aim at the soft pieces of flesh immediately above the collarbone. The inflicted wound would then be further exacerbated by a Muay-Thai elbow bash to the top of their skulls. The saps, now bloody and dazed would always talk, begging for mercy all the while, but were never absolved of their sin.

During her tenure, Dahlia's job-completion percentage neared 98%, and the only jobs she'd failed were on account of lower-ranking partners, peons of embarrassing incompetence. Eventually, this 2% blemish proved a significant enough deficit to prompt her resignation. For a few months after her departure from the hitman federation, she favored working alone under the pseudonym, "razor clam."

Though the two were inseparable now (a dangerous closeness that frightened our dear friend Earl), he had heard that Dahlia originally defied Corporal Davis's recruitment attempts. She scoffed his advances, said she was done working with "crummy, useless men." When Davis tried to retort, tried to boast his marksmanship as among the best in the Marines, Dahlia upbraided his overconfidence, harassing him: "yes, rising from private all the way to corporal surely proves your prowess." Not a man to back down from a challenge, Davis welcomed her defiance, cajoling Dahlia to watch a "corporal's skill proven at the shooting range." She did, but demanded a condition: he must agree to a personally crafted test of her own arduous and dynamic design. So, after Davis's persistence was augmented by his 99.8% target-hit rate, Dahlia agreed to partner up. Over time, the two cultivated intimate feelings, and those feelings served to bolster their efficiency at completing jobs and voracity for killing; only now they'd get a little smooch and a grab and a grope for a job well done.

Earl's rumination over the pervasive rumors did little to calm his sweat glands or dry his shirt. The dotted-saline marks were slowly spreading into a triangular-soak blotch stain. Good thing his darling Dee reminded him to bring a handkerchief to wipe his forehead.

After a few useless swipes of sweat, Earl heard the blasting gun-pop of a Chevy's overworked engine trying to climb the hill to the Institute for Information Dissemination's back entrance. Earl decided it would be a good idea to review the meeting's itinerary to ensure he wouldn't disappoint his Momma Dee.

DO THE FOLLOWING IN THIS EXACT ORDER:

1. Smile with your frogmouth and say, "Hello. We are pleased to have you joining us at the Institute for Information Dissemination."
2. Greet Davis first, then Dahlia.
3. Shake their hands but shake Davis's first.
4. Engage in polite small talk, but not too much small talk. We don't have all day.
5. Apologize that the Deputy Secretary couldn't meet them at the Institute entrance in person.

6. Be sure to mention that Momma Dee (but don't say it like that) has sent you as a liaison since she is very preoccupied at the moment with a very important client.

7. Take them through Institute Hall B2.45 and up the steps that join Hall D5.43 and hop along to Momma Dee's office (but don't say it like that!)

8. If your darling Dee is still in her meeting, wait like a good little frog until she finishes. Do not let the two inside her office. Do not interrupt since Momma is with a very important client.

9. Leave the room since the meeting is private. Don't worry your little tadpole gills — Momma will handle the rest.

Earl wasn't so sure why she had to give such inordinate importance to Davis.

"Maybe she's threatened by Dahlia, since she might not be able to seduce her," he thought and almost giggled, but then shunned the thought from his amphibian mind. Momma Dee wasn't threatened by anyone, especially silly, little frogs.

Chapter 33: A Hawk Forced
to Perch Underground

Outside the Institute for Information Dissemination
August 14, 2035—Davis Meets Earl, the penultimate day

Davis could still feel his ass tingling from a hard, mollusk-slippery-slap. I see Dahlia holding his hand as he leaps up the back-entrance steps to the Institute for Information Dissemination, spreading his powerful legs to skip every other step.

"Hey! I can't quite fly up these stairs like you can, Davey," Dahlia said.

"Little clams prefer burrowing, I heard," he replied, ignoring her request to slow down, and breaking free from her hand.

"At least I can breathe underneath the muck and mud!" she said, tapping up the staircase, padding a few steps behind.

As they approached the top, Davis saw a wee man with large, 1980s-style frames magnifying his eyes.

"Sheesh, what a damn freakshow," Davis thought to himself.

Davis, don't be so quick to insult the poor guy. He is very handsome, just misunderstood.

When the bird-mollusk partner-pair reached the top to greet their amphibian liaison, Davis noticed the wee man's shirt was drowned in sweat. This perspiration only added to the fact that Davis hated formalities, but he extended his hand, regardless. To Davis's irritation, the frogman froze, stupidly staring at Davis's outstretched hand as if it were detached from his wrist. Davis stared, confused.

"H-hello, we are very happ—n-n-no. We-we are pleased to have you j-j-j-joining us at the In-in-institute for Information Dissemination," Earl said, feeling self-inflicted pique at botching the first itinerary item.

Earl, take them away, far away from the Institute. Damn your itinerary, your prescribed list of rules and information! You must break free. Don't you know that you're sending them to kill me and my doctor?

"Oh, he's so adorable. Isn't he, Davey? Such a baby peach!" Dahlia said. "You don't mind if I call you 'peach,' do you? I have a thing for nicknames."

Earl stood silently, wishing he could retrieve his crumpled directions from his pants-pocket, but now that would be improper, unprofessional for the Lead Bullfrog Assistant. After a moment of awkward silence, Dahlia continued:

"Uh okay...I'll take that as a yes. Anyway, Mr. Peach, thanks for coming out to get us. We're pleased to be here—with the opportunity, I mean."

"Th-than—" Earl said, before he shook his head furiously, filled with fear. His eyes started to hurt and roll in his head.

"Hey, buddy—you all right?" Davis asked. "You don't look so good."

"Hello, Corporal Davis. We have been waiting for you, eeek!" Earl found himself saying, feeling good, grand even, a mild state of euphoria at the fact that he nailed item number two of the script. He knew his Momma Dee would be proud.

"Thanks for helping us score this gig. And you ar—"

"Hello, Dahlia, former grade-three assassin," Earl said, mechanically.

"Uh. Yeah. Thought we already did the greeting thing. Hello to you, too?" Dahlia said. She looked over to Davis quizzically, noticing his patience started to wear thin.

Dahlia then reached out her hand, and Earl promptly recoiled at the gesture. He was not about to go off script again. He reached out his hand to Davis.

"Dude. What the hell? Shake her damn hand."

Dahlia pulled Davis aside, concerned. She whispered out of Earl's earshot.

"Fuck this guy, Davey. Weren't we supposed to be meeting the Deputy Secretary? Not a good impression if they want to us to continue the job, especially because they gave us botched information the first time."

Davis nodded, and the two returned to Earl.

"We've got other contracts we could take, you know, Captain Stone Fruit," Dahlia said.

Earl winced, not knowing how to respond to their threat of departure. He did not think he was sexist yet he saw how Davis might think so. Earl reprimanded himself for his apparent misogynistic preference to shake Davis's hand first.

"Uh-uh, n-n-n-no, so-sorry. I-I'm sorry," Earl admitted, as he extended both of his hands to shake Davis and Dahlia simultaneously. Ever the loyal frog, he still carefully ensured that he touched Davis's palm first before engaging in a double-single hand shake with both the corporal and the clam. Then his eyes hurt again, rolling around in his head for a moment.

"I deeply apologize that I have been sent as a liaison for the Deputy Secretary of the Institute for Information Dissemination, but she is preoccupied at the moment with a very important client. We will boost your pay by 5% for our unintentional offense. If you both would follow me, her gracious, Madame Deputy should be finished as soon as we arrive to the Capital T Truth Division offices. Eeek!"

"Ok...ay," Dahlia said, directing another concerned glance at Davis.

As the two assassins reluctantly tailed the stone-fruit frog-man, Earl punched in the back-door code and instinctively led the pair through the winding, networked halls of the Institute, passing only a few scant workers with their heads down, much too preoccupied to greet Institute strangers. The workers surely knew the back entrance was reserved for essential, special-interest guests, typically those planning to serve the Capital T Truth Division. Dee controlled most employees unlucky enough to work in this sector.

Davis felt somewhat esteemed from their sly entrance; he favored privacy, liked the fact that government jobs tended to be hush-gigs. "Plus, not nearly as much potential for legal blowback," Davis thought, walking up the steps to the third floor which housed the Deputy Secretary's office.

As the motely trio passed through the Central Hub, Davis and Dahlia slowed down, distractedly listening to frustrated voices which boomed from an office suite designated with a gold plaque: "Intern Office of The Institute for Information Dissemination."

"What the hell is that supposed to mean? You can't expect us to believe this garbage! He hasn't been home for four days, damn it," a man said.

"I'm bl'uh…sorry sir, but we…bl'uh…believe that's what happened," a blubbering woman said from the front desk.

"Our Danny? A runaway? This just isn't him, isn't them, for God's sake! I refuse to believe it. He and Dina were always happy. This is bullshit! I want my son back, and I know you damn liars have him here. I've been reading up on you. I've figured out what y'all do, here."

"Perhaps at home they were happy, Mrs. Umberto, but ever since I hired them *here*, they kept to themselves, scheming. Insolent of and in their work, never mind how simple the task. They must have been hiding something, I'm sorry to say," a man said, pompously.

"I want to speak to someone with some motherfucking authority here, and I want to speak to them right now!" another man shouted.

"Bl'uh…Sir, I'm going to…bl'uh…have to ask you to calm down."

"Donna, it's fine," the pompous, Intern Supervisor said. "I'm in charge of this office, Mr. Dio. No one else in the Institute knew them half as well as me. Now that I think about it, didn't I hear your van has mysteriously gone missing? Surely you can't expect the Institute to have taken that, too? Listen to reason, my good sir. And I'd appreciate if you'd take a step back and stop breathing on my chin. We don't want to have to call the FiBs in here."

"Why, why didn't we just listen to Danny at dinner last week? We could have taken him seriously. Dina would still be here!" a woman said, beginning to break down.

"Ma'am, I understand your concern for your child, truly I do. But—wait—what was that? What happened when Danny came over for dinner, Mrs. Dio?"

"He…he was nervous about his job, about how people were acting here, that he was scared."

"Don't tell him another thing, Darlene. He'll only use it against you. Think about Dina," Mr. Dio said.

"Oh! Well, that certainly *is* interesting. I do know that, for whatever godforsaken reason, some higher-ups were interested in giving Danny some more responsibility, even though I'd advised against it. But, still, could be the key. It is not uncommon for teenagers afraid of real responsibility to run away. What, exactly, did he tell you?"

"Oh, what does it matter if you won't help us? Don't think I won't have my law offices look into this. Y'all will be fucked!" Mrs. Umberto interrupted.

"Okay ma'am, no need for that. Like I said, we don't need any FiBs in here. Listen, I only ask since we could be onto something. Now that I think about it…maybe we *can* help. Let's just say—and I'm hypothesizing here—Danny formed a little action plan since he was unhappy at the Institute, afraid of god knows what, calculated a little plan to flee from whatever danger he's fabricated in his paranoid head. If that's true, we just may be able to track the two down, or figure out where they're going. At least why."

"And how might you do that? Telekinesis?"

"Information is our trade, Mr. Umberto, if you remember. A little hint goes a long way. I'll tell you what: I'm moved by your passion. I'll talk to my supervisor, the Deputy Secretary herself, and see if we can book an appointment to discuss Danny and Dina, but it will have to be tomorrow morning since she is very, very busy today. Don't worry, if anyone can find them, she can. Does that sound okay to you all?"

"Now were finally getting somewhere, damn it!"

"I-if you'll p-p-p-please keep following," Earl said.

"Yeesh, some fogeys got their panties in a bundle," Dahlia said as the three continued down the hall.

"Can't really blame 'em, Dahl. Their kids are missing. Why I always say we don't hit anyone under 21. Not worth the hassle," Davis commented quietly. "Gets ugly. Loved ones get feisty."

I sensed that Earl again felt guilty and ashamed, unable to rid himself of an overwhelming feeling of responsibility for the fate of the two interns, but he still couldn't place exactly why.

"Oh, please, my honored guests, don't mind them. Regrettably, their supervisor is probably right; those two interns caused nothing but mischief during their tenure. Mischief only breeds more mischief. Luckily, I bet our gracious Deputy Secretary will find them just as she found you two in our time of need, eeek!" Earl said with a robotic cadence and continued to lead Davis and Dahlia around the last corner before the offices of the Deputy Secretary. He stopped for a moment, flinched back his head, rolled his shoulders, and looked around the hallway before saying, "We-we-we're almost to Momma Dee's office. Right th-th-through this door."

He gulped.

Davis and Dahlia stopped before Earl opened the double doors to the office suite. Dahlia couldn't ignore the peculiar behavior any longer, noticing one too many red flags. She looked to Davis and said: "Mr. Nectarine, could you just give us a moment?" Dahlia asked.

"Sh-sh-sure. I need to ch-check if she's ready, anyway," Earl said.

"Good. I only ask because we wanna go over some talking points, you know, to make sure we maintain a solid relationship with your boss," she replied.

"O-ok," Earl said, mindlessly preoccupied that his Momma Dee would be upset with his missteps regarding the itinerary.

The two then stepped back towards the balcony bannister where Earl couldn't hear them.

"I don't know about this Davey, seems pretty sketchy. If I remember this Deputy Secretary at all, she's a pretty crazy bitch."

"Right. And crazy bitches tend to go off the rails pretty quick. Don't I know it," Davis said, smirking while looking into Dahlia's eyes.

"Oh, hush, you silver-tongued feather-brain. Seriously, Davey, tell me. What do you think? Dude is calling her, 'Momma.'"

"Let's at least go in there and meet her. The extra 5% would be a nice cash-grab; might help us get outta this wretched business. Not to mention the double-pay if we catch the guy that reporter is hiding."

"And then pearls, pearls for this little clam?" Dahlia said.

"The biggest in the sea—only the best for my main mollusk, my shelled assassin," Davis said. "And if we feel off about the job, we can always ditch it for another...but then again, the pay wouldn't be as good, might have to do a couple, since a ditched gig ain't great for our reputation."

"Let's hope it works out, then," Dahlia said, mostly convinced. "All right. Let's go for it. The faster and dirtier the better. But we gotta watch each other's backs, yeah? A corporal and his clam."

"Until the end," Davis said.

Satisfied with their decision, the clam and her corporal walked back to the now open entrance to Dee's office suite, mistakenly left ajar by Earl's preoccupation with upsetting Dee. Davis could hear voices coming from the room.

"Now, sweet Daryl, I have a sneaking suspicion that you're keeping something from me. If you want honesty from me, I'll have to ask the same."

"I told you. I've never met that reporter, not once. But you haven't said a word about Danny or Dina. I saw them the day they went missing. And you wouldn't take my meeting request for four days."

"Oh, I've just been *so busy*. I can't say Shipping and Receiving is at the top of my list of to-dos. And I think you *have met* our little fat-cat reporter. How's his wife?"

"All right. I don't need this shit. I don't work for the Capital T Truth Division, and I don't report to you. I gotta get back to work."

"Oh, but Daryl…we're simply not *done with you yet.*"

"Put your tits away. Fuck this. I'm not playing your games," Daryl said.

"Suit yourself. I'll see you very soon, Daryl."

Earl was standing by the door, listening. To his surprise, the door swung upon and smacked him square in the forehead!

"Move," the Head of Shipping said, storming off.

Davis saw Daryl exit the Deputy Secretary's office, fuming. Earl then gestured that the two were welcome to come in to meet with his boss. The hitmen walked in to find the Deputy eagerly waiting in her seat, fingers laced, and elbows perched atop her desk.

"Well if it isn't my favorite deadly pair! So very happy to see you, corporal, yes! Dahlia…" she said.

The rest of the meeting is a bit foggy, but I'm not sure why. Though I'm getting more and more control over my dream-mind— more wits about me as I see at least—I still can't quite decipher the details of the meeting. It moves in and out of view. Suddenly crisp, I hear:

"Well, damn, Miss Deputy, if that's good for you, then it's fine for us. We'll pin down that fat cat, no problem, paws bleeding and all. Definitely will do the same for the Head Researcher if he's there, too. Glad you're so close to finding the address. We were a bit worried," Dahlia said emphatically.

"Yes! Now, that's just what I wanted to hear. I just knew you two wouldn't let me down. And I'll see you tomorrow at O'Hoolihan's, right? For the official address update? I do apologize for the miscommunication," Dee replied.

They nodded. As Davis and Dahlia got up to leave, Dee interrupted their exit:

"Oh, just one more thing. And, let me just say I know, I know how unprofessional this will sound, but I promise I have a very, very good reason, paramount to Institute success and security. I do apologize, very sincerely. I truly am so—

"No disrespect, Miss Dee, but we haven't got all day, here. We've got things to take care of. What is it?" Dahlia said, prompting a quickly hid wince from Dee.

"Yes. Why of course. Well, I really should be apologizing directly to you, little Miss Dahlia. I need to talk to your corporal, alone, talk to him about a very urgent job to be done right this afternoon, right now in fact. There will be very good pay, and on my honor as Deputy Secretary for Information, I will supply Corporal Davis with all the proper and required paperwork," she said. "Better yet, he'll leave cash-in-hand."

"Uh, okay. So long as my little clam's okay with it," Davis said.

"Well, you're right, Miss Dee. It is a bit unexpected, but if the pay's good, I suppose I can suffer through an afternoon without my hawk. It's not too dangerous? He can get a bit hasty without me," Dahlia said and winked at Davis.

"Oh no, no, no! Not too dangerous at all. An inside job. No weapons, and no killing," Dee said.

"So long as he'll be home unscathed by seven, then I'd say go for it, Davey baby. I'll call a cab."

Dahlia shrugged her shoulders and walked out, but not before ruffling Davis's feathered head. After Davis watched (and enjoyed) Dahlia's exit, he asked:

"So, what's this special job you got for me?"

"Oh, Mr. Corporal, it is one of tip-top importance."

"Uh. I don't mean to be rude here, Miss Deputy, but could you cut to it? Who's the target?"

"Oh, right, yes, a very busy man, a very busy hawk who wants to fly back to his little clam, not eager to spend time with me, with Dee. So, you see, you've already met the target, a certain Head of Shipping who just left in a huff. I need you to take him somewhere special, to somewhere secret. If you'd be so kind as to follow me, I'll show you where, yes!"

"I don't like to follow without knowing where I'm headed."

"Oh, a suspicious man, are we?"

"How I got to be who I am. Now tell me or I walk," Davis said.

"Delightful, yes! Utterly scrumptious, your blunt ire. You win," Dee said. "Downstairs. To the underground," she said, and giggled in delight.

Chapter 34: Danny's Saving Grace

Outside Dina's House
August 10, 2035—the day of the escape
Around 4:00 p.m.

I hear the gentle, sparking hum of a mini-van engine. The van coughed into an aggressive exhaust-pop as Danny shifted into drive and revved the engine to race down the street, feeling frantic and afraid.

"I'm not letting her fucking do that to him," he thought.

Danny. You can't go back. I'm not there, damn it! At least I don't think I am... Why can't I wake up? Where's my doctor?

The van whipped through blurry, kaleidoscopic roadways rushing through Danny's eyeballs like a cascading mountain stream.

"Which way? Which way's fastest?" he thought amid the van's tires screeching, committing an illegal left-on-red turn, taking what he decided would be a faster route. Danny's body jumbled in his seat, a victim to the soccer-mom van's poor handling, but he didn't care. He had more important things to worry about—me. As he hurtled through the congested streets of D.C., red meant green and green meant go—no time to waste. Thoughts of his professor's screams creeped into and invaded his mind. Pounding, piercing screams!

"And what she had done to his toenails...sick," Danny thought. "I don't care what happens to me. That bitch is going to pay," Danny said aloud as he pounded the wheel.

After whipping around a corner, his borrowed van screeched to a sudden halt at a red light, where Danny was stuck behind a gray Subaru. His anger boiled, his emotions threatening to make a scene.

"Oh, fucking hell. Don't you know some of us have places to be? Oh, yeah, sip your damn coffee, fat ass. Not like we can turn right on red. Fuck! First 32 in a 35, and now this bullshit?"

Danny punched the center of the wheel, screaming the mom-van's trumpet-horn until he was greeted by a middle finger sticking out of the gray Subaru's window.

This did not make Danny happy.

"You got no idea lard ass! I've a man to save. Get out of the damn way," he shouted back, blaring the horn again. "Fuck. Why am I even justifying myself to you?" he said to himself.

The driver shot his head out, and said: "I suppose we can't read, can we? 'No right on red.' Now calm down. I'm texting my wife and I'm not in the mood for an angsty teenager after the day I've had. A one-minute wait won't kill you, and if it will, perhaps you should have left with more time to spare."

Yes, my doctor, please stop him from going! I'm not even there!

"Light's green, now, ya fat fuck," Danny said, beeping again. The gray Subaru stayed motionless, the middle finger still on display through a crack in the driver's side window. If it weren't for a steady flow of oncoming traffic, Danny might have been able to squeeze by. After the light again turned red, and the oncoming flow stopped, Danny had had enough. He'd been waiting for five minutes, five minutes he didn't have to spare. He throttled the gas, swerving past the gray Subaru as he vaulted through D.C. streets.

As he sped closer and closer to the Institute, frustrated drivers blasted their jarring horns, protesting his perilous maneuvers. His route didn't go as planned; he kept hitting traffic, and his attempted shortcuts cost him an extra fifteen minutes. To make matters worse, about half-a-mile away from the entrance, a typical irritation began nagging at Danny, but this time with a grave importance:

"Where the hell am I going to park? And how am I going to get down there to save him? Shit. Shit. I didn't think this through. Fuck. Not at all. I can't go back for Dina. There's no time. She'd know what to do. He'll be cooked if I waste time like that. I can't park on the street—it would take me ten minutes to run up the driveway. The INFO Guards and FiBs will definitely fucking see me sprinting to the door. They all know me and know what I've done, damn it."

Then, trying to overcome his paralyzed fear from the FiB speeder sirens erupting from the front entrance, Danny remembered something he'd heard last week from Daryl, Head of Shipping and Receiving. Danny and Daryl tended to take their post-lunch smoke break behind the building, out of view. And on that particular smoke break, Danny finally admitted having a crush on Dina. He remembered the underbelly advice from the head of shipping:

"If you ever want to take your sweetie somewhere on a break," Daryl said, between drags, while winking and jostling his arm, "try Garage 21 D. Discreet. Almost nobody goes down there but me, and I'm no peepin' Tom. You can trust me on that. Best part is that you can always make a quiet exit if you're too tossed to go back to work," he continued, pantomiming a woman cupping a man's marbles.

"Nobody parks back there 'cause the door only opens from the inside out, not the other way. Broken. Good thing I'm the one who reports that shit. I'll let you in, D. Just shoot me a text and I'm your man."

"All right, that'll have to work," Danny said to himself as he pulled out his phone and texted Daryl that he'd need to use the back entrance. "I'll have to ditch the van by the door, but at least there will be a shot for us to drive back out of there. Fuck. What am I doing?"

Danny turned into the back-driveway entrance, flashing his Institute ID, smooth as butter, to the indifferent parking attendant. No problems, there. The attendant didn't bother to lift his eyes from his phone; Danny attributed this unexpected behavior to the attendant's lot being used exclusively by Institute no-names. He drove up and parked next to Garage 21 D, trying his best to hide the van behind a dumpster.

"There's gotta be a vent that links shipping to that underground chamber. It's just one floor down. There's just gotta be. No way I can walk through the halls out in the open," he thought.

As he climbed out of the soccer-mom van, someone patted his shoulder, startling him.

"Danny. I see you're fixing to use my back-door spot, huh?" the man said.

"Uh—Daryl? Sorry. Yeah, I was. Sorry. You scared me."

"No problem. I was already down here having a smoke. Don't worry, bud, Daryl's got your back—I won't tell anyone you're tryna get your freak on," he said, winked, and laughed heartily.

"Wh-what do you mean? Nah, I'm not with Dina. I haven't seen Dina since this morning," Danny lied.

"Then you better be careful with whatever other little lady you're meeting here. Dina texted me a little while ago saying she needed to sneak in to the Institute. Said something about love when she got here. There's nothing wrong with a little side action so long as you two aren't exclusive. But be careful with love, D. It can mess with your head."

"She's here? No. She couldn't be..." Danny said aloud to himself. "No. Side act—what? No. I wouldn't do that to her."

Daryl shrugged his shoulders and pointed to Dina's car, parked about 100 feet away.

"She got here a few minutes ago, seemed pretty worried. Didn't say anything but 'I owe you one Daryl.' She ran in right past me as I was coming out to smoke. What the hell did you two get into?" Daryl said, puffing his cigarette.

"Daryl, man. Some scary shit," Danny admitted. "I think the fewer people who know, the better."

"Fair enough. I'll leave you to it."

"Thanks. One other thing...how do I get to the basement?" Danny said, and turned from Daryl to enter the Garage.

"Basement? The hell you want to go down there for?"

"Daryl, please."

"Fine. I said I wouldn't ask, so I won't. There's an entry in the back left of the garage. But you need a special access code. I haven't heard of anyone ever going down there, though."

"I'll figure it out," Danny said. "Thanks, Daryl."

As Danny turned around, Daryl grabbed his shoulder.

"Hey—D. Be careful."

"I will."

As Danny waded into the unknown, he became overwhelmed with concern for Dina, unable to ignore her possible peril. Cursing himself for causing Dina's newfound jeopardy, Danny began to run through the cavernous garage. He had to see for himself. Dina needed to be safe; the professor needed to be safe. If Dina had been caught, he was sure the Deputy Secretary would take her to the underground immediately. Arriving at a heavy, steel door labelled, "RESTRICTED. LEVEL 5 OFFICIALS ONLY," he saw Daryl was right: there wasn't a keyhole, but an electronic, coded lock with a keypad. Feeling he had little to lose, he started punching in numbers, starting with "1-1-1-1." Wrong. "1-2-1-1." Wrong. "1-1-2-1." Wrong. There were too many possible combinations. He began to sweat and curse, and punched in random codes, fearless of if the system would lock him out on account of too many incorrect entries. Angrily, he punched "5-4-3-7." At first the lock buzzed red, but as he took a step back, scanning the garage for vents that might take him into the basement, he heard an air-pressure valve release, cracking open the door.

Too concerned for Dina to wonder if it were more than dumb luck, Danny swiftly stepped down a spiral staircase and entered a dark, winding hallway only lit by tiny, single bulbs every fifty feet. The door closed automatically behind him, and he heard it lock. Cement blocks lined the walls, suffocating, and only served as amplifiers to the eerie silence as Danny trudged carefully into the Deputy Secretary's underground. The air was thin, but heavy, with patches of cold that felt as if you were wandering through the ethereal remains of the dead. Worse yet, the scent of hyper-sanitation stung your nostrils, like a hospital ward just cleansed of a nasty virus. Danny hated hospitals. He began to lose himself in the dank basement, nearly forgetting why he'd come there in the first place.

"Dina…Dina!" Danny whispered as he stepped through the darkness.

All that whispered back was the buzzing of lightbulbs.

"Dina!" he whispered again.

"D-Danny?" a woman's voice said, weak and in pain.

"Dina!"

"It hurts, Danny."

"Where are you?"

"It hurts…it hurts…help me. In here," the voice said from a few doors down.

He ran into the room. It was pitch black, and he felt frantically for a light switch, but before he could find one, he felt a painful thud hit the back of his head. He fell to the floor. Only able to struggle for a moment, soon Danny felt metal vice grips grapple and squeeze his ankles, his hands, his neck.

Moments later, when he regained consciousness, he felt a burning halo gradually heat his head. Looking up, a blaring, white-hot light nearly blinded him as his pupils recalibrated to the room's intense light. It felt like an examination room for the mentally disturbed and dangerous. A devilish woman's familiar voice called over to Danny:

"Oh, Mr. Umberto, yes! I've been expecting you, but I certainly wasn't expecting it to be quite so easy to snatch you right up. I thought I heard some little mice scampering through the vents."

"What the fuck? What is this? Let me go!"

"Oh, my sweet Danny boy, my little intern mite...don't you fret. No, don't you fret one bit. Just look who you're with!" the Deputy said, pointing to Dina, who laid prone and unconscious on a metal table beside him. "This is quite the party. We just *must* have a little fun together. All three of us in fact—with your beloved professor! No time to waste. Oh, a grand reunion it will be! But first, you stay right here. I need to make a special phone call to my assistant, because Momma needs help."

Chapter 35: A Clam and Her Wounded Corporal

Outside O'Hoolihan's Bean Brew and Draught
August 15, 2035—the last day
Around 2:40 p.m.

They're coming. They may be stopped, but I can tell they are close, too close, too close for the doctor to disbelieve...why can't I wake up?

The rusted Chevy parked at the side of the road, about a quarter-mile from O'Hoolihan's. Corporal Davis was bleeding from a new stab wound delivered by a razor clam.

I can feel it, too. Am I bleeding? I wasn't bleeding last time... how much time has passed? Is this now, is... is this today?

"Jesus fucking Christ, Dahlia, what was that? I didn't deserve that shit."

"One. You definitely fucking did with that smug attitude and smug-ass smile. And second, I did it to save our asses. You weren't listening. At all. Fuck, I mean last night you didn't even want to do this job. Scared like a little baby, didn't want to talk about it," Dahlia retorted as she applied pressure to Davis's bleeding thigh. "It's like you're a different person, today, Jesus.

Why wouldn't you want to hit the reporter? To be on time to a meeting? For the Deputy? Fuck that."

"Fucking hell that hurts, Dahl!" Corporal Davis squawked.

"Good. It hurts me too."

She put a little more pressure on his leg. The pain must have snapped Davis out of his anger; he felt remorse and shame for failing Dahlia. Through his winces, he looked to her, appealing to her with sorry eyes, puppy-dog style.

"No. Don't even try it. I'm pissed," she said.

Through the pain, Davis said, "You—ahh!—you know I'm not a l—AH!—liar. Stop pushing down so damn hard. Listen. FUCK! Listen, damn it. You know I'm not a liar."

"Sure. Still doesn't make you *not* an asshole," Dahlia said, beginning to cut away some of the fabric of Corporal Davis's pants so she could clean the wound underneath.

"I didn't fuck her, Dahl. Dahl, please. Look at me. I swear I didn't fuck her. I don't even know what happened just now. It's like I blacked out. There's some shady shit going on here. I don't know what's going on in my head. I'm scared," Davis said.

Dahlia could see he was being honest. "All right. Then what *did* you do for the job? You gotta tell me, or this mollusk goes and takes her clam with her. I'm telling you the truth. I'll walk," she said, and pressed her thumb into his wound. Our corporal didn't much look like a marine with his wailing.

Ouch! No. Stop! It hurts...please...

Davis tried to remember through the pain; he dug into the recesses of his brain-mind for what happened after Dahlia left the Institute.

"Fuck...fuck, that hurt. It's so hazy, Dahl. I don't know what to tell you. I really don't. I went in to talk with her after you left to get the intel, and then... she took me somewhere downstairs to show me something. It was dark."

"Really? That's the best you can fucking do? Am I dumb? Am I just a little bimbo clam for you to stick your dick in?"

"Dahl, don't talk like that. You know that's not true."

"Oh, I do know it, do I? I'm supposed to believe whatever the fuck comes out of your mouth just because you tell me it's not true? Ugh, why am I even doing this?" she said as she wrapped his wound in cloth.

"Because you love me, damn it. And I fucking love the shit out of you, you crazy mollusk. I do. You know I do. I've never loved anyone else, never been with anyone else. Shit, Dahl, have I ever given you any reason, any reason at all, to think that I would cheat on you?" Davis said, his chest tight, and forgetting his wound, forgetting the Deputy Secretary and her hold on him.

Davis looked to her, desperate now, alone and afraid.

"Oh, shut up. Shut up with those puppy-dog eyes. Fuck, why do I put myself through this? Jesus. I hate you so damn much," Dahlia said with a subtle grin while finishing the wound's dressing.

Davis might have felt some relief, some goddamn relief—finally—now that he had his little clam back in his talons. His head felt clearer than it had all day. But he knew that to get his little clam far, far away, that they'd need some cash to fund the trip. He was going to get her those pearls she wanted, damn it. Reporter first, run later.

"Finally, you're finished," he said, relieved.

"Yeah, I usually think that when you do, too," she said and ruffled his hair.

"You fucking mollusk. I love you. Damn it, I do. Fuck the meeting. Let's go take out that fat-cat reporter."

"If we get the hit on him, great, but if not, we're getting the fuck out of here. I don't trust that Deputy."

Davis nodded, and the Chevy roared down the road in pursuit, passing O'Hoolihan's with tires screeching.

No. PLEASE. You don't know whom you're working for! She's a succubus devil. If you think you've outsmarted her, you haven't. If you think she won't reel you right back into her bird trap, she's already left out the bait.

They're coming.

Chapter 36: The Dank Basement Continues

Location unknown
Date unknown, sometime in mid-August 2035

Am I sleeping? Or am I still awake? I keep flitting back and forth. I can't see. I think I know what's happening. These haven't been dreams, no, they haven't been dreams at all. I'm sure now.

I've lived lives I've never lived and died deaths I've never lived. I swear I won't fib; it's unbecoming.

I must be awake. I must be awake and alert to see these trials and traps and laps in others' minds. The one thing I know: it all started on a cold metal square. It all started from a cold metal square, singing and glaring and burning from the harsh fluorescents above. Supine, laying on my back you know, on a cold metal square. That's where I lost my mind, but I gained several more. It's where the Deputy tried to take my mind, steal my knowledge, but she failed.

Sometimes I have pecs, sometimes I have breasts, and sometimes I don't have anything at all. They poke and prod and probe. But I mustn't forget: They're still coming.

"Oh, mister naughty, little rat-a-tat-tat! Does it hurt?" Dee said.

Yes! It hurts! Yes, you ignorant bitch, of course it hurts. The clamps! How long have I been down here? The light begins to fade.

I'm back again, back again laying supine, back again...but looking through glasses? I don't wear glasses...

"Don't worry, my sweet amphibian, this will all be over in a jiffy! Naughty little tadpoles need to grow up into perfect little frogs," she said. "Yes, ease into it, you will be back soon...only a dream...let Momma Dee help. She's so happy you decided to sign your contract. We're going to be the best of friends! Oh, you are a tough mind to crack, a feisty, little, shameless mind! We'll always be together, you and me...yes! Can't have you hopping away now, Momma needs you..."

I'm squirming, squirming. Then it gets dark again…

"This was all your choice, my mousey mouse. You had to go and tell the fat doctor. You just *had* to go and tell him, yes! No! No regard for my feelings, no regard for the good citizens of the country, no regard for anything! Isn't that right? Momma will get those tasty thoughts on the reporter into the cloud, if she's got to clip those little pink feet-claws into a pulp! When one can't win with shame, she can win with pain."

Ouch! Stop! My poor little pink feet-claws. The light burns. It's like a halo around my head. Hot, hot, hot, it gets hot! And my lips are so dry. Ouch! Don't give in. No. Too many thoughts, too many thinking thoughts thinking on top and through and combining together, combining into our zoo! Yes! Fuck! Why did you press that? No. Take them off, take them off! My little feet-claws! No. My feet.

"Now, now, professor, we shouldn't swear. We know it's unbecoming for little rats to swear. Professor, if you would simply stop wiggling those cute little pink claws then it wouldn't hurt so much. So sorry that we're fresh out of cushions. I think we're finally ready for our big finale, yes! We must attach these little nodes here, yes, right here on the temples, to forever link your mind with the Institute's cloud. No, don't worry, yes! Momma Dee will help. She will know your pain and help you. Now don't be afraid, little professor, if you see some places you haven't seen, some people you don't know. It will all be over once we're done. Poof! Poof to all those bad and untrue misleading thoughts once were all done and the little rat is a rat no more, yes! Now, I must attend to one of your students. Earlie will watch over you. We'll have our next session in just a minute."

I see a metal spider holding the light close to my skull. I see the nimbus-web, ever-reaching, churning, inexhaustible, clinging with attached nodes to a bright-red nucleus fastened on the wall. Am I dreaming? I must be dreaming...where is my mind?

Who's that laying on the table? I have breasts?

"Now, ma'am, we can't have that fat doctor telling all those poor people *lies*, can we? We certainly can't. I'm afraid that he'll have to be disposed of, as I'm sure you'd agree. We can't have your staff publishing those dirty, nasty and vile rumors. And, since you haven't been compliant, I've sent an Institute official to serve in your stead as editor of *The Post*. Such a pity…" she said. Click! Snap! "Earlie! Please put our good friend here back in her cell until she complies. Break her mind."

A dream. All a dream. Please. Ouch! The halo burns my head. Fuck! Where is my doctor? Why can't I go back? Help!

"Oh no, remember little rat, you mustn't swear. It's unbecoming. Come now, don't worry, this won't quite burn the hairs off your head. Just a little more, and everything will be back to normal. Tut-tut-tut. Hush, now, we're almost done," she said.

It's light again. Harsh and fluorescent. The halo burns! Please. I feel so strong, my muscles bulging. Why can't I break free?

"What the hell is *that thing*? Dahlia will kill you for this shit."

"Oh, my buff and brawny corporal hawk, it will all be OK. You are just so desperately attracted to me, yes. Oh, what's that? You've fallen for me instead of your beloved? You want to work for me? Ah, yes that's it. Hush now. Momma needs you to help her get a wily Head of Shipping down here before the day is out. We've a little rat and his fat cat to catch, and you wouldn't make poor little me do it all by my lonesome, would you?"

Darkness and light. Again. Darkness and light.

"Let me outta this, you bitch. I told you I don't know anything about Andrea's husband. Why would I know where he is? So what if I screwed his wife?"

"Hmmm. I guess we'll just have to see, my sweet Daryl. No time like the present!"

"Silly little rat, rodents can't fly!"

Wake up, wake up, wake up!

Chapter 37: The Frog Goes Underground

Outside the Institute for Information Dissemination
August 10, 2035—the day of the escape
Around 5:30 p.m.

Earl slowly approached the back entrance to the Institute for Information Dissemination, his powder-blue Toyota Prius inching up the winding driveway. He checked his phone to see a text notification from Momma Dee:

●●●●○ InTel LTE   5:34 PM   ⏰ ✻ 6% 🔋

❮ Messages **Momma Dee**   Details

Oh, and Earlie. Please use the entrance through Garage 21 D. Quickest way from the outside. Hurry, hurry! Hop, hop hop!! Momma will let you in. Just punch in any code and she will open the door.

"Okay, 21 D, it is," Earl thought to himself, maneuvering his sedan up the winding thruways reserved for shipping and receiving. While he ensured his speed did not breach the 10mph speed limit of the shipping driveway, his mind went frantic, concerned for the two interns, and fighting his building will to please his boss. He parked beside a soccer-mom van, and with his head in his hands, thought:

"Earl Eustace Frog, just what do you think you're doing? I know it, I just know Dee is going to do something nasty, vile, something downright *evil* to those poor interns. What if she makes you help? What if you can't resist?

What would be their crimes? Trying to protect one another? *Knowing?*

Yes. High crime that is: knowing something you shouldn't. No! It isn't a crime to know, isn't a crime to advocate for yourself even if those more powerful deem it dangerous for you to know their secrets. If knowing were a crime, Dee would be the first to be served a death-sentence.

This isn't right. No, not right or moral. Not left or moral, for that matter. What she's doing is terribly, terribly wrong. Those two kids are frightened, scared out of their wits. And they should be. Heck, no, *hell*, I'm scared out of my wits too, with no end in sight. I must put an end to this. Now.

How can I live this down? If those interns are hurt, or worse...how will a sorry frog be able to sleep at night? Why must I be so drawn to her seductive, furtive tactics? Seductive? No. She's a damn succubus. No more."

Save them, Earl! I'm not even in there! At least not anymore. Oh, this is bad, bad, this is bad.

Earl looked up out of the corner his eye, observing a tall, buff, slightly graying man saunter out of the door to Garage 21 D. The man walked up to his window and knocked. Earl rolled down the window.

"Can I help you?" the man asked, before dragging his cigarette.

"I-I'm here on o-official c-Capital T Truth Division business."

"I'll say. Why come in back here? No one comes in back here. Shipping and Receiving, only."

"Th-that's none of your business," Earl said, his worry mounting more each second that Dee would be harming the interns. His moment of clarity and compassion brought another welcome realization, too: each moment of gleaned confidence broke the shackles of his stutter. Dee was losing control.

"The Deputy asked for me, specifically. And told me to come in this way."

Daryl gave him a quizzical look, unconvinced, his concern for Danny and Dina rising. Daryl felt uncomfortable letting in a Capital T Truth Division official through the back entrance right behind his favorite interns.

"No chance. Go in the front, bud. This is my jurisdiction. And I'm saying *no*."

"Listen. Don't make me call in the FiBs," Earl threatened, flashing his ID which stated his authority as "Lead Assistant to the Deputy for Information."

Daryl shook his head and scoffed.

"Some place this is, threatening their own employees. Whatever man, but I'm going to keep my eyes on you. You got 30 seconds in that garage. Don't try anything funny."

Earl hurried through the garage, afraid of Daryl tailing him. He felt bad for bullying the Head of Shipping, but he was not about to involve anyone else in Dee's schemes. He arrived at the electronic lock, and punched in the numbers, "3-7-3-3." Though the lock buzzed and the light turned red, a moment later, the thick, sheet-steel door opened, just as Dee had promised. He sighed, but began to feel oddly comfortable, almost nostalgic, as he passed through the door's threshold. He had never been here before, he thought, at least he never remembered being here. But the underground's familiarity was undeniable; his body, mechanical and swift, recalled how to navigate the Deputy's dark abyss.

He stepped confidently around a small platform and felt a railing that led down a spiral staircase. As he descended the dimly lit stairs, he smelled intense sanitation; it was how he imagined a psych ward would smell, painfully clean. After reaching the bottom of the staircase and walking a few feet down the hall, Earl heard a voice, shrill for the first time in recent memory.

"Oh my. Oh my! If it isn't my favorite little amphibian man. Momma is just so, so happy you've made it to our little play date. Come, come! We're just three doors down!"

Earl mustered as much courage as he could. It would not be easy to fool Dee. He'd have to act just like her perfect little frog would. He walked in the door, and hid the horror from his face. Blindingly white lights glared from the ceiling, shining a spotlight on a poor young man, harnessed to a metal table with leather belt-buckle straps on his hands, feet, neck, and torso. Earl couldn't shake the feeling that he'd been here before, and almost salivated at the sight. He had to shake off the urge to assist his darling Dee in her torture chamber, outfitted with medical scanners and equipment, all hooked up to a supercomputer on the left wall.

"As you can see, Danny and I are having so much fun," she said, pointing to the immobile intern with a white-washed complexion. "Aren't we having fun, Danny? Earl's a bit shy. He must know we're having fun."

Danny tried to look toward Earl, but his neck restraints refused him. All over his forehead were wired nodes, sensing brainwaves and displaying readings onto a wheeled monitor which stood to the right of the table.

"You bitch. You fucking bitch! Let me go. Where's Dina? What're you doing to her in there? I heard her screaming!"

"Earlie, can you believe your ears? A trashy sailor's mouth, we have. We shall fix that," Dee said as she tightened the grips on Danny's ankles, prompting him to wail in pain. His feet turned blue and red, being starved of blood, swollen.

"Y-y-y-y-yes. D-dirty sailors," Earl said in agreement, finally stuttering by choice to make his act believable. He winced, wishing he could signal to Danny somehow that he were here to save him, and not to contribute to his suffering.

"Oh, it won't hurt him for long, Earlie. I know how sensitive little frogs can be."

Danny grunted, respiring with short and rapid breathes. Dee's metal clamps continued to dig into his feet, with such force that the bones in Danny's feet looked broken.

"Tut-tut-tut. Hush now, Danny. Your little lover is just over there in the other room," Dee said as she patted the grimacing and groaning intern. "Such a shame you dragged Dina into this mess. I just don't know how you'll be able to live with yourself," she said and feigned a pout. "We're very close to done. Yes, that's it. Think about Dina. Just have to let the cloud suck, suck, suck all that knowledge up, and then you can work for me!"

"Get that fucking thing away from me," Danny said as Dee lowered an illuminated metal ring, which housed the dangling electro-node attachments stuck on Danny's skull. "What the hell do you think you're doing? My mother's a lawyer. You won't get away with this—this—this has got to be illegal."

"Illegal? Why must they always think illegal?". Misinformation *must* be ripped out from the public mind. Now, let me just attach your mind to the cloud, so we can store all those nasty thoughts. In just a moment, I'm going to press this little red button, and then in a few minutes all of this pain will go away."

Earl stared blankly, wide-eyed, shivering and shaking, unable to watch for a moment longer. His memory began to jog, associating, a dull but vivid recall that whispered what was about to happen would forever change the poor intern into a gumption-less zombie, heeding to Dee's beck and call.

"D-d-Dee, m-m-m-maybe we sh-should let him g-g-go," Earl managed to croak. "H-he-he won't g-g-give us any trouble."

That's it, Earl! Don't give up. You're better than her. I know you.

"Don't interrupt me! Close that croaker before you wish you hadn't opened it. I said he can go once we're finished. We're not savages," Dee said and snapped her fingers.

He knew he couldn't be too averse to Dee's wishes or he'd give himself away, and then he would have no chance at setting the interns free. The thought struck him: perhaps he could release Dina and the Head Researcher while Dee was distracted with the laborious process of uploading Danny's memories to the cloud. Yes. Then the three of them could overpower her. That just might work, but he'd have to continue to play the game; Earl couldn't allow Dee a sniff of suspicion.

"Anything you say, boss," Earl said.

Dee eyed him, warily.

"What does my darling need me to do?"

"Earlie, is something *wrong?*" she said and snapped again.

"Nothing at all...eeek!" he said, clumsily appending the sound of acquiescence Dee was looking for.

"There he is! There's my sweet frog. So glad you asked," she said and moaned. "Go through that door there to the room next door, yes, that's it, that's the one, and keep an eye on little Dina. Your fragile eyes shouldn't see this next part. The little rat's in there too; he's all hooked up, but he's very sleepy. We mustn't have anything happening to them before Momma helps push all those bad, untrue thoughts out of their heads, can we?"

"Certainly not. We must push away all those bad and untrue and misleading thoughts," Earl said mechanically as he wracked his mind on how they would save Danny.

"Momma will be ready for them in just a few minutes, yes! The professor is next. Do us a favor and make sure they don't squirm too much, else Danny's upload might be interrupted, fatal to the little intern and our mission."

Danny squirmed all the more, about to shout, but Dee cupped her hand over his mouth and smoothed a thick muzzle of duct tape to silence him.

"Hush, hush, little Danny. Remember, the more you squirm, the more painful the upload process will be. And not just for you. We wouldn't want your beloved mentor upset, would we?"

Robotically, Earl opened the pressurized steel door, and saw two identical metal tables, one gripping a young woman and one gripping a man with a few gray hairs in his beard. Both had a spider's web of neuro-wires spanning out from their heads that led to the cloud's nucleus. Earl thought the man looked emaciated; you could see his ribs through his ripped, white T-shirt.

Is that man, me? Am I really seeing myself? Is this really happening?

Earl now became overwhelmed with a waterfalling rush of memory—he *had* been here before, he *had* been Dee's dutiful assistant, uploading American citizens' minds into the clouds, holding them down as they screamed, torturing them into shame, hurting them until they, too, were dutiful assistants for the Institute's mission. He heard Dina yell from the table:

"Please. You have to let us go! This isn't human!"

"Hush, Dina. Not so loud. It hurts," I hear myself say, numb and curiously accepting of my fate.

"We're going to get you out of here, Professor," Dina whispered to me.

"That last session got me good. I don't even know how many days I've been here. You came just in the nick of time. But now that he's here, I don't know how much good it'll do. I'm done, Dina. A goner, finished. And now you are, too," I whispered to Dina and winced on account of my gashed feet and gnarled toes, imagining the same happening to Dina and Danny.

"Professor! Don't talk like that. You can't talk like that," Dina said through her sobs.

Understanding that Dee probably had these rooms rigged to hear their conversation, Earl continued his act:

"Sh-sh-she only d-does it be-be-be-because she c-c-c-c-c-cares. For the greater good."

"For the greater good. The greater good?! That's bullshit. I mean, just look at what you two are doing—hurting people!"

"Dina," I said hoarsely. "It's no use. He's under her spell. Soon we will be, too. It's why I'm down here. Because I know what Dee does to people. Fuck. It hurts. Danny!"

A voice was heard over the loudspeaker:

"Shut them up in there, will you? Momma's trying to work! Dina's voice is making him wriggle, and wriggling's no good for the memory upload! You, Professor, you did this to yourself. Your negligence and treachery brought Danny here. And

I want you to hear. Earl! Use my special tools on the wall if you must."

"Hey. No funny business. Not on my watch, eeek!" Earl said.

"Not the clippers…" I said meekly.

"Of course not. Nothing funny about the Capital T. Pl—," Dina began to plead.

Earl hurried over and covered her mouth. Dina began to squirm, the fear in her eyes palpable and animal. She darted her doe-wide, jade eyes to the wall lined with medieval instruments of torture.

"Shhh!" Earl said, giving her a revealing look. He was not here to hurt either of them, was not about to risk falling victim to Dee's overpowering influence again, and so Earl Eustace Frog became the bullfrog he was always meant to be. He became the hero he had wanted to be all his life, and leapt over to me, but fumbled with the metal-vice grips on my head, my feet.

Dina realized what Earl was trying to do. "Th-there's a button underneath his left shoulder," she whispered. "That was the release button she used for Danny."

"Right!" Earl said with urgency, bending down to press a little red button to release me.

"No! Not *your* left, damn it, wai—" I cried, trying my best to correct him amid the pain I felt through my mind's connection to Danny's painful memory upload.

I feel intense, terrible pain. My head is burning and blasting, frying, seeing and thinking and believing and remembering and misremembering and feeling and doubting and being. Chaos. Terrible chaos. Ouch! Electric sparking cognitive currents! My mind connected to the cloud in tandem with another! Too close, too close. Two brains cannot merge, cannot know and think and believe and remember and understand and recognize in the same way. Our humanity, our individuality stripped, coagulated into a fabricated system of belief. A common mission, a common understanding cannot be forced and jammed, manipulated spam fucking with who we are and what we know!

Perspectives cannot be milled and shifted and filtered. You cannot make Danny what you want me, or what you want me, Danny! Our minds are individual, and individual are our minds, and we don't prescribe to you, devil woman!

The static. It hurts! My brain turning to mush, victim to an electric uploading bi-way. I see all Danny's memories and feelings and pains, but there's too much to see and hear and believe. His pain is becoming mine, but his brain-mind quiets, getting softer and softer, almost as if I am the wretched succubus, stealing away the knowledge of his soul.

I am everywhere and nowhere and anywhere and somewhere.

"Pull the nodes off. Pull them off, Earl! What the hell? Left, I said. My left!" Dina screamed, watching me convulse and fry on the table, hearing Danny scream from the next room through the intercom.

"I-I-I'm so-so-sorry, I-sh-she b-boggles my mind—sh-sh-shame," Earl said underneath my shrill groans and screams.

"Be sorry later. Fix this now!" Dina shouted.

Earl quickly removed the nodes attached to my temples and pressed the correct release button. The system, unable to handle an incomplete, dual memory upload, short-circuited, and the room flickered from the power surge. Underneath the strobing lights, I was still screaming, beside myself, inside others, shouting, yelping, squeaking.

I saw myself, through Earl's eyes, shoot upright, look around, and sprint out of the room into the tunnels, babbling like a mad man, my bleeding feet drip-dropping a trail behind me.

The power returned to full capacity, running on backup generators, but before Earl could release Dina, he heard a terrible, booming and demonic voice whipping from the other room:

"Just what in the fuck is going in there, Earl? I'm not done with the intern. The process must be uninterrupted. It's a bi-way process! Both streams must remain open. What did you do? My intern is convulsing in here! Babbling something about the Head of Research!"

He heard the metal clanking of the door opening. The door then opened completely, revealing a red-faced, scowling and white-knuckled Deputy Secretary.

"He's—he's gone? No. This isn't happening. You *let him go?* You've fucked with the wrong woman, Frog! You best hope he didn't get far. I'll have to signal the FiBs for this! If I didn't have such foresight…you ignorant, treacherous little man!"

"I'm s-s-s-sorry," Earl found himself saying, feeling ashamed.

"Good. Not that it will do us much. Look what you've done," Dee said, pointing to Danny's lifeless, charred body through the open door.

Dina screamed in terror. Blood-curdling.

"Miss, please, don't hurt me. I just want to go home… please," Dina said, sobbing. "Let me go home. I just want to go home. I won't tell anyone. I promise I won't."

"You're right about that. You certainly won't be *telling a soul*...you can thank Earl for that. He's forced me...me!" she said and snapped, glaring at Earl with her sanguine eyes.

"I'm sorry. I'm sorry. I won't let you down again, eeeek!"

I don't think the squeak was voluntary.

"Better not, or Momma's having fried frog legs. Now, get those hedge clippers. You're going to make her scream and wail until there's nothing left. This is *your fault*."

As Earl slunk towards the wall holding the hedge clippers, Dee walked over to a digital control panel installed in the south wall, typed in a few unknown digits, and said into a wall-microphone:

"Attention Security and Non-Security Personnel of the Institute. Grade 5 Breach. RUN RODENT RUN. I repeat. Grade 5 Breach. RUN RODENT RUN. This is not a drill. I repeat. This is not a drill. All Lieutenants, man your positions. RUN RODENT RUN. All personnel should be on high alert. Rodent must be exterminated on sight."

Chapter 38: I'm Not a Rat
A Professor's Diary #8

Daryl's Basement
August 15, 2035—the last day
Around 3:00 p.m.

To Professor Earnest Gaines:

I am no rat. I am no rodent of any kind. Well I guess I am, in a sense, but I won't listen anymore. There's no time. I'm finally awake!

I remember! I remember who I am. Yes. I have it all written down in my diary, all of it right here, all the demons and heroes. I must go and show my old friend. Maybe now he will finally believe me, finally believe the danger is real.

She's killed Danny! *I killed Danny?* I don't know. No time for that now.

Daryl didn't come back last night. Which means…

I know *they're not coming. They're here.*

We must get out before the hawk swoops and the clam slashes. And the FiBs come after us all. Maybe I can reason with Dahlia, and convince Davis he's been under Dee's spell.

I hear a car parking.

There's commotion upstairs. Don't worry, I'm coming doctor!

Earnest Gaines

Chapter 39: A Confession

Daryl's House
August 17, 2035—two days after the last
5:07 p.m.

I've never been sorrier nor guiltier as I am in this moment, drafting the final entry to the professor's profound and terrible saga. A terrible saga forced into his mind by the corruption and deceit of the Institute for Information Dissemination, a terrible saga that infiltrated and addled his mind, a terrible saga instituted and impaled within him by *her*. His moments of clarity and visions were an unexpected malfunction the cloud's upload process when interrupted. The dual upload short-circuited the system, and the more powerful of the two brains won, winning the memories and perspectives of the other. It fried poor Danny's body and fried the poor professor's mind.

The Institute may have been formed with good intentions, but under the Deputy Secretary's reign, we have truly lost sight of Sherman's mission to help the public trust what information they consume. I have no doubt that Sherman did, *truly*, mean well and good when he passed his revolutionary INFO Act. And yet, under his mismanagement and the corruption of ambition, Sherman unwittingly let a subordinate whittle down his power for good. In its vile stead, Dee, under the veil of the

Institute for Information Dissemination, craftily manipulated the public into disbelieving any information from anywhere else.

The damage will be ever felt as historians mull over the complexity of the Information Age and the Institute's monstrous role within it. I know I am sorry for my part and will accept any and all consequences.

I hope you can find it in your heart to forgive me. Legally, I don't care. Morally, I hope you understand. I know I won't ever forgive myself. I tried to break free from her, truly I did. I was on the cusp of breaking from the whole wretched Institute. Hopefully after reading this recapitulation, you will sympathize with my plight.

The professor sure got quite a lot right in his basement ramblings. I promise to leave all his entries as I've found them with some very minor revisions for clarity. I must confess I felt obligated to add dates and locations, except in the professor's personal diary entries with the intent of providing the experiences directly, as he faced them.

I understand some might feel my bias will inevitably seep into my retelling (I did my best to recreate his experience), but I defend my choices in this way: no citizen will truly be able to comprehend the terrors of the Institute if you cannot see and hear and think and know and remember as the professor did. I hope you find this acceptable.

We must remember that our troubled professor suffered through the memories of our major players, especially me. I feel like I know him, though I've only met him in passing at the Institute. Hell, he was *there* with me, after all, rooting for me despite his pain, rooting for me against the Devil right up until the end.

But I couldn't save him. By the time we arrived at Daryl's house with the FiB Lieutenant's escort, the inside was flooded with the Federal Institute Battalion's elite. Blood was splattered on the windows. There was nothing for a frog to do. Davis, Dahlia, Andrea, Dr. Andrews, and the Head Researcher were all dead.

It was in this moment I finally stripped my mind completely from Dee's powerful influence. I could no longer feel shame at her behest, because my own conscious was too heavy. Woefully scanning the room, looking at the bullet-riddled bodies of the innocent trying to escape Dee's clutches, I lied to her, and said I wanted to take notes for the inevitable paperwork we'd need to submit to coverup the killings. Her ambition and presumption unwavering, she believed me.

I haven't seen her these past two days as I compiled the professor's diary. My only hope is that Sherman still holds enough sway to rid the nation of Dee forever; I try to find solace in knowing that Sherman might act honorably, and restore some public faith to dismantle the Institute after he realizes Dee's toxic tendrils controlled some of his recent, more regrettable moves. I may be able to rely on his inclination toward preserving his reputation. Maybe he'll do the right thing and admit the Institute is no good for America, after all.

I plan to go and tell him. Tonight. If we're lucky, this retelling may garner an unheard of "A+ Institute Accuracy Report." Then the public will surely believe.

I must get this book published to honor the professor and the Doctor's good, brave work in trying to take down such a horrid demon. Their deaths cannot and will not be in vain, and neither can the heroic efforts of Danny and Dina, the two underestimated interns who gave their lives to free a friend in desperate need. They all must be remembered, will be remembered.

If you are reading this, it is my sincerest hope this book will tear to shreds that succubus of an Institute. The American people deserve better. The people must know.

Sincerely,

E.E. Frog

Earl Eustace Frog
Ex-Lead Assistant
Office of the Deputy Secretary for Information Dissemination
Capital T Truth Division
August 17, 2035

ACKNOWLEDGMENTS

As those who write know, publishing books is an unruly beast. It's foolish to think it's a feat to be accomplished alone. I'd like to endlessly and sincerely thank the following people for their unrestrained, compassionate help to get this damn book in your hands.

To Heather M., who is as tireless and vigilant an editor as they come—I won't publish any book without her. I'm not sure I have it in me to publish another narrative that's told out-of-order, ever again, so perhaps we both can rest easy.

To Grace J., who supplied magnificent story ideas and wrangled in my writerly ego with wit and charm. To Tom M., who analyzed the story's consistency amid its chaos and gave unforgiving style advice. To Leah R., who was a bedrock support and connected me with some pretty awesome folk to get this show on the road. To Sam H., who had enough grit to give honest feedback and enough patience to deal with my blathering. To Sofie G., who helped me promote the book, all out of the kindness of her heart. To Jesse T., who was unyielding in advice and feedback. To Matthew R., who put the interior design into hyper-speed so we could publish on schedule. To Lisa S. and Steve M., for proofreading the text with expediency.

To my family for being there for me during these three, hellish years.

And, of course, to my entire book launch team who believed in me, without whom an audience for this book would not have been possible.

ABOUT THE AUTHOR

Sam Sarkisian's
The Institute

Sam Sarkisian is a Lecturer at Boston University where he teaches college writing and introduction to communications writing. This is his first novel, but he has several more projects in the works. He lives in Somerville, MA with his dog, Mango, and likes to play amateur pool.

He hopes you liked the book. If you want to read more, you can follow Sam and his upcoming work, here:

Website: sam-sarkisian.com
Instagram: @theinstitutenovel @samsarkisiann
Twitter: @sammiesark